‖‖ ‖‖‖‖‖‖‖‖‖ ‖ ‖‖ ‖ ‖‖‖ ‖‖‖‖‖‖‖‖ ‖‖

P9-DCA-212

Praise for the stories in *Taking Charge*

Stephanie Vaughan's *Cruel to be Kind*

"With hot action and an enjoyable plot, don't miss the wonderfully fun *Cruel to be Kind.*"

—Patti Fischer, *Romance Reviews Today*

"A wonderfully written BDSM love story, *Cruel to be Kind* captures the feelings of insecurity, hope and love between an established Domme and a submissive who's never known what it is he needs. Erotic, intriguing, passionate and unforgettable, *Cruel to be Kind* is a must read."

—Ayden Delacroix, *In the Library Review*

Lena Austin's *Black Widow*

"Ms. Austin has written one of the best BDSM erotic romances that I have read in a very long time… As a reviewer, I can do no more than give *Black Widow* my highest recommendation."

— Meribeth McCombs, *The Road to Romance*

"In *Black Widow*, readers are introduced to Dom and sub personalities, the frailty of subspace, and the effects of pain and pleasure on the mind and body… I recommend *Black Widow* for the curious virgin and the seasoned Dom in need of a refresher course."

— Melissa Levine, *In the Library Review*

Cruel to be Kind and *Black Widow* are also available separately in e-book format at Loose Id.

Loose Id

ISBN 10: 1-59632-150-4
ISBN 13: 978-1-59632-150-2
TAKING CHARGE
Copyright © 2005 by Loose Id, LLC
Cover Art by April Martinez
Edited by Linda Kusiolek and Karen W. Williams

Publisher acknowledges the authors and copyright holders of the individual works, as follows:
SIERRA SECRETS: CRUEL TO BE KIND
Copyright © October 2004 by Stephanie Vaughan
BLACK WIDOW
Copyright © July 2004 by Lena Austin

All rights reserved. Except for use of brief quotations in any review or critical article, the reproduction or utilization of this work in whole or in part in any form by any electronic, mechanical or other means, now known or hereafter invented, including xerography, photocopying and recording, or in any information storage or retrieval is forbidden without the prior written permission of Loose Id LLC, 1802 N Carson Street, Suite 212-2924, Carson City NV 89701-1215. www.loose-id.com

DISCLAIMER: Many of the acts described in our BDSM/fetish titles can be dangerous. Please do not try any new sexual practice, whether it be fire, rope, or whip play, without the guidance of an experienced practitioner. Neither Loose Id nor its authors will be responsible for any loss, harm, injury or death resulting from use of the information contained in any of its titles.

This book is an original publication of Loose Id. Each individual story herein was previously published in e-book format only by Loose Id and is a work of fiction. Any similarity to actual persons, events or existing locations is entirely coincidental.

Printed in the U.S.A. by
Lightning Source, Inc.
1246 Heil Quaker Blvd
La Vergne TN 37086
www.lightningsource.com

Contents

SIERRA SECRETS: CRUEL TO BE KIND

Stephanie Vaughan

Dedication

To Raven, who talked me down from the ledge too many times to count.

— SV

Chapter One

A prickle of awareness raised the hairs on the back of his neck, and he knew he was being watched. That it was a woman doing the watching he had no doubt, although if pressed he couldn't have said how he knew. He just knew.

Steve Eriksson leaned an elbow on the bar in front of him and let his eyes scan the room.

Goldie's was nothing special as bars went. No sophisticated game room or huge selection of microbrews on tap the way Off Limits did across town. But then, Goldie's didn't cater to the tourist crowd, either. It was just a no-frills working class watering hole where a good burger and a cold beer could be had for a decent price. A pool table in the back and a competition dart board had constituted all the value-added features the regulars needed to keep Goldie's in the black since it had opened.

The group of four women near the front door wasn't the source of his itch. They each wore a variation of the young professional's uniform and had their sights set on the group of equally upscale looking men in suits at the far end of the bar that presently supported his weight. The women looked like the type that Tivo'd *Sex and the City* and rated the quality of their lives by the size and content of their shoe closet.

No thanks.

His eyes moved on past Evan from the custom leather goods shop, looking like he was about to hook-up with the new teller from the savings and loan, to the room's only table of one.

In profile she didn't look old enough to be in a bar in the first place. A baseball cap on her head, a ponytail of dark hair pulled through the opening in the back, Steve could tell only that she wasn't dressed to kill and she appeared intent on whatever it was she was doing. A small laptop computer in front of her, she slowly scanned sheets from the stack of papers to her left, occasionally typing one-handed on the computer.

What made the picture especially intriguing was the rest of the tableau: an arm's-length away a full meal sat untouched. A flat tureen of what had to be Goldie's infamous shepherd's pie and a tall glass of dark beer stood silent watch over her labors. That both had been sitting for a while was obvious from the shrinking track of foam on the beer and the rivulets of condensation, while the pie's crust of mashed potatoes remained smooth and unbroken.

Unable to reconcile the high-powered buzz he'd felt with the slight figure seated at the table, Steve was about to move on. Until she lifted her head and the previously downcast eyes moved from the computer screen and locked on his.

Direct and dark, they reached out and grabbed him by the balls. A jolt of electricity ran through his system, as though he'd stuck a screwdriver into a wall socket. Those eyes snaked down into his soul as though to look around. Size him up. Think about moving in.

And then her eyes slipped past his shoulder, breaking the connection, and he could breathe again.

Holy shit!

A grin spread over his face. Before he could even think twice about it, Steve was standing next to the small table. It must be alien mind-control because he couldn't recall giving his feet the command to move. One minute he'd been lounging against the bar, the next he was there at her table.

"I noticed you're not touching your food. Is there something wrong with it?" Not exactly original, but it was the first thing that popped into Steve's head. He wanted to see those eyes again like he wanted the Red Sox to win the World Series.

Between his height and the bill of the cap, she had to cock her head back to make eye contact. "My waitress go on a break?"

That wiseass half-smile on her face did something to his stomach. She was so perfect and wholesome looking, Steve half expected her to hold up a tube of toothpaste and grin for the camera. He would have thought a blush and a stammered reply would be more her style, sweet young thing that she was. But she hadn't so much as missed a keystroke on her computer.

"No idea. But I'm Steve and I'd be happy to get you anything you want."

He couldn't take his eyes off hers, but he got an impression of casual dress: white tank top, jeans, 'Christa's Catering' stitched onto her cap. But those eyes—dark, chocolaty brown and gazing up at him with not one hint of coyness.

"Good to know. Thanks very much, Steve, but I'm almost done. If I need anything I'll be sure and look you up."

She turned back to her work and Steve felt the rejection like a blow low in his gut.

No way.

This was too good to let go of and she had to be feeling it, too. He refused to be blown off without even getting his shot. He pulled out the empty chair opposite and sat down.

Seconds ticked by and she didn't so much as flick him a glance from those eyes of hers. "You don't mind if I watch, do you?"

Permission or no, Steve watched as she scanned another document, found what she was looking for, and keyed more information into the laptop.

"One of those, are you?" A small surge of triumph surged through him as he congratulated himself on drawing her out. She seemed incredibly self-contained. Self-sufficient. As though she didn't need anyone or anything to complete her. She was happy where she was and with what she had. "Do you like to watch, Steve?"

Caught flat-footed, he found those enigmatic eyes fixed on him like a laser beam. What were they talking about? While he'd been daydreaming the stakes had somehow gone way, way up.

"I'd rather be doing. But watching beats nothing every time."

* * *

He really was too amazing to be believed.

Didn't it just figure? Megan had spent the better part of the past four years looking for the right one. She'd even gone so far as to move to San Francisco—the Big City, to most people in her home town—figuring she'd have better odds fishing from a bigger pond.

Nothing.

Nada, zip, zilch, zero.

But take herself off the market, decide to head back home to lick her wounds and give her poor battered heart a rest, and what does Fate do? Dangle the sweetest hunk of prime male in front of her it had been her pleasure to see in many a long month, that's what.

And it was, very much, her pleasure.

Fate was a real cunt, Megan decided.

She knew Megan had a thing for long hair on men. That Megan had given up hope years ago of ever finding that particular combination of red and gold that made her palms itch to sink her hands into it. But here they both were in one man, standing in front of her.

She'd spotted him the minute he'd walked in, all easy grace and long, lean muscle, perfectly showcased in work shorts and soft old T-shirt. Connoisseur of the male form that she was, she could have wished for that T-shirt to fit a little more snugly across his shoulders, but still... Megan was a total sucker for beautiful male arms and she could see this man had them in spades.

He laughed at something the barkeep said and Megan thought that if there were a God in Heaven, this fine example of His work would have an itch on his belly that needed scratching right about now. She already knew there wasn't, so it only confirmed things for her when it didn't happen. Megan had to content herself with imagining.

He would reach those long fingers under his shirt, pull it up six inches or so and show off the strong musculature she knew it hid. He would score those fingers lightly across those taut muscles... Megan tried sending him the thought telepathically, but it didn't work now any better than it ever had. Still, it didn't hurt to try. She'd like to rake her own nails sharply across his belly while she squeezed his velvety-soft testicles gently—or not so gently—as he writhed in agonized pleasure.

Her instincts must be rustier than she'd thought because The Delicious One had nearly caught her staring. Megan had no intention of starting anything and it would be best all around if she just stuffed her tongue back into her mouth and paid attention to the task at hand. Namely, trying to figure out if she was running her sister's business into the ground or not.

Running Christa's catering truck didn't require any skills she couldn't perform in her sleep—except when it came to balancing the receipts. Her brief college career had taught her that math was not something that was ever likely to be integral to her livelihood. At least, not by choice. Today she had given herself the incentive of a meal cooked by someone else if she could get the month's receipts entered into the accounting program her sister used. Megan had thought she might finally be making some progress when she had become hopelessly distracted by the amazing-looking man who had walked in.

Too bad he wasn't her type.

Men who looked like he did never were.

But then Fate had gotten really nasty by giving the beautiful man she had no business even talking to a hard shove in her direction. She'd seen his long legs with their light furring of hair in her peripheral vision. Megan counted to ten and willed him to give up and walk away. She wasn't sure she had the strength to turn him down. Even if it was for his own good.

But the lamb not only sat down with the lion, he engaged her in play. And her old instincts kicked in, God help him.

* * *

Megan made sure he paid for his interruption by taking a good twenty minutes longer to finish than the work required. At least, that's what she told herself. It wasn't that she was so mesmerized by the exotic beat of the blood in her veins, made thick and heavy by the man across from her, that inserting numbers into a spreadsheet was all but beyond her capability at that moment.

And it certainly shouldn't be necessary to wrest control back from her libido this early in the game. No, she was just setting the ground rules. Making him understand from the start what he was getting himself into. If it turned out that was what they were doing.

"So, Steve." After tucking away her computer, Megan drew the now room temperature meal in front of her and reached for the beer. "What can I do for you?"

She made sure her hand remained steady as her fork pierced the soft crust of the pie. Taking a bite before she caught his eye again, Megan was thankful for the food in her mouth. Anything audible that escaped might be interpreted as appreciation of the food, and not her own groan of helpless lust at getting her first real look at his eyes. Lashes darker than they had any right to be framed eyes as unusual as their owner's hair color, a rare blending of blue and green.

Megan thought she read uncertainty in them as he found his voice. Poor baby probably had no idea how to behave after being kept waiting, as he had. "Let me take you out to dinner."

Keeping any hint of a smile from her face, Megan gestured to the food in front of her. "I've already got dinner, thanks." A two-beat pause. "Is there anything else you can think of to do for me?"

It really wasn't fair of her to tease the poor man like that. He obviously had no idea of the kind of woman he was trying to play with. And it was a bad sign for her how much it touched her to watch him keep swimming when the current was clearly over his head.

"Whatever you need, babe, I can do for you." Someone please tell her that wasn't a catch she heard in his voice.

Megan sighed a little.

There would be no getting around it. Fate, life, pure dumb luck—whatever you chose to call it—was plainly insisting that this man was in her path for a reason. And Megan had learned the hard way that hiding from the inevitable never worked. It would only hunt you down, make you pay double when it finally found you.

Megan folded her hands on the table and leaned forward a little. She wanted to read every gradation of feeling on his face when she rocked his world.

"Steve, I need to explain some things to you."

Chapter Two

Steve flinched.

That didn't sound good. It was never a good sign when the woman told the man, "We need to talk." It usually turned out to be something like she was the last of her high school gal-pal group still not married and, gosh, wouldn't next month be perfect for a garden wedding. Or that her old college roommate, who was neater than you and an amazing cook, hadn't been 'strictly platonic' after all and, not only was he back in town, but she was moving in with him. Or she was finally ready to try a threesome—with another guy as the third.

"Here's the deal, Steve. I don't think you have any idea whose table you picked to sit down at." Her arms as she leaned on the table were slim but firm-looking and he wondered what she did to keep in shape. He let his eyes take a surreptitious flick downward, trying to make out the shape of her breasts. He was betting on smallish—barely a B cup—with pert little nipples. Looking back up, Steve realized she'd caught his every move.

Busted.

But instead of outrage, he would swear he read approval on her face.

"No, that's okay. Don't be embarrassed. In fact, I want to hear what you like. Especially in bed."

Holy— He couldn't have heard that right. "You want to hear what?"

"I want to hear what you like. What you don't like. What your fantasies are. What you've never done but always wanted to...if you found the right person." Her voice had gone soft. Almost hypnotic. Steve thought he could stare into those eyes and listen to that voice all night long. Ideally they would both be naked as part of the exercise.

"This is a pretty good fantasy right here. But I'd really like to be having this conversation somewhere quieter. Maybe without the audience." Steve gestured toward the rest of the room.

She shook her head, her ponytail swaying with the motion, just grazing the tops of her shoulders. "Not yet. Soon, maybe. But we need to get some things straight first."

Steve didn't believe conversations like this happened in real life. He'd always figured those letters in the backs of men's magazines were fake. "Dear Penthouse, I never thought these letters were real until something happened to change my mind." Yeah, right. How many nymphomaniac blonde twins with fireman fantasies were there in real life? But here he was, on the verge of living one. He was afraid to open his mouth and screw things up.

"Like what? Your place or mine?" Jesus, talk about lame. This was where she got up and walked out, disgusted by his clumsy attempt at repartee. What the hell was wrong with him? Smooth was his middle name.

Sliding her hands off the table, she placed them at the neckline of her tank before smoothing them lightly down the shirt. The effect was to bring those tiny but perfect tits into gorgeous relief. As he watched, she brushed the tips of her fingers lightly back and forth until the nipples began to crest.

"No, more like, what does that make you want to do?"

Suddenly Steve was choking on his tongue. Heat washed over him. And his dick, already half-way to hard, completed the trip.

"Touch. Taste…suck on them," He sputtered over the words. His hands, he realized to his colossal embarrassment, were stroking the table, as though those tempting peaks were beneath them.

"That sounds nice." She nearly purred as she leaned back a little, sizing him up through slitted eyes. "I think I'd like that, too. But first, I'd like you to do something for me."

Steve stiffly nodded his agreement.

"I need to hear the words, Steve. Say 'Yes, Megan.'"

He was a parrot, reduced to repeating whatever was necessary. Whatever she asked. But at least he knew her name now. "Yes, Megan."

And then she smiled at him and he felt like he'd done something amazing. Steve realized he'd do a lot to earn that smile. "That's perfect. See how easy that was? Now put your hand in your pocket and stroke yourself. I want to see that pretty cock get harder."

Whoa.

"I can't do that in public. I'd be arrested."

"Well, then I guess you'll just have to be careful, so that no one sees but you and me."

He wanted to look around, see who might be watching. This was his home turf. He knew people here, and people knew him. His arm shook a little with the force of holding back the hand that seemed to have a will of its own as it edged toward the pocket of his shorts.

"Steve. Do it now." The steel beneath the velvet of Megan's voice was close to the surface now and he gave up the fight, slipping his hand beneath the table and into the loose pocket of his carpenter's shorts.

The pants were just roomy enough for him to barely reach his cock, where it now stood at attention beneath the baggy drape of the material. He ran his fingers familiarly up its rigid length and saw her eyes flare.

"Mmm, that's nice. I like the way you do that," Megan murmured approvingly. "I think you need to do that for me without the clothes, though. I want to watch you stroke yourself 'til you get so hard a breeze would set you off. Until your balls tighten and you go off like a rocket for me. I'd like that a lot."

Here?

Her eyes felt like a physical touch. Everywhere her gaze moved, Steve felt the tingle and the heat.

"Do it again. I didn't tell you you could stop."

The table must be smaller than he realized if she could see that.

He drew a long, shuddering breath in through his nose as he let his hand go back to making slow sweeps up and down. The barrier of the material kept him from getting any kind of a real grip and the tantalizing barely-there touches were maddening. Steve knew how to touch himself. He'd jacked off hundreds of times. Pleasure, comfort, boredom—they were all good reasons. Knew to the exact degree how much sensation he needed. But this was different. Something about having her eyes on him while he did it made all the difference, had never felt a fraction as good as it had just now. And the thought of being naked in front of her, touching himself—for her—pulled a groan out through his clenched teeth.

"Sssh. We don't want to draw a crowd," Megan chided him softly. "In fact, I think you'd better stop now. I want you to put both hands—that's right—up on the table where I can see them and keep them there. Don't move again until I tell you."

He wanted to rock his hips, push her down on top of his throbbing cock, savor the feel of her tight little pussy for the first time. And he knew just how it would feel. The thought of forcing his way inside her, an inch at a time, danced at the edge of his consciousness.

Steve watched as Megan gathered her papers, putting them neatly into a colored plastic folder. Calling himself ten kinds of dog, Steve peered under the table as she bent to place her belongings next to the wooden bar chair. He was rewarded when her shorts pulled taut across her backside, revealing a heart-shaped ass he instantly coveted.

Megan looked over her shoulder at him and smiled a little at the look she intercepted.

She stood. "I have to go now."

"What!?" His tortured libido screamed in protest. He was on fire for her. "But what about—"

She turned back to him, as calm and collected as though this had been a business consultation and not a… Steve didn't know what the hell it had been. But to leave him in this condition was nothing short of cruel.

"I want you to do two things for me, Steve." Megan adjusted the cap on her head with one hand, smoothing her ponytail with the other. Again she gave him that look that shot straight to his soul. "I want you to think it over tonight. If you liked this, and you think you'd like more, then meet me back here tomorrow night. That's one. Two is, if you do decide to meet me tomorrow, you may not touch yourself between now and then. And don't think you can fool me, because you can't. I'll know."

Picking up her possessions, Megan straightened and her lack of height finally sank in for Steve. The top of her head probably wouldn't even clear his shoulder.

"Have a good night." And she turned and walked out of the bar.

* * *

Megan didn't allow herself to look back. Not even a quick glance as she pulled the door to the street open and walked out into the crisp evening air.

It had been dusk when she had stopped off at Goldie's for a working dinner before she headed home, and it was now full dark as she walked to her truck. Although Christa had plans to buy a 24-foot full-sized truck in a couple of years, Megan gave thanks that the current operation she had taken over consisted of a light duty truck loaded only with coolers. She didn't think she could handle an unfamiliar vehicle of that size in her current condition. While the law wouldn't recognize it, she might as well be drunk. She was that distracted by the man she'd just left.

Megan hadn't touched the beer she'd ordered and she'd barely made a dent in the abomination Goldie's had the nerve to label shepherd's pie. The only shepherd that disaster had been fit for was the four-legged German variety. Not that she'd noticed from the couple of bites she'd managed. As soon as Steve sat down at her table, her appetite for anything other than the man had fled. Just like the blood supply to her brain, she thought miserably.

Unlocking the cab of the truck, Megan unloaded the computer case from her shoulder and flung the rest of the articles weighing her down onto the seat beside her. She spared herself a moment to bang her head against the steering wheel as she contemplated what she had just done.

Stupid, stupid, Megan.

She had no business beginning anything, particularly with someone this close to home. She knew the risks that came with her lifestyle and she knew the rules for safe play. But she had gotten one look at those long legs and that pale copper hair and she'd been a goner. And those eyes. Even as she'd nearly fallen headlong into them, she had known that they were going to break her heart. She could see it coming already and there was not a damn thing she could do about it.

Megan drove home on auto-pilot. She'd grown up in this town, learned to drive on these streets, gotten her first kiss behind the bleachers at the Fourth of July parade. And just like her friend Jacy had known from the time she was twelve that she loved women, Megan had known from an early age that there was something different about her. Even her Barbie and Ken dolls had had a relationship that in today's parlance would be called 'alternative.'

She was what she was and there was no changing that fact. Just like Steve was what he was. Although she'd bet her best ceramic knife he didn't realize it. There had been that slight hesitancy—that sweet hint of confusion she had seen in his eyes—that told Megan that he knew no more than the average Joe about the lifestyle.

Lifestyle.

God, she hated that word. Why couldn't it just be her life? Why couldn't it be different but accepted, like being left-handed or having eyes of two different colors? Dammit, this was exactly why, before deciding to come back to Remington, Megan had also decided she wouldn't be dating any time soon. Dating. Another word she hated.

Why couldn't she just meet a nice man, fall in love, and settle down? More importantly, why was she beating herself up again over things she had realized a long time ago she couldn't change? Megan knew better. She knew why she was alone and likely to stay that way.

Like so many things in life, it was a numbers game.

Start with all the people in the world. And not that if she were stuck on a desert island with just herself and Ashley Judd, she couldn't learn to go the other way—she knew her core preference was for men. So take away the 51% that were women.

Then start factoring in things like age, geographic proximity, sports compatibility, and political beliefs. And before you knew it your choices for available sexual partners were getting slimmer than Lara Flynn Boyle on a hunger strike. Throw in one more little detail like the need to sexually dominate your partner and Megan was living testimony to a lot of lonely Friday nights.

As she was fitting her key into the front door of her half of a duplex, the phone in Megan's purse chirped. Not that she needed Caller ID to tell her who was calling. It was the same person that called every night to make sure she got home okay.

Punching the talk button, Megan juggled her armload of paraphernalia to get the phone to her ear. "I'm home, Christa. You can go to sleep now."

"Har-di-har-har. Very funny—it's only 7:00 o'clock, you ungrateful little butthead."

"Love you too, sis. And I'm fine. I appreciate the concern but you're supposed to be resting and thinking nothing but calm thoughts. Not worrying about your employees."

Having piled the load of gear she had hauled in from the truck onto the table nearest the door, Megan didn't bother to muffle her grunt of relief as she lowered herself down to the sofa.

"You're working yourself too hard, Meg. All you have to do is keep things going for a little while. I'm not looking to put Martha Stewart out of business, okay? So relax a little and ease up."

Megan had never been particularly close to her older sister. Born seven years earlier and the center of their parents' universe, Christa had been content in her role of princess. Megan's arrival had come as a complete shock to everyone, but even more so to the pampered Christa. It hadn't helped that throughout her teen years Christa had persisted in referring to her younger sister as "Oops." But their mutual hostility had gradually softened over the years until lately Megan had even begun thinking of her former nemesis as something of a friend.

"I'm fine. Really. Although, would it have killed you to throw down the extra hundred and fifty bucks it would have cost for power steering on that pig you call a truck? I'm going to have shoulders like a trucker here, soon."

"More like a thousand. And I mean it, Meg. Your day is over after lunch. Hear me? You shouldn't be getting home this late. What, were you shopping for shallots to add to the tuna salad again?"

"Would you believe me if I said I was having drinks in a bar and flirting like mad with the cutest thing in pants I've seen in a long time?" A picture of Steve as he'd looked sitting across from her, stroking his cock at her command floated into Megan's head. She could almost feel the liquid silk of his glorious hair under her hands as she thrust her fingers into it and drew his head down to her soaked pussy. She closed her eyes and sighed at the picture in her mind. Her still unsatisfied cunt began to throb again.

"You lying little bitch, you did not." Her sister paused, no doubt waiting for Megan to laugh and confess she'd been working on new recipes for the business. When she didn't, Christa began to grill her in earnest. "Did you really? Oh, good for you. You go! Who is it? Do I know him? I do, don't I? So tell me, tell me. Come on, I'm dying here. And you said yourself, I'm supposed to stay calm. Tell me before I hyperventilate."

"No way am I telling you anything. It's too early. I don't want to jinx it. Besides, it probably won't turn into anything. You know my luck with men."

Megan read the concern in her sister's tone. "Meggie, I know how you are with advice. But, can I just say, be a little less picky? You've thrown back some keepers over the years. And try being a little more...feminine. No offense, honey, but not too many guys want to fuck an Amazon. You know?"

Chapter Three

"Hey there, big guy. We don't usually see you in here two nights in a row. What's the occasion?"

"Hey, Jace." Steve smiled and called a greeting as he brushed through the swinging doors and into the familiar darkened interior of Goldie's. "Heard you got a new cook. Word is four people ate here last night and not one trip to the ER."

Smiling at Jacy Ralston, general manager of Goldie's, was no hardship. A few years younger than Steve, Jacy was blonde and gorgeous. Nearly as tall as he was, he'd watched her break hearts from the time she'd left grade school.

"Yeah? You know what you can kiss, pal." The attractive blonde smirked back at him from behind the bar, giving her perfect behind a smack. "A big wet one, right here."

"I'm tempted, Ralston. But I've seen that right hook of yours in action." He grinned at her mock indignant look as he turned to scan the main floor of Goldie's. "Besides, I'm meeting someone." Jacy said something about letting her know when he was ready but his attention was already elsewhere, his eyes taking in the various groupings of tables, chairs, and patrons.

Four twenty-something men about his own age, eyes glued to the game on the big screen over the bar. Three couples. Evan again, looking as though he hadn't hooked up with the cute little bank teller after all. There had to be a story to that one. A big group of assorted ages and types—probably coworkers blowing off steam on a Friday night.

Shit.

No petite brunettes looking dangerously underage.

So Megan wasn't here yet. He'd have a beer and sit down to wait. That she was coming he knew in his gut. The Kings game looked close; he could kill some time watching the boys tank another one.

Steve signaled the waitress and sat down at a table with a view of both the TV and the door. He was just sliding his hand around the frosty glass of pilsner when the hair rose on his arms and he felt the crackle of electricity across his skin.

"Can non-basketball fans sit here, too?"

Looking over his shoulder in the direction of that soft alto voice, Steve's gaze caught and tangled with Megan's.

She looked so serious. He wondered what it would take to get her to smile again. Whatever it was, he knew he would do it. He wanted it. Needed it.

"I don't know. I take my roundball pretty seriously. You'd have to promise to at least give it a chance."

As she pursed her lips, thinking it over, Steve took the opportunity to covertly study her. Tonight she'd worn a skirt and the tight denim hugged her subtle curves, while a good ten inches of smooth thigh showed under its brief length. A snug red T-shirt showed off her slender arms and trim waist. Megan turned her head to gaze up at the television consideringly, her ponytail swinging in counterpoint. When she looked back she seemed to have made up her mind about something.

"I like a man with dedication and loyalty. But I don't think basketball will ever win me over. No consideration for the female fan."

Momentarily puzzled, realization suddenly struck. "Oh. Cheerleaders?"

"Worse. Baggy pants," she deadpanned. "Now, football, on the other hand, has a lot to offer."

The glint in her eye said 'Gotcha' as clearly as if she'd spoken the word.

Steve acknowledged the hit. "That is why I never talk sports with a woman. Sit. I can see we have a lot to clear up."

He stood, pulling out a chair with a guilty twinge over not doing it sooner. He could almost feel the imprint of his mother's hand on the back of his head for his bad manners.

As he stood behind Megan, holding her chair, he noticed again how much taller her bearing made her seem. Standing close to her Steve could easily see the top of her head, the way the subdued glow of Goldie's elderly light fixtures brought out gleams of red and mahogany in her hair.

She sat, her manner almost regal. She seemed to take his service as her due.

When Steve had seated himself opposite Megan at the small circular table, he raised a hand to call the waitress. "Something to drink?"

"Just a Coke, thanks. Make it diet." The waitress left and they were alone again. "I'm glad you came. I didn't know if you would."

"Hey, that's supposed to be my line. Besides, I can't believe you get turned down very often."

Steve slid his fingers along the sides of his beer glass, beads of condensation allowing them to slip easily over its curves. It didn't take much to imagine his hands sliding just as easily over Megan's. He knew already that they would be understated and elegant, her skin firm and resilient under his hands. Raising his eyes from where they followed the path his fingers were making on the moist glass, he let her see the heat he knew was there.

He wasn't surprised when Megan didn't respond immediately, instead letting the tension build.

"You might be surprised. It happens." Her gaze continued to hold his, steady and dark—so direct it was like a touch. His dick responded.

The waitress returned with Megan's soft drink, taking her time placing it just so. Steve wasn't sure why tonight was different, but he couldn't recall the staff at Goldie's ever putting so much emphasis on presentation. She left finally and the tension, momentarily forestalled, began to build again.

"So, did you have a chance to think about it last night, Steve?" Megan watched him even as she lowered her head to take a sip of her Diet Coke. Her tongue lingered on the straw just long enough to make him wonder if it was deliberate.

"Yeah, I did." He smiled. "Once or twice."

"That's good. And since you're here, I hope that means you're interested in exploring a little more tonight."

It was all too fucking unbelievably good to be real. His cock was rising to full attention and he could barely think to form words. "Oh yeah. Definitely. More." Steve reached for her hand, but she drew back, only slightly out of reach.

"Good."

Wordlessly Megan stood and Steve stood up with her. With an offer like that on the table he was sticking close on her tail. Picking up a small backpack purse he hadn't noticed, she brushed past him, heading toward Goldie's back door. So casually it might have been accidental, her hand brushed his fly, where his burgeoning erection tented the front of his shorts. A bolt of lust so powerful it nearly brought him to his knees blasted through him.

Momentarily stunned, by the time he could piece together a coherent thought Megan was halfway to the door. As he caught up to her, she gave him that smile that made him feel like he could stop a speeding train or leap tall buildings in a single bound.

"Ready?"

* * *

Down, girl.

Megan reminded herself for what felt like the tenth time that night to slow down. If it was meant to be, it would happen. But it might happen a week from now, or even a month. There was no need to inhale him like a rich dessert that might be whisked away before she'd had a chance to indulge. She needed to get a better grip on herself before the evening spun completely out of control.

But he was so completely incredible.

Taking the last turn before the back door that led outside to Goldie's overflow parking area, Megan paused to unhook the chain guarding a small, inconspicuous staircase. She barely glanced at the metal sign hanging from it announcing to the public that it was for staff use only. Megan palmed the key she'd pulled from her pocket and glanced back at the man following her, careful to keep her inspection brief.

Being two steps below her on the stairs put Steve's head just slightly below hers. A flash of upraised eyebrows told her he'd never been up here before. Good. Megan didn't like the twinge of something uncomfortably like jealousy that flashed through her at the thought.

This might be something or it might be nothing—it was too soon to tell.

The early signs were good, though. His energy had called to her from the first second she'd spotted him across the room last night. He made her heart beat faster and her blood pound in her veins. Something in the way he moved and talked and looked roused the Domina in her. Like a tree in spring, she could feel the Domme force in her rising. She was flooded with a sense that had been dormant so long she had begun to question herself.

"I didn't know this was up here. What is it?"

"The old manager's office. Jacy doesn't use it much—too far away from the floor. She said we could borrow it."

"How long have you known Jacy? And how is that we've never met?"

Megan stepped into the room and felt for the light switch. Jacy had given her the key and shown her the room earlier that day. The room was small, measuring probably twelve by twelve, and, like the bar below it, had been built in the 1800's. Unlike the public sections of the building, the little manager's office had been allowed to age naturally, if ungracefully.

The desk alone occupied close to nine square feet, its large surface area unadorned save for a banker's lamp and a desk calendar three years out of date. A bookcase containing old ledgers as well as a motley collection of paperback books, two mismatched chairs, and a black Naugahyde sofa so old it was the last word in retro cool were the extent of the room's furnishings.

"I don't know. It does seem strange. I've been asking myself the same question. A while, though. Since about junior high." Pulling her backpack off her shoulder, Megan shoved a hand inside it, fishing for her phone. After calling up its phone book, she handed it to Steve. "Would you mind ordering the pizza? Number four on the pre-sets. I'll eat anything except bell peppers. Tell them to have it here in exactly one hour."

When Megan looked up Steve was just standing there, phone in hand, looking at her. This could be it—when he told her what he thought and where she could get off. Before slamming the door on his way out.

She hadn't expected the moment of truth so soon.

Megan stilled. Blue-green eyes searched hers for...what? What did he see when he looked at her? An unnatural freak? Or a strong woman who could do things for him no one else could?

"Sounds like you know what you want."

"You're right. I do." Deciding it was best to get everything out in the open, Megan let what she was feeling show on her face. She let her eyes roam over him, from that glorious fall of bad boy hair, down strong shoulders and muscular torso, all balanced on long, tanned runner's legs. "And if you do, too, after you've ordered our pizza you'll take off your shirt and sit in one of those chairs."

Eyes kindled and nostrils flared, as though he were trying to catch the scent of her. Steve looked away long enough to find the number on the unfamiliar telephone and press the appropriate buttons. After ordering a large anchovy and onion, he ended the call and handed the telephone back to her. Except for the time necessary to dial the phone, he hadn't taken his eyes off hers during the call.

"Anchovies? That's taking a little bit of a chance, don't you think?"

It was a ballsy move and she was inwardly thrilled. A lot of men would have opted for something plain and non-offensive. The fact that he'd taken a risk kicked her pulse up a notch. She kept her face neutral as he pulled a chair away from the wall with one hand and reached for the top button of his shirt with the other.

His fingers slid the buttons from their fastenings quickly and efficiently. Not a lot of show, just taking care of business, which was fine for a first time. If things went the way Megan hoped, there would be plenty of time for slow, teasing strips and leisurely bindings later.

Completely unbuttoned, Steve parted the material with both hands and shrugged out of it. As he did so, his back arched slightly with the movement, thrusting his well-defined pecs forward, displaying two flat male nipples pierced with small horizontal barbells.

Megan allowed a small tilt of her lips to signal her approval. He was beautiful to look at, with a dusting of red-gold hair tapering down to a small trail that arrowed toward a taut belly lightly cobbled with muscle.

"Nice," she encouraged. "Now lose the shirt and sit."

Hesitating a little first, Steve tossed the shirt on the sofa and sat down slowly in the wooden chair he'd selected. He sank down, his legs widening naturally to give himself room, watching her as he went.

"Not bad. We can work on speed later. I want you to reach your hands through the back of the chair and clasp them behind you. And hook your feet on the outsides of the legs. Do it now, Steve."

She kept her tone calm and even, but with the ring of authority. Megan could tell he was doing things he'd never done before. Intellect warred with instinct and the battle showed clearly on his face. His body recognized the call and wanted to comply. But a lifetime of conditioning fought his natural impulse to obey.

The chair looked like a '40's era office chair, heavy and armless, with slats evenly spaced across the back. The openings looked just wide enough for a man of Steve's size to be able to slip his hands through. Megan admired the play of muscle across his chest as he did, the small movements of his metal-pierced nipples drawing her eye like a magnet and making her teeth and lips itch in anticipation.

Reaching once again into her backpack, Megan retrieved an envelope. She pulled the remaining chair in front of Steve, just out of reach were he to change his mind and pull his arms from where they rested behind him. Megan removed the contents of the envelope and sat down.

"Before we get started, we need to go over a few rules first."

Chapter Four

Rules?

What the hell was that all about?

Steve was puzzled as hell. And more turned on than he could ever remember being before. Turned on. Shit. He was practically panting with anticipation. He'd been stiff as a lead pipe since Megan's hand had 'accidentally' brushed his fly. And like mercury on a hot day, he'd risen with the heat.

She was sitting just out of reach, holding a business-sized envelope. The way it bulged told him it held more than just a single sheet of paper. The hands that held the packet were neat with short, unpolished nails. The eyes that looked down momentarily were equally free of enhancements. Her clothes were nothing special, either. So why did he find her the most attractive woman he'd ever met?

The whole package that Megan presented looked wholesome and clean. Good enough to eat. Steve moved his hands, gripping the chair to keep himself from reaching for her.

He wanted to dive into her. Bury his head between her legs and eat her sweet little pussy until she came, screaming his name.

And he could do it, too. If only she'd let him.

A grin breaking through at the thought, Steve was momentarily distracted from the matter of the envelope and the papers they held. It took the dry flick of Megan opening the envelope to draw him back.

She unfolded the mass. "I want you to have these. They're copies of my driver's license, my work information..." She peeled pages off the stack, coolly efficient as she ticked them off. "And a summary of my last physical. Here, go ahead and take them. You should look them over."

Steve unwound his hands from the back of the chair to take what Megan was holding out to him.

The driver's license told him she was older than she looked. Twenty-five to his own twenty-eight. He'd bet that baby face got her carded any place they didn't know her, though. The W-2 form was dated less than six months ago and showed her to be an employee of Bonner Food Service, d.b.a. "Christa's Catering." The health summary was printed on letterhead from a major health plan in San Francisco, declaring Megan Mussina to be healthy and negative for any sexually transmitted diseases.

"We won't do much tonight. I'd like to see the same information from you first."

He might have thought it was a joke—something Megan had been put up to by his older brother Rick. But one look in her burnt chocolate eyes told him she was stone cold serious.

"What the fuck is this? You've got me hot as hell, lady. But I've gotta tell you, this is the weirdest fu—first date I've ever had."

God knew he'd done a lot in the name of getting laid. Steve had been shoe shopping. Been grilled by suspicious fathers. And he'd been dragged to more chick films than he could come close to remembering, let alone name. But he'd never—ever—been stripped half-naked and asked to submit paperwork.

"What is this? A date or a job interview?"

"Mmm. How about a little of both?" She didn't fidget or drum her fingers. The woman who looked back at him had the kind of calm he associated with surgeons and fighter pilots.

"It's also about safety. And trust. And maybe the most intense sexual experience of your life. But you've got to trust your partner. And know that, no matter what, you're safe. There are a lot of nutballs out there and bad things can happen. So I want you to know who you're dealing with. Just like I want to know who I'm dealing with. Anyone who isn't willing to give you that should make you walk away in a heartbeat."

Steve couldn't help the shout of laughter that erupted at that last bit.

"Ha! About the worst thing that I can imagine happening would be not getting to fuck you blind. If that's what we're talking about, show me where to sign, sweet thing. I am more than ready."

"I'm serious about this, Steve. And you'd better be, too. If you don't feel what I feel—and I'm talking some pretty incredible chemistry here—that's okay. No harm, no foul. We walk away right now. Because nothing is more important than safety. If you can't live with that, we'll just say good night and goodbye."

A knee-jerk rejection to the idea arose in him and Steve opened his mouth to protest. But whatever he was going to say was squelched in an instant with one look from Megan.

"Stop." She silenced him. "Before you say anything, stop. And think. Think about what you want."

He felt the weight of her words press down on them both. The seconds of silence spun out between them as Steve did as she directed. He wasn't sure exactly what he was supposed to be thinking about, though. He knew he wanted her. Wanted her with a fierceness he couldn't recall feeling for any other woman and didn't pretend to understand. He wanted to drive himself into her, over and over. Take her. Make her his.

A series of pictures of the two of them sprang fully-formed into his head. One after another, like a series of stop-action photos, they flashed across his mind.

Both naked. Sweaty. Limbs tangled. Two bodies so hot you could feel the steam rise off them. Droplets of moisture running down her torso. One hand grips her pussy, thumb on her clit. Another hand holds her ass, driving her down on his rampant cock. Her head thrown back as she comes, screaming his name. Back arched, frozen in time, her hands clutch his chest. She slumps forward along his body, limp and satisfied from something only he could give her. A contented—okay, smug— grin breaks across his face.

Steve pulled himself back mentally from the scene playing out in his mind. He wasn't sure exactly what Megan was asking him. What she expected from him. But he knew he couldn't live with himself as a man if he backed away from her challenge. And that's exactly what it had been.

He looked that unflinching gaze square in the eye. "Okay. We'll do it your way. Because babe, you haven't got what I can't take. Where do I sign?"

* * *

Megan watched the struggle resolve itself inside the man in the chair and savored the thrill that rolled over her. She'd won and she knew it.

A lot of men would have flipped her off, verbally if not physically, on their way out the door by now. She knew because it had happened more than once. It happened sometimes that a man responded to the particular energy Megan knew she projected. Only to find that when it came right down to it, he couldn't give up control.

Megan didn't blame them. She knew what she was asking ran counter to every bit of cultural training they'd ever learned in their lives. Even the ones she could sense had a powerful need to surrender. Sometimes the fear was greater. Fear of the unknown. Fear of what it meant to their image of themselves as a man. Fear of what their friends would think if they found out.

"Good." A smile broke slowly over her face as, at last, she let herself enjoy the moment. It was always a little like the first dance with a new partner and Megan luxuriated in the feeling. As powerful, as erotic, as a first kiss, the first time a new partner submitted was a special rush no roller coaster could duplicate.

Although it was doubtful Steve realized it, he had just placed himself completely in her hands.

"Tonight we'll play a little. But mostly we'll just talk. We'll get to know each other a little bit. I want you to sit in the chair and tell me what you like. And what you don't like."

Blue-green eyes looked back at her while her fingers itched to run themselves through that incredible hair that drew her like an irresistible magnet. To keep herself from reaching for him, Megan leaned forward in her chair and sat on her hands.

"Unzip your pants for me. I want to see that pretty cock I know you've got in there." A shiver of anticipation ran down her spine at the thought. Megan had imagined it, and she was ready to reward herself with her first good look at him. Steve's hands moved slowly to his fly—too slowly for her taste. Besides, it was time begin. "Now, Steve!"

Both hands reached for the snap; the left popping the button free while the right lowered the zipper in one smooth tug.

"Now show me." No underwear impeded his progress as Steve shoved aside the now open fly of his shorts. The cock that sprang free was thick and long, its head already flushed purple. So beautiful. Megan wanted to fall to her knees and worship its silken perfection. "Nice. Wrap your hands through the back of the chair again and let's have that talk."

"Lady, you are definitely something else." But he did as she said, inserting his arms through the chair's wide slats and gripping the seat behind.

"Thank you."

"I'm not so sure that was a compliment."

"I am." She couldn't sit still another second. She had to move before the energy building inside her exploded. Controlling her movements through sheer grit, Megan stood slowly. Making sure Steve's eyes were on her, she crossed her hands and gripped the hem of her shirt, pulling it slowly over her head. When his shoulders bunched, as though preparing to release his grip on the chair and launch himself at her, Megan stopped him with a shake of her head. "Ah-ah."

Bracing her legs, Megan reached around behind her back to release the catch of her bra. She wasn't overly-endowed on top and didn't really need to wear one, but the ceremony was important. Men loved that sort of thing and it was important to keep his attention focused, so she drew the moment out.

The red lace she'd chosen especially for the occasion came off without a hitch. Not that her modest curves were anything to brag about.

Except for the rasp of their breathing it was so quiet in the room that, for the first time, Megan was aware of sounds from the bar filtering up through the floor. It was Friday and it sounded like Goldie's had a full house, the whiskey-rough voice of Melissa Etheridge belting one out a signal that Jacy was in charge downstairs.

"You like doing that. Don't you?" His voice was raw with desire. In that moment Steve was any woman's wet-dream. Big, half-naked and wanting her.

"Taking my bra off? Yeah, I do. I hate 'em. I wore it as a special gesture. You should feel honored."

"No. Controlling the action. Making me sweat."

"Don't worry, baby. I'll make sure you have a good time. Just trust me to take good care of you." Megan smiled as she dropped the scrap of lace and stepped in close to him. She stepped between his widespread legs, his breath gusting warmly over her bare breasts. Megan reached around behind his head to find the elastic band that held his ponytail and quickly pulled it free. She dropped it without another thought, impatient to finally—*finally*—touch that amazing hair.

Thrusting both hands greedily into the silky depths, Megan used it as a grip, tugging Steve's head forward to her breast. The contrasting sensations of cool silk in her hands and hot mouth on her breast wrenched a groan from her. Steve didn't waste any time as he latched on, easily drawing her nipple deep into the moist paradise of his mouth.

His tongue laved the soft underside of her breast, while his teeth grated lightly over her skin. Unleashed from its confinement, his hair slid like heavy satin through her hands, the citrus scent of his shampoo underlain by his own unique scent invading her nostrils. Irresistibly drawn, Megan lowered her nose to Steve's head, drawing the intoxicating scent deeper into her lungs.

Surrounded by him on all sides, the heat of his big body, the strength in his long runner's legs, the power of his broad shoulders—all at her command—thrilled her. The mouth drawing hard on her flesh was making her toes curl. She wanted all of him and she wanted him now.

"Easy there, big fella." Using that sinfully seductive hair as a control again, Megan tugged firmly on it, pulling his mouth away before she lost her mind. It half killed her, but she made herself release the handfuls of hair she'd been gripping like a drowning woman. His lips were slick with the same moisture that clung to her nipple and Megan had a sudden, powerful urge to see them bruised and full from her kisses.

Without breaking his gaze, she reached down between them for his neglected cock. Wrapping a hand around as much of it as she could, Megan gave it a preliminary stroke.

"Tell me a fantasy, Steve. What's the hottest thing you've never done?"

Chapter Five

It was heaven.

It was pure fucking torture.

It was the hottest thing he'd ever done.

And neither one of them was even naked yet. It took a few seconds for the meaning of her words to work their way through the fog of lust that shrouded his brain. She'd asked a question. And she expected an answer.

"You. I want to fuck you."

As soon as the words had left his mouth, Steve wanted to call them back. He could read the disappointment on Megan's face. Shit. He needed to get this right.

Usually he was the smooth one with women. Ever since he was a kid he'd been next in line behind his brother. Taller, stronger, bigger—Rick had attracted women by just existing. Steve had had to learn to compete, and he'd done it with charm. By the time he'd reached high school he could talk a girl into his car and out of her panties. But just when it mattered most, his entire lifetime's supply of smooth had deserted him. It probably had something to do with one small hand wrapped around his cock.

"We'll get to that." His pulse skyrocketed at her words, spoken so matter-of-factly. "But I want to find out more about you first. You must have some fantasies. Tell me a fantasy."

As she talked Megan resumed stroking him, one hand on his dick, the other tracing circles on his chest. The hand holding his cock slid authoritatively toward the end and a thumb pressed sharply into the tip. His moan of pleasure was strangled at birth as Megan's other hand pinched a nipple. Ever since he'd had them pierced they'd been extra sensitive—almost an electric connection to his cock—and the twin sensations brought him up off the chair.

Or would have if Megan hadn't countered his movement by bracing a hand against his chest and squeezing harder on his cock.

"Easy there, big fella. Here..." Releasing her grip on his rigid flesh, Megan stepped back. "I'll stop distracting you and let you concentrate. How's that?"

Letting her hand trail over his arm and shoulder, she moved around him. Never completely out of contact, Megan now stood directly behind him. His hands still pushed through the back of the chair, Steve stretched his fingers, instinctively seeking her flesh. Whether by accident or design, he could just nearly skim the smooth skin of her thigh with his fingertips.

Megan's hands moved to his head again, fingers grazing his scalp, and began sifting rhythmically through his hair, tugging with an erotically firm touch. A shiver raced up his spine, reached across his shoulders and circled his head, as her hands again and again combed from crown to shoulders.

"I have no intention of repeating myself, Steve. I'm waiting."

It might have been accidental, but Megan's use of his name was accompanied by a tug so sharp his eyes watered. As another shiver swept his body his cock gave a corresponding twitch. How could he be expected to answer questions when he burned so hot for her he wasn't sure he could still form words?

"I'll just go sit over there and give you a minute to think."

"God, no!" He amazed himself that he was able to squeeze out that much. "Don't stop."

As fingers slowly raked his scalp again, Steve's eyes closed in pleasure and the floor tilted. Or maybe he was the one leaning. Either way it felt so damn good he'd say just about anything to keep her hands on him. Waves of sensation washed over him as magic hands alternately tugged and soothed. A thought nagged at the edge of his consciousness and he tried to focus. But the sense of well-being that flooded all the empty places inside him effectively shut down everything else.

He could no more form words than he could fly. Except he was flying. Steve floated on the wash of sensation. Until his nagging conscience overtook him with the awareness that the sizzle of warmth that had surrounded him was gone. He was floating in his bubble alone now.

And with his next breath the bubble was gone.

Reluctantly, Steve opened his eyes to see Megan standing over him, her expression unreadable. As he mentally searched for the cause of her displeasure, he had a moment's panic when he realized she was no longer touching him. How to get her back?

He held his breath and blurted the next thought that popped into his head. "Two women. At once."

Began to breathe again when she responded. "And?"

"And they're both really into it. Really want it. They want it bad—from me." The words began slowly, but picked up momentum as Steve described the half-formed idea taking shape in his head. "I take care of them both. One with my mouth. One with my dick. It's so fucking good. The best they've ever had. They can't believe it."

He stumbled a bit over the last word, half-expecting to be whacked upside the head for letting her see what pig he was deep down.

"Mmm, yeah. That's a classic." Megan didn't seem upset, though. Or disgusted. Just the opposite, in fact. "And you probably wouldn't fight too hard if one of them was a bi-racial underwear model, either. Would you?"

"I'd tough it out."

"You're so brave. I'm in awe." The lightest touch, so light Steve couldn't be sure it was there, brushed his forehead. "So, what else?"

"What else? You want more?"

"Oh yeah." Coming close again, Megan hiked up her skirt with one hand, using the other for balance. Then slowly, heart-stoppingly slowly, she lowered herself across his knees. "I want to hear what else you fantasize about." Releasing her skirt, she once again wrapped her hand around his cock.

"Shit. Like I can think about anything but your hand on my dick right now."

"Really? So this is working for you?" Using both hands now, Megan began to slowly pump him, fingers rolling over his flesh like a constricting python. *So fucking good!* She was killing him. But what a way to go. "Has anyone ever tied you down?"

Sitting on his lap the way she was, their eyes were about even. Hers were such a dark brown, almost black, that her pupils were nearly swallowed up by them.

"No."

"Ever thought about it?" Another double pump of his cock had him groaning his denial.

"Huh-uh."

"You can't lie to me, Steve. I've got the ultimate lie-detector in my hands and it says you *have* thought about it."

Sure enough, his dick gave an involuntary twitch. His gut clenched and he could see himself tied down. At her mercy as she took her pleasure from his body. His cock.

Someone moaned and her mouth slammed down on his in a wet, devouring kiss. Steve opened to her, tried to inhale her, their tongues tangling wildly. The hot mouth that meshed with his took no prisoners. The hands working his helpless dick were merciless. He couldn't fight the feelings as he was lashed between the brutal pleasures of her fingers and mouth.

Megan's body shifted and the burning moist heat of her pussy brushed the base of his shaft. God, he wanted inside of her! It would finish him off, but he wanted it. Needed it.

He wasn't going to get it. The irresistible rhythm of his cock inside the prison of her fingers pushed him to the edge of a towering cliff. And then over.

*　*　*

This is not love.

You are not in love. It's way too soon. What you're feeling is the result of hormones and chemistry. And the fact that you haven't gotten off with anything that wasn't powered by Duracell in over a year.

Still hadn't, for that matter.

Megan looked again at the face before her and pondered the unknown. What were the odds that someone so responsive, so intense, so *perfect* for her had been placed in her path? What were the odds that someone like him even existed? And living in her own little podunk town. She wouldn't have believed it herself if she hadn't just experienced the unexplainable. Steve was every Domme's most un-secret dream brought to life in every exquisite detail.

No, that wasn't true. Not every Domme's.

But definitely this one's.

Megan was ready to swear that he'd slipped into sub-space for a few minutes there. And she doubted he even realized it. Probably didn't even know what it was. Which made what an incredible natural he was that much more amazing.

"Are you all right?" Her voice sounded husky and awkward to her own ears. What had passed between them was powerful and she wasn't ashamed to admit she was a little shaken. And more than a little touched.

Opening his eyes slowly, it took Steve a few moments to focus on her. His gaze had the dazed look of someone who'd had too much to drink.

"Yeah. I'm good." His eyes closed again briefly until he roused himself with a noticeable jerk. "Wrecked, but good."

Reaching into her back pocket, Megan removed the clean handkerchief she had placed there while dressing for her date.

Her plan for the evening had been a loose one and she hadn't been certain whether she would need it or not. But what might as easily have served as a blindfold became not just a matter of good manners, but an expression of caretaking. And tenderness.

She took the square of soft, white cloth with its edging of old lace and gently wiped away the sticky semen that covered her fingers and Steve's cock. She couldn't resist a last, fond caress as she returned it to its resting place behind the placket of his carpenter's shorts. Her aching cunt clenched in regret, as though it knew it wouldn't be making the acquaintance of that magnificent specimen tonight. Her clit throbbed in time to the blood that still pounded in her veins. Her head told her she wouldn't die from frustration. But the hollow core of her that continued to pulse in readiness wasn't so sure.

"You were...amazing." Steve looked back at her and it tugged at Megan's heart to see the doubt in them. "I can see you've never had anyone who appreciated how special you are. You're incredible."

As if of their own accord, her lips had eased closer to his, her breath whispering across Steve's. It was the most natural thing in the world to close the distance and press her lips to his tenderly.

It felt like a first kiss.

Whereas before their mouths had clashed in a ritual of passion and claiming, this was a breathtakingly gentle meeting. Megan's tongue stroked the seam of Steve's lips in feather-light brushes. But something was missing.

"Put your arms around me, Steve. I want to feel you holding me."

Faster than she would have thought possible he untangled his hands from the back of the chair and strong arms clamped around her waist and back. Megan responded in kind, wrapping her own arms around Steve's neck. His kiss somehow caught her by surprise, but it felt completely right to angle her head to meet him and take the kiss deeper.

The kiss went on, tongues stroking, lips tasting, until Megan realized she had begun to rock her hips against him. The white-hot encounter just ended might have brought Steve some relief, but it had created quite the opposite condition in Megan. And clamor though her body might for a long, hard ride, her mind understood that she had to stick to her plan. She needed to cool things down, not heat them back up again.

Breaking away, Megan drew a long, steadying breath. "We'd better stop there for now."

"Stop? I don't think so. I finally got my hands on you and I've got a whole laundry list of things I want to do with you."

Steve's hair was still mussed from Megan's fingers. The light glinted off the golden barbells through his nipples and drew her eye. But the slow, thorough exploration of his body that she had planned would have to wait. Rules and cautions existed for a reason. They were there for everyone's protection. No matter how she might ache to roll those flat, male nipples through her teeth while she tormented his luscious cock—moving too fast would only endanger them both.

"Good. We can compare lists, then, because I have plans for you, too. Later. After you get me those papers." She paused as she climbed slowly off the large lap where she'd been so comfortable. "Besides, looks like our pizza is right on time."

* * *

"You did *what?!*"

"Jeez, Jacy. You could call dogs with that shriek." Megan glanced around the Motherlode Diner, trying to judge how many of the morning's customers were reacting to her friend's cackle. It was hard to tell how many were looking because of the volume and pitch of Jacy's yell and how many were staring because that's what people always did when Jacy was around.

Wondering for the two-thousandth time what life must be like for the six-foot-tall, blonde, model-gorgeous ones in life, Megan realized the description could just as well describe the man she'd been with last night. She realized she liked the phrase 'been with' in relation to Steve and let it roll around her mind. There was something a little bit illicit and a whole lot thrilling about it. It had been a long time since she'd been with anyone for anything more than a casually social evening.

She'd had dinner with Evan Coughlin once, but they'd been more passionate about their respective businesses than each other. She loved ice skating and she'd gone out for drinks with an ex-pro hockey player she'd met at the rink. He was a nice enough guy, and Megan had enjoyed skating with him and listening to the stories of his playing days with the Vancouver Canucks. But there'd been no spark on her side and she'd let him down as gently as she knew how when he'd pressed for more.

"Girl, you did *not*. Tell me you did not stick your fingers up your pussy and paint his cheeks with your...your 'dew.'"

"Okay. Have it your way. I didn't." Megan toyed with her coffee cup, spinning it in place in its saucer to give her hands something to do. What she had done last night with Steve in the office above Goldie's had felt as natural as breathing. Like hearing music you hadn't heard in years or remembering the steps of a dance you had once known by heart. Being with Steve had felt effortless. After the first couple of hesitant steps, they had danced together like they'd done it a hundred times before.

But from the minute she'd closed the door to her little Toyota hybrid, leaving Steve to watch her pull away, Megan had begun second-guessing herself. What if she'd gone too fast and freaked him out? He'd never been dommed before, she could tell. His actions were too awkward and hesitant. She'd bet any amount of currency that he knew nothing about Dominant/submissive relationships.

"Oh my God, did you really? You actually striped his cheeks like a bad '60's TV Indian? You are something else, girl. You know that?"

Megan looked up in time to see her friend's eyes stray toward the door. The bells above it tinkled as an elderly couple left. Looking from Jacy to the door and back again, Megan responded. "Yeah, I get that a lot." From the corner of her eye Megan saw her old friend Evan walk in and take a seat at the counter and Jacy's million-dollar smile dimmed by a few thousand megawatts. Curiouser and curiouser. "Maybe I wanted him to have something to remember me by. So sue me."

"So. You and Steve Eriksson." Her friend picked up the thread of the conversation again. "I never would have predicted that. You're so big city and he's so...so Remington."

"Meaning?"

"Meaning... I don't know what it means, Megan. Okay, I guess what I'm saying is, I don't see what the attraction is. I see what your attraction is for him. You're my friend and you're beautiful and smart and interesting. But Steve? Oh, sure, he's got the long hair and the great bod and he's a partner in his own company but... Hey, when I put it like that *I* might even be interested." Jacy's grin was back full-power now.

"Forget it. He's taken. Besides, you play for the other team. Remember?"

Chapter Six

Steve stepped out of the shower and glanced at the clock on the bathroom sink. With numbers so large they were easy to see even without his contact lenses in, the clock read 5:10. He had twenty minutes before Megan was due to arrive. Toweling himself off, he stepped into the bedroom, giving it one last visual inspection. He had finally convinced her to come to his place for the evening and he had high hopes for the bedroom later.

Pulling on a clean pair of shorts, Steve glanced around the room. While he didn't figure he'd get tapped for any magazine spreads, he liked to think it was a step above the usual bachelor dump. He'd spent enough years bunking with Rick before Dad's construction business had taken off to appreciate his own space, and he'd put some time and money into it.

The bed was a pine California King and Steve liked being able to lie in the middle of it and not be able to feel an edge. He'd even overcome his embarrassment enough to ask the sales girl to help pick out the colors for the bedding. Being color-blind, he didn't trust himself not to pick something that would make the first woman he brought over run screaming. And asking his mom just seemed too pathetic.

He wasn't a pig, but he wasn't anal about cleaning, either. He'd been around enough women in his life, though, to know that most of them put a higher priority on things like an absence of dirty underwear on the floor than most men did. Maybe it came from working in the construction industry, but Steve figured he was at least partially responsible for Oro County's perpetual water shortage. He was addicted to showers. He *had* to take one when he got home from a job—the dirt and the grime on his skin that came with working in, under, and around old houses made his skin crawl. He'd been known to take another one in the morning, as well.

Cutting his hair would probably be a time saver, but he hadn't been able to bring himself to do it for a couple of years at least. Chalking it up to laziness and a dislike of change, Steve realized that it had all been for a reason the instant Megan had slid her hands into it, though. He closed his eyes and let the memory wash over him, like he had at least a dozen times a day since. The prickle of awareness, the way the tiny hairs on the back of his neck lifted, the blood that rushed to his cock. It all felt *so freaking good* it was almost better than sex. Almost.

From thinking about her hands in his hair it was only a small jump to think about Megan's hands on his cock.

Shit. He'd never get things ready on time at this rate. Steve could just imagine Megan walking in on him fisting his cock. And explaining that he'd been fantasizing about her sounded even worse.

He combed his hair quickly, leaving it to dry in the still-warm evening air while he pulled on his favorite blue and gold

Hawaiian shirt. Besides liking the colors, it had the advantage of not fitting too tightly. The piercings that felt so amazing during sex could be a dead give-away in a snug knit shirt. He figured Megan would have enough clues about how turned on he was. There was no need to advertise it.

Involved in pulling the take out containers from the oven where they'd been keeping warm, Steve nearly didn't hear the knock on the door. Trying not to look too eager, the anticipation building in his system all week nearly boiled over when he pulled the door open and saw her.

Megan, while technically still on his doorstep, was leaning over the railing—peering into his living room window. The short sundress she wore rode up the backs of her toned thighs, a brief few inches of flowered material blocked his view of heaven, while what he now recognized as her favorite blue backpack hung from one tanned shoulder.

"Hey, there. If you want the tour, come on in."

She turned, smiling her rare smile that never failed to turn him inside-out. "Hey, yourself. I was about to give up. If you didn't want me to come over, all you had to do was say so."

"Fu— uh, hell, uh, I mean..." Suddenly his tongue wanted to do anything but form words. "No. Absolutely I wanted you to come over. Come on. I'll show you around." He stood to one side, motioning Megan in.

She walked in and something primitive turned over in Steve's chest. She was in his home. He'd had women over before, of course. But this felt different. He wanted her to like where he lived. He wanted her to be comfortable here. He knew instantly that he would be taking mental note of her reactions to everything. What she liked and didn't like. He'd never much cared one way or the other what a woman thought about his place. But he sure as hell cared this time.

"Mmm. Smells good. What's cooking?"

"I picked up dinner from Mama Rosa's. Lasagna and fettuccini Alfredo. Everybody loves lasagna. And fettuccini in case you don't eat meat."

They were standing close. It would take only the smallest hint from Megan and he would fold himself around her. He'd always been partial to tall, leggy girls before Megan. But he thought she might have permanently changed his preference now. He liked the feeling of being physically larger. Her protector.

"You're talking to a chef. The only thing chefs like more than cooking is eating. There's not much I don't eat. Hey, this is nice. Did you have help decorating?" Megan did a slow turn and Steve tried not to grin like an idiot. It was stupid. All she'd done was compliment him on his furniture and he felt like he'd just won a major award.

They were in the hallway, with a good view of the living room and dining area. The entertainment center dominated the living room, with the big flat-screen TV and kick ass stereo. He might have gone a little overboard on it but, hey, he liked sports. He liked being able to see the droplets of sweat flying off the athletes in high-definition. So what? He didn't have to answer to anyone. If he wanted to spend big bucks on state-of-the-art electronics, he would.

"You mocking my he-man clubhouse?"

"I wouldn't dream of it."

"Good. You'd better not be playing with me. A man doesn't appreciate having his big-screen mocked."

Megan's eyelashes made a slow sweep downward before eyes like bittersweet chocolate flicked him with a sidelong glance. "Oh, I'll play with you, all right..."

Time shifted into slow motion. The measured beat of his heart echoed in Steve's ears, while the breath he'd been drawing skidded to a halt at the back of his throat. He had the eerie sensation of his blood halting its flow through his veins.

Only his eyes moved, and they locked on Megan's—

"...later. Let's eat first. I'm Starvin' Marvin."

* * *

Megan had purposely kept things light while they'd eaten their food. Although they had met twice since their evening at Goldie's, this was their first real 'date.'

The two times she had seen Steve since that night—once to get the papers and once for lunch—had both been at the restoration project his company had going. It hadn't been hard to rearrange the lunch truck's route to end up in the neighborhood of the old Swann mansion, with its large white and green sign proclaiming it "Another Quality Restoration by Eriksson and Sons" boldly planted out front.

Megan had never understood the appeal of other women's fascination with construction workers. But after walking in on Steve stripped to the waist, a light sheen of sweat highlighting the ridges and valleys of his lean musculature, she was learning. He had been stretching for some wires just barely within reach and then pulling them through a hole in the plaster wall. Watching him standing up on his toes, arms outstretched, Megan had spent a delightful thirty seconds imagining the rest of his clothing gone, his arms tied. She decided she would let him leave the boots on.

The meetings had served a purpose, though, giving them both an opportunity think and evaluate. Strong as the attraction was, it was important to find out if they liked each other aside from their obvious physical compatibility. Did they like each other for who they were? Was the other person someone they would like to spend time with in the outside world? Megan often thought that dating in the D/s community was a lot like dating in the so-called vanilla world. The characteristics sought, like honesty and integrity, were the same. There were just a few bonus questions at the end of the questionnaire.

While she couldn't speak for what Steve felt, Megan was positively smitten. Not only was he so close to her physical ideal that the differences didn't matter, but he was a good guy. He held down a responsible job. Spoke of his family with obvious affection. He probably even helped little old ladies across the street.

Like right now, for instance. He was picking up the plates they'd eaten their dinner off of.

Megan called his name and he looked up. "Yeah?

"Steve, you're scaring me. I'll tell you right now—if you rinse off those plates and put them in the dishwasher I'm walking out of here."

He actually stopped what he was doing. "Why?"

"Because it's unnatural and it's freaking me out, that's why."

He grinned. "But is it impressing you? I'll go back to burping and scratching my nuts as soon as I'm sure of you."

Rising from the beautiful oak table Steve had confessed over dinner to having made, Megan moved around it until she stood in front of him, inches away. Reaching out, she gripped him through the denim of his shorts, squeezing a handful of his cock and balls.

When she knew she had his attention, she softly gave him his orders. "You'll do exactly what you're told, Steven. You'll start by licking my pussy until I tell you to stop." His eyes widened and his breathing hitched erratically, whether from excitement or pain Megan couldn't be sure. "And if you're very good, I might—and I stress *'might'*—allow you to come, too."

Let the games begin.

* * *

Thankfully it was a big table and Steve had already cleared most of the debris of their dinner, because Megan had plans for it. Made of hundred-year-old oak salvaged from one of his jobs, Steve had shared the story of its origins during dinner. But, more important than its provenance, the legs looked sturdy enough for what she had in mind. After taking the plates from his now paralyzed hands and ditching them in the kitchen, Megan returned to the dining room where Steve still stood, frozen to the spot. Hoisting herself up onto the table, she spread her legs and took the hem of her dress in her hands.

"Here's what we're going to do. You start by taking off your clothes. For every item you take off, I raise my skirt. That was a wonderful meal and I'm feeling generous, so we'll say I raise it two inches for every piece of clothing. Does that sound fair?"

His Adam's apple did a double-clutch as Steve swallowed, then nodded. Megan shushed him when his lips parted as though to speak. "Ah-ah. You speak only to say 'no' or 'I don't understand.' You don't need to say 'yes'. Just do as you're told.

Say 'no' at any time and the game stops. Do you understand, Steve?"

He nearly forgot himself immediately, and Megan realized she hadn't made enough allowance for Steve being new at the game. When the first 'ye—' sound came out of his mouth, she reminded him. "Just do as you're told."

Fingers reaching for the top button of his shirt, Steve fumbled the first one, working it free only with difficulty. Having the same problem with the second, he snorted his impatience, grabbed the shirt by its hem and pulled it off over his head. The beautiful pattern of gold hibiscus on a blue background did wonderful things for his eyes, but the second he had it off and Megan could feast on the sight of his naked torso, she was nevertheless delighted it was gone.

"You are so beautiful. It's a crime for you to wear clothes. If I could, I would take you to a desert island and you would never wear them again." Her voice was tight with emotion. The words came from her heart, but she struggled to get them out. Clearing her throat, Megan nodded to his shorts. "Keep going."

Steve didn't speak—*good boy!*—but his eyes darted to the edge of her skirt.

He was right, she needed to keep her part of the game going. But she needed to reinforce who issued the commands and who was the willingly commanded.

"For that little piece of insolence you'll be punished later. Now you'll be begging twice as long before you'll be allowed to come. And for being slow to respond to an order you forfeit half the distance I raise my skirt. One inch instead of two, this time. Now, do you want to risk any more or are you going to take off those shorts?"

Megan thought she detected a faint hint of movement, as though he wanted to shake his head. But Steve obviously had a feel for the game and stopped himself, instead stripping off his shorts and underwear, until he stood in just his socks and running shoes.

Long and flushed with a deep rose tint to its head, Steve's erection curved a little to stand tall against his belly, nearly reaching his navel. Beautiful in its arousal, it bobbed teasingly, as though calling to her. Megan wanted to kiss it like a shy boy's first experience. She lusted to suck on it and treat it like her favorite ice cream cone, swirling her tongue around it until the sweet syrup trickled down her throat. She wanted to hold herself above it, her juicy slit poised for the long, slow glide down it.

The anticipation was killing her.

Raising her skirt well past the two inches the game called for, Megan could feel the heat of Steve's gaze on her barely covered pussy. She'd begun creaming the moment she'd grabbed his jewels and hadn't stopped since. The thought of that delicious mouth glued to her swollen clit had her hotter than a firecracker and it took a major effort on her part not to squirm.

Instead she rewarded him with a small smile. "Too bad you're not wearing your work boots. I seem to have developed quite a fantasy of you in them and nothing else." She heaved a little sigh. "Go ahead and take your shoes off."

Steve obeyed faster than Megan could remember seeing a man move before and it was finally time to give the nice man his reward.

Hiking her skirt the final two inches revealed a pair of Megan's tiniest thong panties. So small they barely qualified as a garment, the miniscule scrap of daffodil yellow eyelet was held to her body by delicate filaments no thicker than the floss that gave them their irreverent nickname.

"Come here, baby," Megan called softly as she indicated the chair in front of her. "Help me off with these. It's time for dessert."

Chapter Seven

Yes, ma'am!

As though released from a spell, Steve practically dove for the chair Megan indicated. Holy Mary, mother of God, was she trying to kill him?

He hoped so.

Like a lighthouse calling to a lost ship, the scrap of yellow that shielded her sweet flesh from his view beckoned.

"Sit down and make yourself comfortable. You're going to be there a while." Her voice was a velvet whisper, like fine old scotch.

Her thighs were beautiful. Not too long, but slim and toned. And, like the gates of heaven, Steve knew paradise lay just beyond them. His hands slipped along their smooth length, reverential lest he be expelled before he'd even entered. When he reached the tiny strings holding the material in place, he slipped his thumbs under them and tore his gaze away to find hers.

Steve watched as her eyelids drooped low, then lower still, before she gave a brief nod and lifted her bottom to allow him to slide the material away. But before discarding them, Steve took a moment to raise them to his nose and draw the exotic perfume deep into his lungs. Like a connoisseur appreciated the first hint of a fine wine by its cork, so Steve's own eyes closed briefly as he savored the unique medley of scents that was Megan.

Placing the panties safely aside, Steve reached for that sweet bottom, intent on sinking his fingers into its satin flesh and losing himself in her.

"Since when do you eat with your hands? I'm going to have words with whoever taught you. Hands behind your back, Steve. Grip your forearms."

Megan issued orders like an old-school drill sergeant. How she managed it without raising her voice, though, escaped him. She never spoke above a soft conversational tone and always sounded like such a lady. But the authority in her voice was unmistakable.

Steve hadn't figured it out yet, but something about it got him *so fucking hot.*

He didn't know what kind of sick fuck that made him, but with that plump little kitty—all nicely shaved with only a neat little ruff showing, thank you, Jesus—staring him the face, Steve didn't much care. He'd drown in her flesh tonight and sort out the details tomorrow.

Leaning forward about to make contact, Steve was leading with his tongue when hands gripped the back of his head. Threading her fingers into his hair, Megan let him know that this would be done at her pace. Her way.

She guided him the final few inches until, at last, his mouth was on her. Hot and spicy, a little salty, Steve let the flavors roll around on his tongue. Tasting. Savoring.

Truth was he loved going down on a woman. Everything from the throaty sounds of passion, to the unique flavor every woman had, to the texture of their skin in their most secret place—Steve loved it all. His own aching cock faded into the background noise of his consciousness and he was alone with his awareness of *her*. Aware only of how natural, how incredibly good, it felt to be filled with the taste of her—to be surrounded by the scent and feel of her—something deep inside him was satisfied. He wanted to freeze the moment in time and never lose it

He slid along the slick channels to either side of her pussy, circling her clit before drawing that tender flesh into this mouth. Eyes closed, mouth working, drinking her juices like a man dying of thirst, Steve realized that was exactly what he was. A man dying of thirst and he had finally found a woman who could quench his craving. Why the realization settled on him with such ease, he didn't know.

Steve didn't have enough active brain cells left to figure out why, so he gave up the fight and lost himself in the moment.

So fucking good! Her hips were pumping a gentle rhythm now and the only thought Steve could identify repeated itself over and over inside him. *So fucking good!* He licked and sucked, first circling around Megan's hard little clit, then sucking her labia into his mouth where he worked them gently with his teeth. Using suction, he drew on her clit, then thrust hard with his tongue into her slick pussy. Back and forth, clit then pussy, over and over.

The hands that had been tugging rhythmically on his hair suddenly grabbed hold and pulled hard, mashing his face and nose into her slippery flesh. Megan gasped and drew in a series of short panting breaths, each deeper than the last. Just as Steve thought he might be about to smother, the hands in his hair went slack and the table reverberated with the thump of Megan falling backward in a boneless heap.

Steve couldn't hide the triumphant grin that spread over his face.

He was a god!

He had slayed her with just his tongue.

Now, if only someone would tell it to his aching cock and balls.

* * *

"Not bad. You lick pussy pretty well, in fact."

Megan had recovered quickly. Steve had given half a thought to picking her up—she was just a little thing, really—and carrying her to bed. He'd been mulling his options, every second that ticked by punctuated by the pulsing of his neglected dick. He hadn't checked, but he was pretty sure if he did his balls would be turning blue enough to match his shirt by now.

Megan had shoved herself up until she rested on her elbows, though, and awarded him the equivalent of a C+ in pussy licking. He didn't think so. That had been an A performance in anybody's book. His outraged ego wouldn't stand for it.

"Not bad? That must be one hell of a curve you grade on. That was—"

"Steve." Megan interrupted what was shaping up to be a pretty good rant, fueled by one-third bruised ego and two-thirds frustrated lust. "Unless you want this game to stop right now, your options are still 'I don't understand,' or do as you're told. Now, which is it going to be?"

Her dark mahogany hair, usually so shiny and neat, was mussed. Probably from when she'd hit the table after her climax. Other than that one telltale sign Megan looked no different than she had when she'd been working on her spreadsheet that first night in Goldie's. Her eyes should have been sleepy with that just-got-laid look every man liked to see and know he was responsible for. Her lips should have been puffy and wet from his kisses. But they hadn't kissed.

Her eyes looked direct. One hundred percent pure business.

What the hell was this they were doing?

He didn't know. Megan fucked with his head until he didn't know up from down. He only knew he hadn't gotten laid yet and no way was he ready for it to end. And he didn't doubt for a minute that if he said the wrong thing, she'd turn on her heel and walk out of there.

Jesus, could he be any more frustrated?

"I. Don't. Understand."

The only visible sign Steve could read from Megan was a slightly deeper than usual intake of breath as she pushed herself the rest of the way up. Hopping off the table, she picked up her backpack from the empty chair where she'd tossed it earlier. He consoled himself that her first few steps hadn't been completely steady; what on any other woman he would have called a wobble in her walk.

Reaching into the bag, Megan retrieved a fistful of nylon rope.

"I want to tie your hands. May I?" A shiver skated up his spine at her matter-of-fact announcement. He looked back at her a long time before speaking, a million thoughts tumbling through his head.

"I don't understand."

"I want to finish what we started. To do that, I need to bind your hands." Megan looked back at him, eyes steady, breathing even. "And I think you want me to."

* * *

Megan knew she was rushing things but, damn, it was hard to control the want. Instinct told her that she had what he needed. That he needed to go to the next level and she was the only person in his life who could take him there. Her gut told her that if he backed down now he would retreat back to his safe vanilla existence and never challenge himself again. What kind of life would that be?

Deep inside her, Megan knew with everything she was that Steve was a sexual submissive.

Whether it was due to DNA, birth order, or the result of being breastfed too long, the truth was nobody knew the why of it. And at the end of the day, what difference did it make anyway? It just was.

He was.

He could either face it and choose to accept it. Or he could turn his back on it and deny it even existed. That doing so would mean turning his back on her was only part of it. Ask any closeted gay what giving up a basic part of your identity meant.

She could have wept in frustration because he was so close. So close to trusting. He needed to trust not only her, but his own instincts, as well.

Megan understood the fear that kept him from accepting her challenge. All his life he'd been taught that what he was feeling right now was wrong. That a real man didn't let anyone tell him what to do. Real men called the shots. In everything from what he did for a living to where and what he ate for dinner. But most especially in the bedroom.

She knew the kind of names men gave to anyone who was different. Faggot. Ball-less. Pussy-whipped. And those were the nice ones.

Clutching the rope in her hands to keep from reaching for him, she worked to keep the emotion from her face. It had to be his choice. Like coaxing a wild animal, Megan knew that the key was to project a calm exterior. If he sensed even a fraction of how tense she was…how much his answer meant to her, she would lose him.

"Okay. We'll do it your way. Let's keep going."

* * *

"Lie down on the bed. Face up. Hands over your head."

Now that Megan knew Steve wasn't going to walk out—or worse—her calm had returned.

The play of muscle sliding under skin drew her eye irresistibly as Steve lowered himself to the big bed. The navy coverlet repeated the clean lines evident in the rest of the house. A wing chair sat in the corner, covered in an improbable plaid combining maroon, dark green and navy. Either Steve had surprisingly sophisticated taste in decorating or he'd had help.

An unwelcome clench in her gut at the thought of the source of the presumed help reminded Megan that no matter how much she might want to own him, body and soul, in the present, he would always have a past. A past that existed without her.

Steve lay back on the bed, the dark comforter making a fine contrast, like an artist's drape, behind the graduated shades of his skin. He obviously worked outdoors fairly often, because the skin of his torso and arms was darker than that of his lean flanks. His Scandinavian heritage showed plainly in the fair skin there, while the sun-bleached hair of his legs and forearms was several shades lighter than the red-gold of his head and groin.

Having separated the bundle of rope into the three smaller lengths that made it up, Megan now drew the longest of the three through her hands as she circled the bed. Never taking her eyes off Steve's, she moved slowly, enjoying the slightly nervous, obviously excited sight of him, displayed as he was on the bed.

Not displayed quite enough, though.

"Spread your legs for me. I want to see every inch of you."

Eyes on her face, Steve cautiously did as he was told. Although she stood behind him, Megan knew that while his cock continued to strain upward toward his belly, his balls would now be visible when she eventually moved back between his legs.

"Now put your wrists together. Mmm, yeah, that's it. Excellent."

The soft nylon rope slid between her fingers as she took a doubled length of it and laid it across his wrists. While she could feel the weight of his gaze on her, Megan kept her movements calm and deliberate. Wrapping the rope around his forearms a second and then third time, she drew the tail portion between his wrists and tied it off.

"Is it comfortable? Not binding anywhere?" She knew it wasn't, but Megan nevertheless ran her fingers between the rope and Steve's skin to confirm it.

"It's okay."

"You don't sound too sure." Megan leaned on the bed, bending low to caress his face with her lips. She kissed his broad forehead first, then the upward slope of one cheek.

"It's...different." His lips skimmed her ear as she continued to drop small kisses on his upturned face, his breath carrying the scent of her own excitement back to her.

"It's perfect. You look wonderful." Megan only needed to turn her face slightly to bring her mouth in contact with his. She tasted herself on his lips as their tongues began to explore and the memory of his mouth on her pussy shot a fresh bolt of lust through her. When Steve tried to deepen the kiss, Megan let him for just an instant before breaking it off. "I'm going to put the ends of the rope down here, between the mattress and the box spring. Unless you really pull, they should stay put."

Matching actions to words, she tucked the lengths of nylon under the mattress before returning to his feet and shaking out the two remaining sections of rope.

Before things in San Francisco had gone so disastrously wrong with Damian, she had developed an interest in Shibari, the Japanese art of rope bondage. With its emphasis on visual presentation and the comfort of the one being bound, it was as beautiful as it was effective. Steve's height and coloring would make him a dream to work on. But that would have to wait for another time. One step at a time.

After securing Steve's feet in the same manner as she had his hands, Megan climbed up beside him on the bed.

"How do you feel?"

As turned on as she was, her voice came out low and husky. She couldn't explain it, but when she was truly excited her voice took on traces of a southern accent. Holly Hunter meets Kathleen Turner at her sultry, sexy wildest.

"Exposed."

"Poor baby." He sounded worried. She'd have to do something to put him at ease.

Taking his lovely long cock in one hand, she used her other hand to catch the pearls of fluid that had been collecting at its tip. Megan trailed two fingers through the salty liquid and brought them to her mouth as she ever so gently began pumping him. Letting him see her tongue as she swiped at the tips, Megan closed her eyes as she drew them into her mouth to suck them clean.

"Oh, God. You're killing me here. You know that, don't you?"

The strain in his voice would have told her he was on the edge, even if she hadn't been holding his cock in her hand, a visible throb pulsing through it.

Kneeling at his side, Megan continued stroking him with firm, easy sweeps of one hand. She brushed a few hairs off his face, where they had caught when he had begun tossing his head from side to side, and caught his chin in her hand.

"Look at me, Steve." He forced his eyes open with noticeable effort. Megan stared at him hard. "Don't come until I tell you to. Got it?"

"What—?" Megan continued pumping ruthlessly on his captive cock. Unable to hold her gaze while she worked him, Steve's head dropped from her grasp.

"Don't come until I give you permission."

With that Megan turned her back on him as she re-gripped his gorgeous fat cock, lowered her head and deep-throated him.

Chapter Eight

Shit. Oh, fuck! So good. Fuck. Dammit. Shit. Oh, fuck, no.

Steve tried, but there was no way he was holding this back. No way to keep his mind off the incredible hotness of her mouth on him. Sweet and dark, swallowing him down. God, so fucking good!

One cool hand on his balls squeezed pressure down on him, but it was like holding back the sea with a sandcastle. It couldn't hope to stand before the crashing pleasure that swept over him. The heat and pleasure retreated for a moment, but the second time her mouth covered him and he felt her lips part to accept him, he was lost.

He tried to grip the sheets, but his hands were held uselessly over his head. He was powerless in the face of it and he cursed himself as he shot helplessly into her mouth.

Fully expecting Megan to pull off him in disgust, his sanity exploded as she stayed on him, riding out his orgasm. His brains were sucked out his dick as Megan swallowed him down, the tight constrictions of her throat triggering him again and again.

Aftershocks were wrung out of him as she continued to draw him down, tongue wrapping languorously around the underside of his sensitive flesh, mouth suckling gently.

Megan released him at last, the furnace of her hot little mouth pulling away with a little pop, leaving him bereft.

"That's some mouth you've got on you there, sailor."

She sounded downright smug. As though she knew she'd ripped the soul right out of his body, taken it apart and rearranged it. He'd have to do something about that. Later.

"Mpfh."

Seconds ticked by. Steve tried to form words, but nothing came. He floated in a perfect place. Content. Fulfilled. *Complete.*

The bed shifted and warmth pressed in on him along one side. A welcome weight came to rest on his chest. Puffs of moist air gusted intermittently over his sensitized skin. He drifted.

Time was relative. He had no idea how long he lay there, Megan's head pillowed between his chest and shoulder. Until the weight shifted and moist heat closed over his nipple.

"Fucking a—"

"There you go again. Does your mother know you talk like that?"

"Dunno. Maybe you should ask her."

"I just might, at that. That would be some conversation. 'Mrs. Eriksson, your son Steve has an appalling lack of self-control. The absolute second I began going down on him... Well! You simply wouldn't believe the words that came out of his mouth. And not a one of them polite, let me tell you.'"

Megan chuckled at her own joke, her laughter vibrating along the wall of his bare chest.

Steve pried his eyes open as realization dawned and he became aware of her movements drawing her away from him. When had she taken the rest of her clothes off?

"Where you going? Get back over here and untie me, woman."

"Oh, I'm not going anywhere. I am far from done with you. You'll just have to stay right where you are for a little while longer. You came before I gave you permission. It's time for a little lesson in control."

* * *

Jesus, was she joking?

"What, are you fucking kidding me? You were going down on me. Lady, I was so damn hot for you…"

The peace and contentment of moments before was gone. The injustice of it all… Pissed him off? You betcha. It was fucking insane.

"I know you were excited. But that's not the point."

"Yeah? Then what is?"

He felt like an idiot. Tied up like a chicken on a spit. Teased out of his mind and then beat up for doing what any man would do. He might have to listen, but he didn't have to like it. It didn't help that she just sat there, resting on her heels, calmly looking back at him. Why was it the more pissed the man got, the calmer the woman became?

"This is all new to you, I know, what I'm asking of you. But for it to be as good as it can be, I need you to try."

"Try what? *Do* what?" Frustration boiled up and poured out of him, but he couldn't help it. "Megan, what the hell is it we're doing here, exactly? Tell me, because I'm not getting it."

What was going through her head? Steve laughed bitterly at himself when he caught that thought flickering through his head. What man ever knew what a woman was thinking? Supposing that they were. Megan looked so calm, just watching him from behind those inscrutable eyes of hers.

She was so different from any other woman he'd ever been with. So calm and controlled. She was the only woman he could think of that wouldn't be cuddling right now, planning their next date and picking out a color scheme for the wedding. If he hadn't seen her swallow his cock like a wet dream and drink his cum without missing a drop, he wouldn't have believed it of her. She looked like she was more ready to talk about mutual funds than mutual orgasms.

"Steve, let me ask you something. Haven't you always felt different? Like you needed something you weren't getting? That you weren't getting the same thing that everyone else was? Maybe the sex wasn't all that, either? Did you ever feel like that?"

"No. Shit, no." Although… He wondered sometimes what was different between him and his brother. If he tried half the things he'd seen Rick pull… He'd tried copying Rick's style when he was younger, but he hadn't liked the feeling of going down in flames. So he'd adapted. But, still. "I don't know. Maybe."

Megan seemed to decide something, because she rose up off her heels. Dropping to hands and knees, she crawled over him, straddling his chest. She ran her hands up his sides, beginning with his torso. Not tickling. Just gently running her hands from his chest and belly, stretching up to reach his arms, her small pert breasts almost within range of his mouth.

A shiver ran through Steve and his nipples stood up, almost painful where the barbells touched nerve endings. His cock began to stir.

Letting her fingers trail down the inside of his outstretched arms, Megan left a trail of fire in their wake. Her hands traced circles around the pierced flesh, trapped the sensitive skin between thumbs and forefingers and pinched. Steve was nearly erect now, the head of his dick reaching for the warm flesh of her tender backside. She took a nipple in her mouth and sucked hard. Never quite releasing him, her teeth slid down to the barbell, gripped the metal and tugged.

Steve's body bowed up off the bed, taking Megan with him, as a bolt of sensation shot through him in a direct line from her mouth to his cock.

"Ah, God!"

"I don't think you've ever truly gotten what you needed." Megan blew a small stream of air over the skin her mouth had just covered and another jolt of lust rocked him. "You're special. Different. And I don't think anyone has ever known quite what to do with you."

She was licking his other nipple now, giving it the same attention she had treated the first to. She worried the tip with her teeth, rolling the metal back and forth. Bit down slightly harder on it than she had the first. Her eyes swept from watching the effect of her clever tongue up to his face. "But I think I do. I know what you need. The question is, will you let me give it to you?"

* * *

Hoo, boy.

She hadn't meant to go there.

Not at all.

Megan's plan had been to tease Steve. To play with him—keep him teetering on the knife-edge of wanting but never quite getting. Until he admitted the truth. About himself. And her.

But she had looked in his eyes and seen the frustration. More than that, she'd seen the pain and the memories it masked. And in that moment she hadn't been able to Domme Steve. Instead of being strong and putting his well-being first, she had stepped completely out of role and poured her heart out to him.

She was such a dope. Maybe that was why she always came up short. When push came to shove she never seemed to quite have what it took. Damian had shown her that. No, that wasn't true. It wasn't fair to blame him. He'd only confirmed it for her.

"I know exactly what I need. My dick in your cunt."

Okay. So maybe he wasn't quite as down and out as she'd thought. Or maybe he'd learned to take what he could get since he never got what he really needed.

"Relax. We'll get there eventually. I think."

"You 'think'?"

"Sorry, sweet pea, but your dick in my cunt, as you so delicately put it, is a privilege—not a right. You'll have to earn that."

"Let me guess. More pussy licking."

"I like to think I'm not quite that predictable. Not to mention repetitious. No, this will be something a little harder for you, I think." Megan narrowed her eyes a little. "I want to know your secrets."

"Secrets? Like, what did you have in mind?"

The wary look was back in Steve's eyes now. To counteract it, Megan resumed the stroking she had momentarily forgotten.

"Do you remember that first night when I asked you about your fantasies? I want to hear more about that." Crouching low over Steve's outstretched body, Megan let the tips of her breasts brush Steve's. Already tightened in anticipation, when they touched his they beaded even more tightly into aching little points. To see his skin, so tender and sensitive, penetrated by hard metal did something primitive to her. Shaking off a shiver, she went on. "And about what you've never done, but always wanted to."

"I want to fuck your pussy. Hard. I've never done that."

"So noted. We'll put that on our list of things to do." Grabbing a pillow, Megan lifted Steve's head and shoved the pillow behind it. "There. That should give you a better view." It raised his head just enough for him to be able to see what she had planned next. After taking a quick check on the ropes again, she moved on.

Megan turned, taking a slow deliberate visual tour of the man stretched out before her. His color was good. His breathing was a little quicker than normal, a little more shallow, but that was to be expected. Eye contact was good.

"And your ass, too. That'd be sweet."

She adored the way those chiseled lips curled up at one corner in a bad boy grin of anticipation. It only added to his appeal. Steve had so many sides to him. The last thing she wanted was a one-dimensional relationship based solely on a man's need to be dominated. Sure, it made her hot as hell that he was turning out to be the most natural sub it had ever been her pleasure to know. It lit her up like Founders' Square at Christmastime to be able to give him an order and see him submit—to see the pleasure he took in being controlled. To know that his need coincided with hers and that, together, they could find a rapturous pleasure they could never hope to find separately.

But it wasn't enough.

Megan wanted more than that. She wanted something she wasn't even sure existed. Something lacking that had destroyed her last relationship, surely, and probably every one before it, too.

"Oh, really?" She arched an eyebrow at him. "Hmm. I'll have to think about that one. You'd have to be an awfully good boy to earn something like that."

Slithering backwards, Megan kneeled between Steve's knees and, pushing her breasts together, used them to press on his straining cock. The tang of sweat on his belly calling to her, Megan took a swipe with her tongue and tasted saltiness as she rocked back and forth, using her own flesh to stroke his.

Megan accepted the tribute of the low growl that rumbled up from Steve's chest without comment. It meant her plan was working. She wanted him mindless with wanting.

"How about it, Steve? You a breast man?" She loved teasing him. "Would you like me to keep this up for a while? You could fuck my tits—give me a pearl necklace. What do you think, babe?"

"Fuck, yeah."

Giving him a few last strokes for good measure, Megan sat back a little and took his shaft in both hands. The big plum head of it was stretched tight and beaded with fluid again. Her self-control went down without a fight to temptation. Another few swipes of her tongue took care of the pre-cum and had Steve flexing his hips, trying to drive for the solace of her mouth.

Megan pursed her lips and let the satiny skin push past the entrance of her mouth. But only a little. Using her double-fisted grip on his cock, she made sure only the tip entered, and that just barely. She swirled her tongue around the corona, using it to stimulate the sensitive spot just below the bulging mushroom-shaped head.

As Steve groaned, Megan dropped one hand to his scrotum, and beneath it to massage the area behind. Slipping lower still, she held his cock in the firm grip of one hand and let the fingers of the other drift into the crease below. She kept her strokes short and light until she reached the small, puckered opening of his anus.

"What about this, Steve? How do you feel about ass play? Have you ever explored how good it feels to have your G-spot stimulated?"

If his vehement "No! No way." hadn't been enough for her, the way his ass cheeks tensed up and his whole body jerked away from her hand confirmed it. His eyes that had been squeezed shut, lost in his own pleasure, popped open.

Although she didn't take time to pout, a little frown of disappointment still found its way to her lips. But she backed off immediately.

"That's okay, babe. Maybe some other time."

Still working his cock with one hand, Megan tore open a condom with her teeth. Sheathing him quickly, she drew herself up until she kneeled over Steve, her slick opening poised above him, and stared hard into his eyes.

Aiming him, Megan lowered herself until she could feel his rigid flesh begin to nudge her drenched channel. She'd been wet and ready for this moment for what seemed like her whole life. As slowly as she could, she pushed gently down over him, her murmured "Easy, babe" the only sound in the suddenly deafening silence. Like a bull rider settling onto the back of a particularly unruly bull, she eased cautiously downward. Her inner muscles parted as Steve's meaty cock forced its way in, inch by inch. Until at last he was in to the balls and Megan would swear she could feel him kissing her womb.

Finally.

Belly to belly, gazes riveted, time ground to a halt.

Hands outstretched above him, mouth pulled back in a grimace, muscles straining to keep from thrusting—Megan's heart turned over in her chest at the picture of wild masculine beauty before her. He was perfection.

She wanted to hold the moment in her hand forever, never leaving, eternally caught in this intricate dance.

"Now fuck me, nasty boy."

Chapter Nine

Holy Mary, Mother of God and all her cousins. So good. So good. Tight and hot. She gripped him like a closed fist that clamped from all sides and somehow managed to touch every single nerve ending he had. Just being inside her was fucking incredible. She was so damn hot. She knew what she wanted and she wasn't afraid to take it.

Take him.

Hands and legs tied like a pagan sacrifice. Teased until he thought he would explode. Then used for her sexual pleasure. Shit, yeah! Woman-on-top had always been his favorite position. But it had never been like this before. She was sexier than any woman he'd ever been with. Riding him like it was her right. Like he was her sex slave, born to serve her.

"Hey, numb-nuts! How much longer is it going to take you to wire that *chingazzi?* Yeah, Steve-o, I'm talking to you."

Steve shook his head and the job at hand faded in as the vision of Megan faded out. That had been happening to him a lot the past couple of days. Since that night at his house, he'd relived that moment a hundred times. In one night he had set three new personal-bests with her. The table. The blow-job. The...he didn't know what to call it.

"Yeah, yeah. I've got it, Robert. Go back to playing with yourself for a few. I've got a couple more connectors to tie off."

Pulling his face back from the hole in the floor he'd shouted through, Steve wiped the sweat from his face. It was hot as hell on the second floor of the Swann Mansion where he was finishing up the wiring for an elaborate chandelier the crew was ready to hang. The restoration on the old house was a long way from complete and the fixture wouldn't stay up long. But a mixed group of baby-kissers from City Hall and history wonks from the dead poets' society Catherine worked for were coming through tomorrow for a look-see and Catherine wanted as many of the big pieces in place as they could make happen on short notice.

Ms. Catherine Thompson of the Oro County Historical Society was one hard-assed bitch when it came to getting things right on the resto'. That she was also his brother's fiancée as of last week made it hard to say no to her. That he could still remember what her lips felt like wrapped around his dick made it just that much trickier.

Man, had that only been six months ago?

His brother Rick had met Catherine in this very house. They had come together like fire and gasoline and on one memorable afternoon Steve had very nearly gotten caught in the inferno. Funny how the memory of that day, that had been so vivid in his mind until recently, was fading fast. His sense memory had been rewired like he was rewiring the old bordello. Something had yanked out the old and replaced it with new.

The last of the wires capped off, Steve headed down to the first floor, using the bandana he had tied over his hair to wipe the sweat from his face and neck as he went. Descending the staircase, he twisted the square of colored cloth to wring the moisture from it. But just the action of stretching the handkerchief between his hands brought to mind Megan's hands as she had used a similar motion when she had bound his hands and feet. That quickly, the tingle of blood rushed to his groin, reminding him that he was working and hardly in a position to do anything about it.

Steve rounded the corner into the foyer area where his brother Rick stood talking to a smaller, dark-haired man. In his early twenties, slim and wiry, Robert Karabedian had done the cleaning and refitting on the chandelier Eriksson and Sons Construction had pulled down from the rotting ceiling. Steve's theory on Robert's success could be boiled down to 'sink or swim.' Smaller than either Rick or Steve, Robert had the personality of a wolverine coming down off a crack binge and the people skills of a DMV clerk. Steve maintained that the little man knew he could never hold down a job that depended on anyone actually liking him and threw himself into his one-man lighting restoration business body and soul.

Rick and Robert had had enough go-rounds that Steve had lost count of the number of times Rick had sworn never to use him again. So it shocked the hell out of Steve to see the two men talking and laughing like old buddies.

"Dude, so I'm telling you, she goes into the other room to get her coat and I'm, like, standing by the door waiting. And I, you know, I look over at the DVDs and tapes all piled up by the TV. I'm, like—she had the stuff laying out, okay? It's not like I went pawing through her drawers or anything."

"And? You found out she has a secret addiction to *Lord of the Rings* videos? So you dress up like an elf while you're banging her. It's a win-win." Catherine must not have shown up yet, Steve decided, if Rick was using his full adult vocabulary. Steve had noticed a tendency in his brother to tone things down a little when his now-fiancée was in the room.

Robert gave a nod, acknowledging Steve's presence, and went on with his story.

"So, she didn't have any fucking *Lord of the Rings* videos, okay? She can call me Robin fucking-Hood for all I care. As long as she follows it up with 'Can I swallow now?' No, I coulda' handled that. She has a little something called *Babes Ballin' Boys* on hand for her viewing pleasure. And right next to it on the shelf is another gem called *Bend Over, Boyfriend*. Dude, if I want to get poked up the ass I'll do something illegal and get sent to prison. At least there I'll get three hots and a cot."

Rick was laughing his butt off. "Oh, that's beautiful. *Babes Ballin' Boys,* huh? So did you search her purse for any strap-ons? Make sure she wasn't carrying?" His brother could hardly get the words out, he was laughing too hard.

"Fuck that!" Robert didn't have much of a sense of humor when it came to his manhood. Sensitive with a hair-trigger, both brothers knew it and weren't above needling him. "If anybody's getting fucked up the ass, it ain't gonna be me."

Winking at Rick behind Robert's back, Steve couldn't resist getting in on the ragging. "Well, I don't know there, Robert. Maybe you'd like it. I hear that after you get used to it, it feels pretty good. You know. 'It's only weird the first time.'"

"Yeah, I guess if anyone would know, it would be you, Steve-o."

"What the hell's that supposed to mean, Robert?" He wasn't pissed. But his arms unfolded from their formerly relaxed position across his chest. He was just flexing his fingers, that was all. He wasn't going to hit the little cocksucker.

"Nothin', man. Just, if it's got hair like a chick, and tit jewelry like a chick..." The little shit was enjoying himself way too much. The smirk on his face made Steve itch to put his hands around ol' Bobby's greasy little neck and squeeze. "No shame in being a catcher in a world full of pitchers, man."

Rick's face was suddenly in Steve's and his brother was holding him back. "Don't do it, Steve. It's not worth it. C'mon, you shit bigger than he is."

When had he moved? Steve didn't remember reaching for Robert, but the piece of cloth in his hand matched the dark patch of a pocket missing from the other man's shirt.

Without turning away, Rick dismissed Robert. "Robert, I think we can handle things from here. Why don't you take off?"

"Hey, I'm sorry if your brother doesn't like looking in the mirror. I'm just surprised it took him and Manly Megan this long to hook up."

* * *

"So how's the romance going?"

Megan looked up from the yellow summer squash she was slicing into half-inch pieces. Her sister watched from a chair nearby as she cut the last of the vegetables she was chopping to make a Ratatouille.

"What romance?" Trying hard for an innocent look, Megan concentrated on slicing the various vegetables into bite-sized pieces.

Christa had called as Megan was finishing clean-up from the day's rounds with the catering truck, claiming an uncontrollable craving for the spicy vegetable stew that was a summer favorite in the Mussina house. Megan had stopped at her favorite produce market for the ingredients she didn't have on hand and headed over to Christa's. Besides wanting to go over the week's receipts, Megan was looking forward to the chance to prepare something more challenging than tuna salad.

"Don't play coy with me, girlie. I may be under house arrest but I still have contacts in the outside world. I made a few calls. I know what you've been doing."

Megan's stomach turned over at her sister's comment and she nearly blurted out the truth. The off-hand tone gave Christa away, though. It was a little too relaxed. A hair too studiedly casual. It was an old trick of her sister's, Megan remembered, to pretend more knowledge than she actually had and wait for the victim to spill.

Catching herself just in time, Megan parried. "Oh. Well there's no use denying it, then."

"Nope. None at all."

Years ago she might have fallen for it. When they were both still kids living in their parents' house she had. Many times. But she'd been around the block once or twice since then and, this time, used some of her hard-won calm. She picked up the last zucchini and sliced it lengthwise first and then into quarters. "Well, then."

Christa was a seasoned campaigner, though. She only gazed back at Megan and rubbed her charmingly rounded belly. "Indeed."

Adding oil to the big pan on the stove, Megan scooped up the vegetable mixture and dropped it in by handfuls. She adjusted the heat slightly and watched her sister stew. "You don't have squat, sis. Nice try, though. By the way, I'm using turkey ham instead of Tasso in this. You don't need the extra salt."

"Megan!" The pitiful wail would have never passed Christa's lips in the old days. Marrying Doug, having babies to look forward to—it had softened her sister to a degree Megan never would have believed. "I'm stuck here in this house. I don't see anyone but Doug, you, and sometimes Mom or Dad. And the mailman. And he only comes by because he's forced to. Give me some details. I need to live a little, even if it's only vicariously. Please?"

It was the last plaintive request that cracked the armor of Megan's reserve.

"It's too soon, Christa. I... It's only been a couple of weeks. Just a few dates, really. But—" Her mind flashed back to another kitchen. Steve's face across the table from her. His expressions as they'd eaten and talked. "I really like him. He's different. Special."

"Wow. It's serious then."

Self-conscious at how much her sister had divined, Megan could feel the weight of Christa's gaze on her as she stirred the vegetables sautéing in the pan. "I didn't say that."

"You don't have to. I can see it on your face. You are gone, girl. I don't think I've ever seen you like this. What about him? Is he serious?"

Megan opened her mouth, but no words formed. She tried again with the same result. On the third try she got it. "I don't know, Chris. How do you know what a man is thinking?"

Her sister laughed. "That's easy—they're usually not. As a veteran of nearly five years of marriage, I can say this much about what's on a man's mind: sex, cars or sports. In that order. Or nothing. If you ever make the mistake of asking and he says 'nothing,' believe him."

* * *

"You've reached Steve Eriksson's phone. I'm not available to take your call right now. Leave a message and I'll call you back."

The tone signaling that it was time to leave a message jarred Megan out of her trance. She'd been busy going over her last conversation with Steve in her head while she listened to the business-like tone of his voice on the machine. Not at all like she remembered him in her head. In her favorite mental image he was swearing and begging. "Please, baby. Please."

But what to say?

"Hi, Steve. It's Megan. We must have gotten our signals crossed—I thought we were meeting at my place. I'll try you at the restaurant. Talk to you soon. Bye." She didn't bother to leave her call back number. She knew he had it.

Twenty minutes later, driving down Sutter Street, Remington's version of Main Street, USA, Megan searched for a parking space. Not as bad as in high summer when the sleepy little town in the Sierras was packed with tourists. Tuesday night this time of year shouldn't have been a problem. She puzzled over her bad luck until she spotted the hand-painted A-frame sign in front of the Elks Lodge. "Tuesday Night Bingo! 7:00 p.m. until ???" That would explain the heavier than usual accumulation of cars.

As she circled the block for the third time a spot opened up near the new Ph? restaurant Steve had agreed to try with her. Megan had been introduced to the Vietnamese noodle soup while she'd been attending culinary school in San Francisco and had become a near addict to the stuff. Coming back to Remington, with it's abundance of diners catering to the tourist trade and featuring 'down home cookin',' had meant going cold turkey on her passion for Ph?. Until she had seen the sign go up for Phat Phuc's, as she had discovered it was called. Megan was still cringing at the unfortunate name even as her mouth had watered.

Pulling in to the parking spot, Megan grabbed her backpack and headed for the restaurant. Although the business was new, the building it inhabited wasn't. Most of the three blocks that made up the main drag were filled with authentic original architecture dating to the 1800's. It was what gave Remington its historical feel and what drew the vacationers. The big picture windows of the building revealed that two of the six tables the little eatery contained were filled. It took all of two seconds for Megan to see that Steve wasn't there.

She stood, mulling her options and absently scanning the street when something caught her eye. It wasn't the ratty old sign on top of Goldie's, with its ugly yellow light bulbs. Lately driving by and seeing its familiar red door, or even just thinking about it, made her smile. But the black Dodge truck parked two doors down from it was familiar.

It was Steve's truck.

Oh, yeah—definitely his. She knew, even from this distance, that the antenna ball perched atop it advertised his beloved Kings basketball team.

Without conscious thought Megan's feet began moving in the direction of Goldie's. Either she'd gotten her signals crossed or...she couldn't think of what else it could possibly be. Steve must have arrived early and stopped in to wait for her there. Was there a game on? She had no idea.

Pushing through the door, Megan smelled the familiar mix of odors that seemed uniquely Goldie's. Equal parts beer, popcorn, and kitchen smells, it never failed to put a smile on her face. Not like the one that came over her when she thought about the old manager's office upstairs, though. Her smile grew as she spotted a familiar back, bisected by a ponytail of a particularly fetching shade of red-gold.

The music from the jukebox—the Rolling Stones, Jacy must not be on duty—made calling Steve's name pointless. Megan crossed the floor, running a finger down his arm when she reached him to alert him to her presence. "Hey, there." Butterflies flitted in her stomach, like this was her first high school dance.

Steve turned on his stool and Megan's hand fell away. He looked down at her.

"Oh. Hi."

"I must have gotten things backward. I thought we were meeting at my place. I hope you haven't been waiting long?"

The man on the seat next to Steve turned to look. Too similar physically to be anything other than Steve's brother, he looked her up and down before casting an equally assessing eye on Steve.

Things were getting stranger by the minute. Why would the brother be checking her out? And why was Steve looking at her with all the enthusiasm of a man greeting the IRS? Megan didn't necessarily expect a kiss in public, but would it kill him to smile?

"Sorry. I should have called. I can't make it tonight."

"But—"

She looked from one face to the other, and then back again, while a sick feeling settled in the pit of her stomach. There was no mistaking the coldness in his tone and it felt all too horribly like *déjà vu.*

Eerily similar to another time and place.

"Steve, could I talk to you outside for a minute?"

"No. Sorry. No can do, babe. You can talk in front of my brother."

Her mind raced, running through their last conversation. Their last three conversations. What could she possibly have said? What signs had she missed? Why was he doing this? He looked like the same man who had trusted his most vulnerable feelings to her. But he didn't talk like him. And he certainly didn't act like him.

"I'd really like to talk to you alone. It's important, Steve." God, would you listen to her plead? She was pathetic.

"So's this." He took a slug from his beer and looked back at the TV screen behind the bar. Experienced in the art of the public kiss-off, Megan knew one when it was handed to her.

"All right." Things were most certainly not all right. "Some other time, then." She searched his eyes, tried to read his thoughts on his normally expressive face. But it was no use. He had closed himself off from her.

Well, then. If this was going to be it, Megan decided, then she wanted her kiss after all. She wanted to leave knowing her taste was in his mouth. Let the other women watching know he bore her mark. The barstool Steve sat on brought him low enough that she didn't have to reach as far as she would have had he been standing. Taking his chin in her hand, Megan leaned in close and spoke softly in one ear. "Be well." She slid down to press one last kiss on his tempting mouth.

At the last second, though, he turned away. Her kiss fell on empty air.

Chapter Ten

Steve didn't think he could handle watching her walk away so he kept his eyes fixed on his beer as he drank it down. That didn't mean that he couldn't still see Megan with his peripheral vision. He concentrated on breathing through his nose as he drained the heavy glass schooner with steady swallows. He told himself it was drinking too fast that made his stomach knot up and twist like pythons mating. It had nothing to do with Megan stopping at Evan Coughlin's table, exchanging a few words, and Evan leaving with her.

How could she even think of going anywhere with that slimy fuckwad?

Everyone knew that Evan was a player. Evan changed women like most men changed their shirts. Steve was sliding off the barstool in pursuit when he remembered. He didn't care. Megan was free to do whatever she wanted with whoever she wanted.

His stomach rolled over again.

Glancing over to see if Rick had caught his move, he realized his brother was no longer seated on the next barstool. There were now two empty seats between them and Rick was frowning into his beer.

"What's with you?"

Rick looked away, out the big picture window to Sutter Street where Evan could be seen dropping an arm across Megan's shoulders as they disappeared from view.

"I'm getting out of the way. Just in case."

Jacy came out of the back room and Steve caught her eye. Nodding in the direction of his empty glass, he held up one finger before turning back to face Rick. "In case what?"

"In case 'dumbass' is contagious."

"Shut the fuck up. You don't know what you're talking about."

"Of course not. You've obviously got it all under control."

"Thanks. I do."

Steve concentrated on the Kings game until Jacy appeared with his beer. The jukebox thumped along with a k.d. lang tune now, drowning out the television. "Here ya go, babe. Hey, Rick. Long time, no see."

Steve took a long pull off his beer and watched Jacy make small talk with his brother while the Kings tried to come from behind. Why couldn't he fall for someone nice and normal, like her? She smiled that cover girl smile and reached across the bar to ruffle Rick's hair. She was so pretty, with her big blue eyes and her perfect features. Why couldn't he be turning himself inside out for Jacy?

He drank more of his beer trying to drown the sick feeling he got when he thought of Megan's face. Steve thought he might twist the handle off the mug as he'd held it, trying to keep from reaching for her. It tore him up inside when he thought about how he felt when he was with her. How much he wanted her. What a sick fuck he must be for needing her the way he did. And wanting the things she did to him.

"So what do you say, Steve?"

While he'd been off in his own little fucked up world he'd completely tuned out the conversation going on around him.

"Sorry. What was the question?"

Jacy smiled as though she knew the nature of his thoughts. "Another beer there? How about something to go with it?" Steve started to protest, only to find that his mug was empty. Not a good sign. When had he pounded the last of it? "How about some nachos? Or, have you tried the potato skins yet? They come covered with cheese, sour cream, bacon pieces…. You'll love 'em."

Steve's stomach roiled at the thought.

He thought of Megan's face. "Steve, could I talk to you outside for a minute?" "No can do. Talk in front of my brother." The voices picked up speed in his head, until they ran together. "I want to fuck your pussy. How do you feel about ass play? If anyone would know, it would be you, Steve-o. Fuck me, nasty boy."

"What's it going to be? Potato skins?" Jacy looked first at Rick and then back to Steve. "Or nachos?"

His gut heaving, Steve bolted for the bathroom.

* * *

He lasted three more days.

Rick had driven him home after he'd puked his guts out in the toilet at Goldie's that night. Just to torture himself, he'd insisted they go by way of Megan's place. He'd told Rick he just wanted to make sure she got home all right. But they both knew he was looking for that pervert Evan's convertible in her driveway.

It had been there, all right.

Fuck, he was an idiot. Full of drunken self-pity, he'd said as much aloud as his brother drove him home. Rick had cheerfully agreed.

"If you're looking for an argument, you came to the wrong place. She looked at you like you were better than shoes and chocolate rolled into one. And you kicked her to the curb. Way to go, asshole."

Steve had stopped asking for advice at that point.

For the next two days he had thrown himself into his work, the first to arrive every morning and staying after everyone else had gone home. Steve had hung sheetrock, spackled joints, taped over them, then spackled some more. He had had some half-baked idea that relentless physical labor would keep him from thinking. That was a joke. He'd had nothing but time to think.

With every nail he pounded or seam he sanded, Steve had thought about other women. He had tried to remember every female he'd ever been intimate with. From Sophia, the foreign exchange student and older woman who'd helped him lose his virginity in his fourteenth year, to Rachelle Billingsly, his first steady girlfriend, to Martha Cho, who he'd dated off and on for a couple of years before she'd moved to Oregon. And all the ones in between.

What had Megan asked him? Something about feeling different? Like he wasn't getting what he needed. And maybe the sex wasn't all that?

Not that it had been bad. It was fine. He'd never had a bad orgasm. Every single one of them had been right on the money.

But they'd been nothing compared to what he'd found with Megan. It was like a shoe dropped. Like a normal orgasm multiplied times ten. An 'a-ha' moment when suddenly everything had changed. And suddenly everything was right in a way it had never been right before. When he had been with her, nothing had ever felt so perfectly natural, so fulfilling, so un-fucking-believably hot. It still gave him a shiver to remember how it had felt to be stripped down to nothing but his most basic, elemental self. To live completely in the moment, nothing but a sexual creature.

Steve had been working in one of the second story bathrooms, cutting tile when it had come him. He had repeatedly measured the piece he needed to replace. His old man had drilled into him 'Measure three times, cut once' from the time he could hold a hammer. After measuring and cutting, particles of tile dust floating in a shaft of afternoon sunlight, he had shifted back to place the new piece. In turning, the irregular triangular shape that was part of the black and white star design had been rotated by ninety degrees. As Steve rotated the sliver of tile and dropped it into place something clicked.

The piece dropped into the hole like it had been specially made for it—because it had. Steve sat back on his heels and stared at it. And stared.

It was a perfect analogy for his life. Something was missing from him and not just any piece would fill the empty space. It required something very special. Something unique.

Megan.

He was different and so was she. But together they fit.

Too bad he told her to take a hike.

* * *

She'd done it.

She had made it through the week.

Except for the gaping hole where her heart used to be, Megan felt pretty okay. Normal, almost.

Too bad her overdeveloped sense of responsibility wouldn't let her pull the covers over her head and sleep the hurt away like she'd like to. There was still Christa's business to tend and customers who relied on it.

Besides, she should know by now that some things just weren't going to happen for her. It shouldn't come as such a shocked surprise that she was so dispensable in the lives of the people she most cared about. Maybe it was connected to the broken thing inside her that needed something different than most women needed to be happy. It made sense. It seemed reasonable that the two were connected.

But she kept hoping... Was it so hard to believe that somewhere out there a man existed who could love her the way she was?

She was in a maudlin mood, Megan realized, and the music she'd chosen didn't help. She knew she had a tendency when things got her down to give in to her sentimental side. This definitely qualified as one of those times. Megan had loaded up her CD changer with her favorite heartbreak singers and planned to wallow in her misery all the way to San Francisco.

It was a measure of her pain that she had called Patrice. She hadn't talked to her old mentor since she'd come home to Remington, tail between her legs. Megan knew the fault was hers that they hadn't stayed in touch. Patrice had never been anything other than an utterly calm eye in the storm of her life.

A small, delicate woman in her 40's, Patrice came from one of the city's proudest Chinese families. The oldest of five girls, she had traveled with her businessman father from an early age. Raised on two continents and educated in Paris, her speech still contained a hint of both the French she'd spoken in school and her family's native Chinese accents. A tiny woman weighing barely one hundred pounds, Megan had seen her bring down the strongest men, taking them apart piece by piece until she owned their very souls.

While Megan had attended culinary school in San Francisco, her nights and weekends had belonged to another type of education altogether. Patrice had served as her mentor and guide into San Francisco's Dominant/submissive lifestyle and Megan had spent over a year learning the submissive role under her tutelage. She had barely graduated to the Dominant role when she had met Damian Ruiz.

Although close to Megan in terms of age, in every way that counted he had proven to be much older. Active in the D/s community for years, Patrice had known him, of course, and had done her best to warn her pupil away from him. But Megan had been sure she knew better and wouldn't be persuaded. She had been eager to stretch her Domina wings and fly. And a willing, eager submissive with a little more experience had seemed perfect.

But what had appeared just right had proven to be too much over time. What had looked at first like an eagerness to please had begun to feel like overwhelming neediness. No amount of mental and sexual dominance had been enough for Damian. And when Megan had introduced limits to the relationship, Damian had reacted by becoming more clingy and submissive. Flowers and gifts had begun to appear, both at home and at school. What her classmates had seen as wildly romantic was, in fact, mentally and emotionally exhausting. Bombarded by emails and phone messages, Megan began to avoid him. Until the night she had gone to a D/s club solo and found Damian tied to a St. Andrew's cross, his body covered with welts, being caned by one of the scene's most physically punishing Dominas.

If you can't give me what I need, then I'll find someone who will. I want a real Domme, not a little girl playing dress-up.

And he had been right. Megan didn't have that in her. Barely six months past her debut and she was a failure already.

She hadn't been able to face Patrice in the wake of her catastrophe with Damian. She had left school without a word to anyone, packed up a U-haul full of her belongings and come home to Remington. Megan hadn't had the courage since to check into her status at the school. She had been less than four months from finishing her certificate when she left. Her roommate Michelle had probably made Megan's picture the bull's-eye on her dartboard for taking off and sticking her with one hundred percent of the rent. She had trashed every relationship she'd had with her immature behavior. You could span a continent with the bridges she'd burned.

And here she was again, running away from disaster. Maybe that should be her motto: When the going gets tough, the tough leave town.

Megan had her weekend all planned out. Friday night would be spent at her favorite hotel near Union Square, where

Patrice had agreed to meet her for dinner. Saturday she would spend the entire day at a spa she knew in Burlingame, being massaged, mud packed, and steamed. Sunday would include visits to all the stores small town Remington couldn't support, from the chain department stores to the big name designer boutiques. Megan would blow some of the money she'd been saving to open her own restaurant. She throttled the pragmatic voice in her head that squawked at spending a dime of her nest egg, telling herself there was nothing wrong with a little retail therapy. Sunday night was soon enough to start putting herself back together.

Her only chore still left undone was to stop by Goldie's on her way out of town. Jacy wanted to borrow Christa's truck to move some furniture and, since Christa had given her permission, Megan had agreed to drop off the keys. Fully expecting to have to pull around back and use the employee parking, Megan was pleasantly surprised to find a parking spot directly in front of the pub. 'Charlie's Angels' parking,' Jacy called it—her term for anytime she found an unusually lucky close parking spot. 'Because they never had to look for a place to park. Get it?' she'd explained when Megan had to ask what it meant.

Palming the truck keys, Megan pushed her way through the heavy red door of Goldie's. Welcomed, as always, by the sound of the jukebox and the smell of popcorn and cooking, she carefully made her mind a blank, blocking out the memories of the last time she'd visited her friend's business. It was still early for the Friday night happy hour crowd and the place was relatively quiet. Just Joe, one of the back up bartenders, Natalia, who would make two-hundred dollars in tips tonight with her amazing memory and even more amazing body, and a middle-aged couple enjoying a late lunch kept the place from being deserted.

"Hey, Joe. Where's the boss?" Megan had to raise her voice to be heard over Tony Bennett singing about San Francisco. Huh. What were the odds of that? Momentarily distracted by the music, Megan had to ask Joe to repeat his response.

"Which one? Everybody's my boss, right, Stretch?" He directed the last comment to Natalia who, at 6'1" was taller than even Jacy.

"You bet. Now do my bidding and get me two glasses of Chardonnay for my customers, eh?"

Nat's Russian accent was a big part of her success. The fact that she could bend over backwards and press herself into a handstand was another.

"I'm looking for Jacy, Joe. I'm supposed to meet her here to give her some keys."

"Sorry, doll. Don't know nothin' about it. Nat?" He turned to the waitress who only shrugged before loading the two glasses of wine the bartender had produced onto her tray and heading back to take care of the couple at the window table.

"Jacy's not here, Megan."

The voice came from behind her. Megan turned to see Steve emerge from the game room in the rear.

Dressed in work clothes, hair tied back, a fine layer of sawdust covering most of him, he must have just come from the job site. The region in her chest that had been numb for days turned over and thumped to life. The dirt on his face only made his blue eyes stand out that much more.

He looked wonderful.

But he didn't love her, Megan reminded herself. He didn't want anything to do with her. So what was he doing here, then?

Whatever it was, it didn't matter. She had to get out before she did or said something really stupid. Like, "Are you absolutely sure you don't want me?" The thought of those words slipping out and his probable response kicked her into action.

Megan turned on her heel and walked out.

Chapter Eleven

"Megan, wait!"

Dammit! She was getting away. Leaving before he'd even had a chance to apologize. Crawl if he had to.

She was already out on the sidewalk when he caught up to her. Keys in her hand, she repeatedly pressed a button on the electronic fob. She didn't even look up when he came closer.

He pressed closer still, caging her against her car with his arms, surrounding her small body with his. "Megan, wait. Talk to me. Please?"

Still trying futilely to get the automatic door lock to work and allow her escape, she finally looked up at him from over her shoulder. The cold, blazing fury in her eyes made him back off a half-step. But only for a second. Then he was right back at her. Maybe he could bypass her intellect and appeal directly to her body. He knew her body liked him just fine. The hurt he'd seen behind the anger made his gut twist, reminding Steve of the last time they'd seen each other. Please, God, give him the right words to make it up to her.

"What's the preferred greeting here, again? Give me a second—it'll come to me. Right. 'Oh. Hi.'" Steve winced. "I've got to go, Steve. Don't worry, I got your message. You were more than clear the other night. You don't have to worry about me showing up places and embarrassing you. Jacy can come to my place if she wants to see me."

Standing this close to her, he caught tantalizing whiffs of her hair, the shampoo she used, the underlying scent that he knew belonged only to her. He closed his eyes and pressed a kiss onto the top of her head. Steve realized that in her present frame of mind she might not appreciate the gesture and braced for an elbow to the ribs. When it didn't come he relaxed a little. But only a little. Standing this close to her, feeling the way he did, it was all he could do not to press himself into her tempting backside. Now that really would earn him a body blow. And to something more vulnerable than the ribcage.

"Megan, please."

"Trust is a funny thing, Steve. Easy to lose." Her voice trailed off so that he had to strain to catch her words. "Hard to win back." When he heard it break a little on the last word a wave of tenderness swept over him. He gave up the fight and wrapped his arms around her slender shoulders, pulling her close against him.

"Oh, baby..." She felt so good in his arms, cradled gently against his body. He gave himself strict orders that this was about comforting her, not copping a feel. "I am an ass."

As close as he was, Steve didn't hear a sound. But after a few moments her head nodded unmistakably in the affirmative.

Huh? She was agreeing with him? That was a good sign. Right? It was progress. Sort of.

"What can I do to make it up to you? Please. You've got to talk to me, Megan."

She shook her head slightly. "No."

"No? Baby, you've got to talk to me. What do I have to do?" His spirits plummeted. God, if he'd jacked this up beyond repair... Steve didn't want to think of the possibilities. He had to be able to fix this. Where was his famous charm when he really needed it?

Another slow shake of her head struck another blow to his hopes.

Looking away as Megan was, her graceful neck was left vulnerable. Steve was a desperate man—he couldn't afford to overlook an opening. He pressed another kiss on the spot where her pulse was visible. Open-mouthed, his tongue rested against her soft skin, tasting her flesh as he moved slowly to the tender area behind her ear. He listened to the instinct urging him to bite down and was rewarded by the low moan he coaxed from her.

By barely-perceptible degrees Megan softened. The stiffness gradually gave way until her body rested fully against his, without so much as a millimeter of space between them.

"Megan, please. Baby, please talk to me. Tell me what you want me to do." Plastered up against him the way she was, she had to be able to feel his erection pressing eagerly against her backside. The promise of satisfaction made by the tempting crease of her bottom was more than a man with his tenuous grip on his libido ought to be faced with. Regardless of whatever she told him, he knew what he wanted to do.

When she pulled away to turn in his arms Steve had to choose between crying in relief or frustration. Relief because temptation had moved out of reach—frustration because relief had moved out of reach. But one look into her tortured eyes and his own problems were forgotten. He would do anything to wipe that stricken look from her face.

"I want your total honesty. I want to know what's different now. What's changed between now and Tuesday night? You couldn't get away from me fast enough then. Why the change?"

"I... I..." Steve looked down into her earnest, almost solemn face. The freckles over the bridge of her nose gave her a waif-like quality and made her look years younger than he knew her to be. He could drown in the depths of her eyes. Maybe it was some kind of hypnotism, because he knew in that moment he could never lie to her again. Tuesday night in Goldie's had been a lie. He had let her think he didn't want her and that wasn't true. It wasn't true then and it would never be true. "Okay. Total honesty? I'm scared of what you make me feel. I guess I thought that if you were gone I could go back to the way things were before I met you."

She gave him a searching look. She looked deep into his eyes and he thought of the first night they'd met, when he'd thought she could see into his soul.

"Is that what you want? To go back to the way things were before we met?" She squared her shoulders and lifted her chin, as though she needed to brace herself for his answer.

A motorcycle rumbled by, the distinctive sound of its punched out baffles violating city sound ordinances and momentarily pulling him back from the emotional brink he teetered on. Self-awareness flooded back and Steve was suddenly conscious of being in a very public place. To his surprise, not only didn't he care, he was actually glad. He wanted the world to know that she was his and he was hers.

"No. Not at all. Lady, you scare the hell out of me." Steve squeezed his eyes shut in desperate concentration. How to explain what he felt inside? "But, you get me. Like no one else ever has. And I can't wait to see what you'll do next."

* * *

Oh, sister, were you ever right. Whatever her sister had seen in her face that night, Megan couldn't deny that Christa had called it. She was a total goner. She didn't like to think of herself as shallow, but looking up into those eyes, not quite blue, not quite green, the sun turning his hair the most incredible shade of red-gold, all she could think was, *he is so beautiful.*

"Next? I'm going to get into my car and drive to San Francisco."

She saw his grin, which had been tilting ever so slightly into the cocky right up until the moment the words "San Francisco" had come out of her mouth, slide right off his face. Disbelief sparred with frustration, with disbelief the eventual winner.

"You can't."

"Actually, yeah, I think I have to."

Frustration got up off the mat and made a feverish comeback. Steve braced himself against the roof of her car and watched her closely. "What's so important in San Francisco, all of a sudden?"

"I'm meeting an old friend for dinner."

"Is this old friend a him or a her?"

Megan could tell that Steve was working to maintain an even tone. But she could also see that jealousy was riding him and sought to reassure him. "It's a her. An old teacher of mine from when I lived in the city."

The two vertical lines between his brows relaxed immediately. "Oh. Okay." Steve moved closer, straddling her legs as he dropped his hands from her car to her shoulders. "Can you call and reschedule?" The rasp of his calloused fingertips against her bare skin made the small hairs on the back of her neck stand up. Steve smoothed his hands down her arms, from shoulders to hands and back up again, a sensual promise made with every stroke. Despite her resolve not to weaken, Megan couldn't keep her eyes from drooping in pleasure. Or from closing momentarily when Steve allowed his thumbs to graze the underside of her breasts on his upstroke.

"I made a promise, Steve, and it's important to me to keep it." Her hormones shrieked in protest, but Megan held firm.

Taking her hand in his larger one, Steve brought it down to press against the fly of his jeans. The feel of his erection through the well worn cloth made her smile. "What about a promise made a little closer to home?"

Deciding two could play that game, Megan pressed against him before raking her nails across the tip. "I don't remember any promises being made." She tried for her sunniest, most innocent smile.

Steve's hips flexed, as though seeking to follow the movement of her hand. "Maybe not in so many words, but those present—" He drew her hand back down to his straining erection, in case she was having trouble deciphering his meaning. "—definitely heard something."

Smiling up into his face, desire sharpening those already impressive cheekbones, Megan hooked her thumbs in his belt loops and pulled him closer. "I won't change my dinner plans, but I wouldn't say no to some company on the drive. If you don't mind finding something to do while I meet Patrice for dinner." While his hips drove her backward until she pressed against the warm metal of her car, Megan used her grip on his pants to pull herself up and whisper in his ear. "I have a hotel room. With a queen-size bed."

"When do we leave?"

* * *

After stopping by Steve's place long enough for him to throw some clothes in a bag, Megan pointed her little Toyota south and headed out of town. It didn't take long for the twisting four-lane road to give way to the interstate that would take them west to San Francisco. Never a bad drive, with Steve keeping her company Megan found the time passed even more quickly than usual. The green hills of the Sierras were left behind and they passed through the flatland of the Sacramento basin before reaching the hillsides of Napa and its endless rows of immaculately manicured vines. The stress and sadness of the previous three days was slipping away with every mile that passed under the wheels of her car. Relaxed—lighthearted, even—Megan's head was beginning to fill with thoughts and plans for the weekend ahead.

Trading stories of their college careers, Megan laughed repeatedly as Steve kept her entertained with stories of his time spent in San Diego. Even his choice of colleges had shocked her. She would have figured him for a local boy, and was surprised he had chosen far away to the south. While she could easily picture him in the laid-back atmospheres of Chico or Santa Barbara, San Diego would have been far down her list of guesses. His grades just good enough to keep from being thrown out, Steve had confessed that he had spent nine of every ten waking hours not in class learning to surf. The thought of how he must have looked, throwing back his long hair as he emerged from the surf, board tucked under his arm, snug half-wetsuit hugging his lean muscles, nearly caused her to drift into the next lane. It took the noisy thumping of the lane demarcation buttons to startle her from her daydream.

Much sooner than she expected, the skyline of San Francisco was looming ahead of them. Megan had fallen in love with the city on her first visit, a family vacation when she was probably nine or ten. The smell of the ocean, the people, the colors of the city lights at night, all thrilled her. As a child she had loved all the things her classmates at the cooking academy had dismissed as hopelessly touristy: eating clam chowder from a sourdough bowl, feeding the raucous seagulls that inhabited every corner of the city—even visiting Alcatraz had delighted her. And of course the food. It was probably her exposure to the diverse cuisines San Francisco offered that had begun her fascination with food and cooking.

Making her way around Union Square to her favorite old hotel, Megan pulled the car to a stop in front. A twenty-dollar bill and her keys to one of the doormen took care of parking. They probably wouldn't need the car again all weekend. If they wanted to go anywhere it was usually easier to take public transportation or walk than deal with the traffic and the hills. Although Megan really couldn't imagine where they might want to go that would be more entertaining than their hotel room. After one critical stop first, that is. A quick stop at the

Concierge desk inside to deposit their bags and Megan was ready for an adventure.

"Do you mind if we take a little walk and stretch our legs before we head up to the room? I have a place in mind I'd like to take you to, if you're game."

"Can I go like this?" Steve frowned doubtfully at his soiled work clothes. "I didn't even shower."

Megan took her time taking visual inventory. From his battered Wolverine work boots to a frayed and obviously favorite gold DeWalt T-shirt ("Real men do it with 18 volts") he was a picture to make any red-blooded woman's heart flutter. And something told Megan it wouldn't be just the women looking. "You'll be fine. The only question is will I be able to fend off all the competition?"

Turning to head out the hotel's double doors to the street, Megan was spun around on her heels as Steve's hand snaked out to pull her back. Using his free arm to pull her close, he hauled her up on her toes and stuck his face close to hers. "No competition. Just you and me." Before kissing her breathless.

Oh, my. Well, wasn't that interesting?

"Okay." Megan saw from the corner of her eye that the concierge was studying his computer screen with more diligence than she remembered ever seeing before. Tilting her head the other direction, she noted that the doorman was staring fixedly at ceiling moldings he'd seen every day of his working life. "Ready, then?"

The hotel she had chosen was located in the heart of downtown, thick with other historic old hotels and first-class shopping. They wove their way between the late afternoon pedestrian traffic, a predictable mix of business people, shoppers and tourists, occasionally enlivened by the kind of exuberant individuality that alternately chagrined and delighted the natives.

A short walk past Nordstrom's, a left turn at Starbuck's and up two more blocks. Megan smiled to see one of her favorite old haunts was still in business. The window display of lingerie was surprisingly tasteful—until the viewer's eye was drawn to the shoes on the mannequins' plastic feet. Three-inch clear Lucite platforms with seven-inch spike heels began to tell the real story. The discerning observer might notice the not-quite feminine bulge behind one mannequin's thong panties. But it was the tail made from authentic horsehair dangling artistically from the rear of another's that really put it over the top, Megan decided.

There had been a time when she had known all the staff at Too, Too Sullied Flesh—better known to regulars as Sullie's—by name. Too many times she had subsisted on nothing but Ramen noodles and classroom projects from the culinary academy because she had spent her week's pay on some toy or other from Sullie's. Although Patrice had a playroom full of equipment that cost more than Megan could ever hope to make as a chef, Megan still hadn't been able to resist the lure of buying as many of her own as she could afford. Or not afford, as the case might be.

The bells over the door announced their arrival and as she stepped through the door, one hand still firmly clasped in Steve's, Megan was awash in memories. The sultry sound of a Rosemary Clooney CD and the smell of expensive leather brought back the times she and her mentor had capped off an evening out with a trip to Sullie's to expand Megan's toy box. The exotic looking African-American woman behind the counter looked up from the magazine she had been flicking through to greet them. Her perfunctory 'Good afternoon, darlings' ended in a high-pitched shriek when she recognized Megan.

"Girlie *girl!* Oh my God, where have you *been?!*"

Megan always enjoyed first-timers' reactions to Raven and Steve didn't let her down. Taking in her friend's low-slung hip huggers—so tight they appeared painted on—waist-length hair and extreme make up, Steve's mouth gaped open. But only for a second. When he got a look at a pair of 34 double-Ds few people ever forgot encased in a low-cut pink T-shirt, he recovered enough to smile appreciatively.

"Hey, babe." Megan was swept into a hug, Raven bending low to greet her height-challenged friend.

Releasing Megan as quickly as she'd embraced her, the other woman immediately launched into her rant. "Don't you 'hey, babe' me, Miss Thing. I want to know why you didn't leave a number where anyone could reach you. Some of us were worried about you, you selfish little wench." Pink lipstick that was a perfect match to the T-shirt was expertly painted on full lips that now formed a pout bordering on ostentatious. Perfectly manicured brows arched over equally perfectly made up eyes that narrowed accusingly in Megan's direction. The hands on the hips were the ultimate punctuation to her friend's snit.

"Don't make the scrunchy face at me, please? I'm in town. I'll leave you my number and email, I promise." Knowing the hurt feelings were ninety percent show, Megan added what she hoped would be the peace offering that would soothe the last of the ruffled feathers. "I've come to spend money."

Looking Megan up and down, Raven turned her attention to Steve. "All right. And are you going to introduce me to this tall drink of water, or will a girl shrivel up and die an old maid first? Hmmm?"

Chapter Twelve

"See anything that looks interesting?"

Megan spoke softly, approaching from the side so quietly Steve hadn't realized she was there until he heard her question at the same time a hand caressed his ass. A slow, open palmed massage of his butt wasn't something that happened to him every day. Especially not in public. But the hypnotic feel of her hand moving in circles over his flesh was making the hair on his arms and the back of his neck stand up. He wanted to feel more of that. But without clothes and somewhere he could do something about it.

"Huh? Uh, yeah. Everything."

"Anything in particular catch your eye?"

After the introductions had been made he had wandered off to look around the store while Megan and Raven had spent a few minutes catching up. While he had been in the Adults Only back room of Remington's video store plenty of times, Steve had to admit this was the first store he'd ever seen with a six foot section devoted strictly to butt plugs.

"Does that—" He'd spoken without thinking. Just said the first thing that had come into this head. But he cut off what he'd been about to say. He wasn't sure he could handle the answer.

Megan looked from the display that stood before them to his face, nothing but curiosity showing on her face. "Does what?"

Trying for casual, Steve looked around to make sure they weren't overheard. Seeing that Megan's friend had returned to her magazine, only occasionally looking their way, he finished his thought. Since there was no one else in the shop at the time he wasn't sure who he was afraid would listen in. "Does that feel good?" He followed Megan's eyes as they glanced at the display and back to him.

"If you do it right, sure. Start small. Use plenty of lubricant. And it helps to be really turned on first. It can be amazing." Steve didn't know whether to be relieved or disappointed when Megan took his hand and led him away. "Any time you want to experiment let me know."

At a side counter was a collection of bottles. "Are you fussy about scents?"

Steve picked up the one closest to him. It smelled like roses. "For who?" He reached for another. More woodsy, like juniper.

"Me. You. Whoever. It's massage oil."

That didn't sound bad at all. It sounded slippery. Slippery could be nice. "Yeah, okay. Just don't make me smell like a girl."

Adding the woodsy one to a small pile at the register, Megan gave him a smile before turning back to Raven, who had begun totaling the sale. Since he hadn't seen her pick out anything but the oil Steve took note of what went into the bag. When, in the midst of the oils and small sample-sized tubes a box was slipped in, it caught his attention. Judging from the price on the digital display, it wasn't something small.

"What's in the box?"

"Just a little something for my hope chest." He wasn't sure exactly what one of those was, let alone what went into one, but it sounded like a chick thing. His curiosity quotient about tripled when Megan gave him a wicked grin and said, "I hope I get to see you in it someday."

* * *

Steve lay on the bed, mindlessly clicking through channels with the TV remote. The Kings weren't playing and nothing was holding his attention. How could it?

The walk back to the hotel had been uneventful. Megan had slipped an arm around his waist and it had felt completely natural to drop one of his across her shoulders. Besides making it easier to protect her from the bumps and jostles of a crowded sidewalk, it gave him an excuse to hold her.

And a good thing he'd taken the opportunity because as soon as they'd gotten to the room Megan had disappeared into the bathroom. Sounds of a shower were making him nuts. He could picture the water sluicing over her lithe body, running in streams from her tits, her mound, her ass. Did she want him to join her? In his imagination he did and she welcomed him into not only the over-sized shower stall, but her body as well. But he could also imagine her glaring at him, ordering him out of the bathroom. So he did nothing.

When she emerged a short time later, she was so transformed Steve had been shocked into silence.

Gone was the casual girl he was used to seeing. In her place was a stranger. A black suit replaced the denim and sundresses he was familiar with. A blindingly white shirt was buttoned up to her chin with some kind of black pin holding it closed. She'd put her hair up into a twist, pulling it off her face, accenting her cheekbones and adding about ten years to her look. Even her shoes were different. Some kind of wicked stepsister jobs with pointy toes and vicious-looking spiked heels took the place of her usual sandals or sneakers. Most shocking of all, though, was her mouth. She had painted it scarlet.

"How do I look?"

Oh, mama. Fuckable. Do me now. Totally fuckable.

"Uh, great... Different. But great." He was babbling. Steve knew he sounded idiotic, but what did she expect?

"Good. Why don't you have room service send up some dinner? Take a shower. Relax." Stepping between his legs as he'd sat sprawled in a chair, unable to move or speak, Megan had leaned over to brace her arms on the chair next to his. "Think about what you'd like to do when I get back."

And then she had kissed him.

A self-assured kiss, as powerful as the image she projected in her severe black, it was a kiss of ownership.

And then, before Steve could react and kiss her back, Megan was walking away. Opening the door. Stepping through. "I was going to say don't touch yourself while I'm gone. But I changed my mind. In fact, I think you probably should. When I come back I want this to last more than thirty seconds. Got it?"

"Yes, ma'am."

But he'd been talking to the door. She was gone.

That was nearly three hours ago. He'd done as she suggested, ordering a burger with everything from room service. A salad, too. Extra fries with Thousand Island dressing. Steve was hoping he'd need the extra carbs and fat for energy.

He'd done the other thing she'd suggested, too. In the shower, after scrubbing away the dirt and grime from the day's work, he had washed his hair with the hotel's shampoo. Then, while the pulsating waves of water had pounded his back, Steve had soaped his hand and thought of Megan.

What would she do when she came back? Tie him up again? A jolt of excitement shot through him as he remembered what it had felt like. So what if he was a sick puppy? He'd never felt anything like it, before or since, and he wanted that feeling again. He shoved himself into his fist over and over, pretending it was Megan's sweet pussy that was clasping him so tightly. "Fuck me," she'd said and it hadn't been a request. Steve closed his eyes and remembered what it had felt like—imagined what it would feel like tonight. It was nothing like the real thing, but it would have to do until Megan got back.

* * *

Thank God that was over.

Megan startled herself with her uncharitable thought. She loved Patrice. Patrice knew her in ways probably no other person on the planet did. And cared for her the same way. Megan didn't like this side of herself. She should be able to put other things aside long enough to have dinner with an old friend.

But the siren call of what was waiting for her upstairs had her ear and wouldn't stop whispering in it. It was exquisite torture and Megan drew it out as long as she could, even asking Patrice if she would like to order dessert. Her old friend had graciously declined, though.

"No, I'll let you go. As wonderful as it is to see you again I can tell you have other things on your mind."

She had started to object, but Patrice only looked at her with those patient, worldly eyes.

"I never could hide anything from you."

"It is no great trick, my dear. I think even the waiter, he knows you have somewhere to go. You glow, Megan."

After that Megan had waited with Patrice while the valet brought her car. The twenty-year-old Mercedes was like everything belonging to her mentor, top quality and redolent of quiet, old money. They embraced and Patrice brought tears to Megan's eyes with her farewell.

"Take care, my dear. Listen to your heart—it is wiser than your head."

"Thank you. I will."

"And if it is more than one month before I hear from you again, be warned. I will take a crop to your backside the next time I see you. Don't think I won't." Patrice might have been laughing when she said it, but Megan didn't doubt her for a minute.

"No, ma'am."

The walk back to her room gave Megan time to reflect. Seeing Patrice had helped Megan turn a corner in her mind, she realized. Seeing her old friend, being in the city of her biggest disappointment, and knowing she had not only survived but moved on, was freeing somehow.

So that when the aged elevator finally deposited Megan on her floor and she found herself in front of her door, all the old energy that had been locked up inside her with nowhere to go came flooding back. When she opened the door, it felt like the start of something important.

He was on the bed, naked save for a pair of boxers, one hand on the clicker, one hand in the shorts. Maybe it was her imagination, but Megan liked the idea that she could still see the stain of her lipstick on him from their last kiss.

"Ready?"

His eyes had been on her the second she'd stepped into the room. He nodded.

"Really?" She infused her voice with just a hint of skepticism—disapproval, even. She had to remember, though, that he was new to role playing. She would have to watch him carefully for any sign that it had stopped being fun. "You don't look ready. Why are you wearing those shorts? Why are you dressed at all, for that matter? Take them off. Then come over here and serve me."

Steve hustled off the bed with an enthusiasm that was most pleasing. Stripping off the offending garment, he tossed it at a nearby chair, not noticing when it missed and landed on the floor. His erection jutted forward eagerly as he came to stand in front of her. "Yes, ma'am. I'm ready."

"I'll be the judge of that. And for future reference, the next time I tell you to wait for me, I expect to find you naked. Is that clear?"

"Yes, ma'am."

Megan loved the twinkle in his eye even as he uttered the subservient words. He thought he was playing. But she could tell it was turning him on just the same.

"We'll have to teach you a proper greeting, including a decent bow." Let him stew on that for a few seconds. "But that can wait. Help me off with my clothes, slave."

A little pent-up breath was expelled when Steve moved to obey. Megan could tell, like most men, he was at a loss when it came to women's clothing, so she held her arms away from her body, indicating she wanted help with the jacket. He unbuttoned the single closure the suit possessed, easing it cautiously from her shoulders. The title had been a risk—he would either love it or hate it. Since he hadn't walked out in a huff she concluded he liked the little buzz it gave him and moved on to her skirt and blouse.

Removing her skirt had taken several long minutes, with each miniscule tug downward on one side matched by another on the opposite side. All the while he had breathed hot, moist air across her dripping pussy, as he dropped easily to his knees for the task.

By the time they got to her blouse, Megan had concluded she had an impudent slave on her hands. No one could possibly fumble that badly that many times with buttons, taking so long she'd had to grit her teeth to keep from moaning in frustration. Each attempt at the buttons—particularly the ones near her breasts—was accompanied by maneuvering that somehow managed to brush the tips of her nipples, teasing them into taut little nubs.

Finally down to nothing but her bra, thong and shoes, Megan led the way to the bed. "I think I'm ready for a backrub now."

With more energy than technique, Steve went to work on her naked backside. He had drawn a little gasp from her when, instead of warming the oil in his hands first, he poured it directly onto her back. Her bra was removed next, strictly for safety reasons, he assured her, not wanting to risk getting oil on the delicate lace. The rosemary and lavender undertones came out gradually as he worked it in to Megan's skin, his hands sliding wonderfully across her back and shoulders. The bed shifted and squeaked as he moved from side to side, using his thumbs and fingers in short, circular sweeps.

Straddling her backwards, Steve massaged the long muscles of her butt and legs. Megan was feeling wonderfully relaxed as he continued to rub the aromatic stuff into the back of her thighs, so it took her a few moments to realize he had stopped rubbing. Stretching out on top of her, warm, oil-slick fingers slid the T-strap of her thong aside and a warm tongue began to explore her pussy. Her senses lulled by the drugging effect of the oil and hands stimulating her skin, her face mashed into the coverlet, there was nothing she could do. Nothing she wanted to do. She could only lie there and take it.

As that skillful, wicked mouth went to work on her, Megan wanted to grind her hips, but the weight of his body above her gave her no leverage. She was helpless. Steve used his lips and tongue to woo her, with little bites and licks, until she was arching and shifting and chasing an orgasm that remained stubbornly just out of reach.

Fingers entered her soaked channel, pressing on her clit it seemed from the inside out.

And then suddenly the fingers were gone and the weight was lifting off her back. Strong arms lifted her limp body and tucked a pillow under her hips.

"I know what Mistress needs now," a low masculine voice rumbled in her ear.

"Mmpfh?" She would never get anywhere with that wimpy protest. Not that she was altogether sure she wanted to.

"Mistress needs a good, hard fucking from her slave." A hot, hard cock slid into her and proceeded to match deeds to words.

Chapter Thirteen

Oh, yeah.

Just like coming home. Only home had never felt like a hot, tight fist squeezing his cock before. It could, though. Steve thought he could get used to it in a hurry.

It seemed like forever since he'd been here, instead of just days. God, he wanted it to be good for her. Steve wanted it to last forever, but he was afraid he wouldn't last five minutes.

Arched over her, hands holding hers to the mattress, Steve realized how small she was. Without her gaze on him, the power of her personality wasn't as obvious and he could appreciate the lightness of her frame. How much shorter her legs were than his. Because when she turned those magical dark eyes on him he couldn't see anything else. The world narrowed until it was just her and him.

Steve wanted to go slow, but it felt too damned good. The vise-tight grip of her pussy. The visual, still burned into his brain, of her ass in the air ready to take him.

He pulled out as slowly as he could force himself to go, the firm grip of her sheath giving up its hold reluctantly. When he was nearly free, only the tip of him remaining inside her, Steve reversed direction and began to slide back in, one agonizingly slow inch at a time.

"Am I going too fast for Mistress?" It gave him a charge to call her that. He wasn't sure why. But it made him feel strong. Powerful. At her service.

The oil he had so lovingly worked into the skin of her back made the sensation of slipping across her a completely new sensory experience. His nipples, sensitized by the metal that pierced them, were electrified by the merest graze across her slick skin.

"Mmm. No. Just right." Her voice was a barely recognizable mumble. Like she was dazed with pleasure. He slowed down. In and even more slowly back out.

"Like that, you mean?"

"No!" A shake of the head for emphasis. "Faster. Like before."

Good thing she couldn't see his face. He was probably grinning like a fool. But he'd never been more aroused. Or more in tune with a partner. He knew what she needed. And he had never felt more uniquely equipped to be the one to give it to her.

He grabbed another pillow and added it to the one already supporting her upper body. Fat and with plenty of loft, they raised Megan's body into near perfect alignment.

His cock now able to slide even deeper, Steve took one of Megan's hands and brought it back to her plump little clit—let her fingers show him the rhythm and direction she needed. As he let the momentum of his thrusts push her forward into their joined hands, Megan began making urgent, frustrated noises as she rocked her hips along with him. God, but it turned his crank in a big way to know he could do that to her. When her rhythm began to pick up speed he pulled her hand away and back down to the mattress.

"Dammit! Let go."

Her tone was lethal. If he knew women—and he was beginning to think he did this particular one—Steve recognized the sound of thwarted lust when it spoke. It took everything he had not to obey the authority in her voice.

The regret wasn't totally faked when he had to deny her. "I'm sorry, Mistress, but I can't. You're not ready yet."

Her language took a turn toward the gutter, but Steve didn't relent. He just continued working himself in and out of her tight, creamy pussy. The only problem was it felt too freaking good. He'd have to start thinking of roundball. The critical three-pointer Bibby missed in the '02 conference finals. They'd need a good outside shooter this year if they wanted—

Megan slammed her hips back into him, trying to find the angle she needed to put her over the edge. The slap of skin on skin, the sight of her slender neck, bared by the angry toss of her head as he thrust in and out, triggered something primitive in him. Feeling the intensity already, the sight of her bare neck seemed to call for another kind of possession. Already pinned under his weight, held in position by his hands and cock, Steve didn't question the need that rose in him to secure her further. To mark her. Taking aim on the graceful transition of neck to shoulder, he reached down and bit her neck. Gripped gently, but firmly, and held on.

Her sweet moans and little grunts morphed into one long wail of need. Longing and lust melded into one. Steve couldn't hold back any longer. Megan needed what only he could give her as much as he needed to give it to her.

Her body shook as he slammed into her, their skin slick from oil and sweat. The feel of her slender hips as his cock drove deep taunted him. He wanted it all and part of it remained elusively out of reach. Megan pushed back on him with his every thrust, her hands clenched tightly in the coverlet. Steve was lost in the wonder of their two merged bodies and the urgency that drove him. The overpowering need to be as close as humanly possible. No, closer than that, even. Inside her. Surrounding her. Part of her.

Jesus God, but he needed her. Wanted her. Loved her.

Teetering on the jagged edge of his own release, Steve took Megan's hand in his again and guided it back to her clit. "Now. Come on." He wanted to be the one to give her everything, including her orgasm, but instinct was in control. He dropped his hands and focused on rocking her world. "Give it up. Come on."

"Oh. You bastard. Fuck me. Harder. *Fuck* me. Now!"

She was yelling now and they were both out of control, bodies colliding. Two elemental creatures, wild things, stripped bare by instinct and passion. "Oh. OhmyGod!" Her cries were the only warning he had before the ecstatic ripples of her cunt gripped him and dragged him with her headlong into oblivion.

* * *

The time on the clock read 5:13, its red digital display subtly anachronistic in the otherwise charmingly decorated old hotel room. Where the furnishings weren't authentic reproductions of the art deco that had been the probable choice of the original management, they were at least old looking. So the glowing red numbers of the clock on the nightstand were disturbing, jarring to Megan's already restless frame of mind. She stretched in the dark, her foot brushing a hairy, masculine leg.

The room's curtains, typical hotel issue, completely blocked all light. At this time of the morning Megan knew the lights of Union Square would be winking off, one by one, as the man-made glamour of San Francisco after dark gave way to the soft grays and blues of the morning. Her body was exhausted but, perversely, Megan was unable to turn off the thoughts running through her head. Like random particles bouncing around in a super-collider, they could still all fit under the *Jeopardy!* heading 'What to do next?' She knew what she wanted to do. She wanted to keep him. Any way she could, whatever it took.

After the mind-blowingly hot turnabout of the evening's first encounter when Steve had so effectively turned the tables on her, they had made love twice more.

Her desire for a shower hadn't worked out when the shower stall had proved to be prohibitively narrow. Not that it absolutely couldn't have been done, but Megan had been feeling mellow and replete and totally unwilling to leave Steve even long enough to shower. The bathtub, though, with its deep draw and wide old-fashioned sides had fit the bill. The tub had been filled and the lights turned out, leaving the room lit only by lamplight from the adjoining room. It had been heaven to lie in each others' arms, alternately soaping and rinsing one another.

Megan had to admit that sex in the bathtub had definitely been her fault.

Running her hands down his neck and shoulders, she hadn't been able resist planting a kiss on Steve's chiseled jaw. Just one kiss couldn't hurt. But one kiss had led to another, the next on his strong neck. Which then called for a small bite. Her fingers had found his nipples, given them a pinch and it had snowballed from there.

Although the water was deep, she hadn't needed her eyes to guide her. Every feminine instinct she possessed told her his cock would be rising and they hadn't failed her. One hand stroked his awakening flesh while the other played with his balls. Steve had remained still, letting her arouse him, slowly teasing him to the breaking point. Until finally, his eyes asking and hers answering, he had lifted her onto his erect cock. Only to halt, his hands frozen as they had been about to lower her body, his lips stopping in mid-kiss.

"Shit."

"What?" Megan closed the distance for him and completed the kiss. He tasted delicious, his skin slightly raspy beneath her tongue.

Water rippled as Steve pulled back, banging his head lightly against the wall. "I forgot the condom. I didn't use one the last time, either."

"Don't worry about it." She linked her fingers with his and let her friend gravity force his lovely fat cock to fill her up. Closing her eyes, Megan held onto Steve's hands for balance and slowly rotated her hips, savoring the sensation.

Lost in her own pleasure, she was startled when he effectively stopped her movement by grasping her around the waist. "Do you *want* to get pregnant?"

She stopped and blinked at him. "No. I only meant I use the patch. Birth control. It's okay." Megan began to move again, still a little spooked by what she'd read on Steve's face and in his eyes. She didn't take believe in taking chances with anything that might require a college fund some day. But she would swear that had been a hopeful spark she'd seen light his eyes, if only for a moment. If she was going to be honest with herself she would have to ask herself why that thought thrilled her so.

After falling asleep still damp from the bath and wrapped in each others' arms, Megan had awakened to the sensation of her legs being parted and a hard penis nudging persistently at her opening. Steve must have been stroking her as she slept, because she had already been wet and ready for him. Their loving that time had been slow and tender, filled with long pauses for nothing but kisses and gentle caresses.

Megan stared hard into the darkness, straining to pick out the smallest hint of Steve's elegant profile. She scooted closer and wrapped herself around his back, slipping an arm around his waist to hug him close. She knew what was keeping her awake.

Somewhere along the way she had fallen in love.

Probably early on, maybe even that very first night when he had presented himself at her table in Goldie's. But what about him? What did he feel? She knew he liked what she could do for him. To him. He was infatuated with the buzz he got when she controlled the moves and made him bend to her will. But was that enough? Was she enough? Or would he need more?

Leaning in close to breathe in his clean manly smell, Megan held him a little tighter and pressed a kiss to his muscular back. *"I love you."* She was a coward and only whispered the words softly. So softly that, even were he awake, he wouldn't be able to hear. The power of the words terrified her, but she wanted to speak them so that maybe, on some level, his subconscious would get the message.

A long arm reached around behind him and gripped her ass, Steve's big hand able to palm it neatly, and pulled her closer. "Me too, babe. Just don't expect me to do anything about it until I've gotten some sleep, though."

* * *

Two weeks later.

"What is it?"

"It's a present, genius. Open it."

Steve looked at the box, a little bigger than a deck of cards, that Megan had left on the recently made bed. It was Sunday afternoon and they were expected at his parents' house for dinner, where his folks were meeting Megan for the first time. Having spent most of the day apart, when they had come back together at her place they had left a trail of clothes that led from the front door to the bedroom. "If I have to share you with my family, I'll need a little something to get me through until tonight. A fond memory to tide me over," he had told her. The afternoon's lesson in obedience had wrecked the bed, but left a smile on his face.

And now this.

"What's in it?" He was pretty sure he recognized it. It looked suspiciously like the same box he'd last seen disappearing into the purple bag with gold lettering in Sullie's. The box for Megan's hope chest. What had she said? Something about hoping to see him in it? Which made it sound like apparel. It was an awfully tiny box for anything a man his size would wear.

Her voice was low and silky. "Something I plan on seeing you wearing in approximately two minutes. Open it."

Still a little reluctant, Steve picked up the box. He picked it up and shook it. The rattling told him it was small. Whatever it was, it wasn't going to unwrap itself. But there was no arguing and very little negotiating when Megan wore what he'd come to think of as "the face." He checked. Yup. Very definitely had "the face" on. Steve ripped the paper and pulled off the lid.

Sitting on a bed of white cotton was a....he didn't know what it was. Black leather straps attached to a stainless steel ring and...a lock? What the...?

Genuinely puzzled, he had to ask. "I'm challenged. How am I supposed to wear—oh, no. In your dreams, doll. In your dreams."

How the hell had she gotten from naked to that so fast? Dressed all in gray, Megan looked like a candidate for the Young Republicans club. She wore tailored pants and a sweater set in a lighter shade, topped off with a pearl necklace that would have done the current First Lady proud. And she was bearing down on him with what could only be a cock harness in her petite hands.

"No fucking way." He felt the need for additional emphasis.

"Oh yeah, way." She had it unlocked and unsnapped now, but there was no adjusting the stainless steel ring that was held by two straps of riveted black leather. And the strap that joined at a ninety-degree angle could only be meant to torture his poor balls. "You are going to look so freaking hot in this. Do you have any idea what it will do to me, to know you're wearing this while we're having dinner with your family?" Her half smile was truly wicked and her eyes were slitted in what looked very much like ecstatic pleasure. "I don't know how I'll stand it all night."

All night?

His cock, which had been milked dry just minutes before, showed traitorous signs of going along with the perverted plan. Steve was appalled at the tingle of interest he felt shoot through him at the thought. Disgusted though he was with himself, the devil on his shoulder was whispering in his ear. *"Yeah. Oh yeah. You know you want it, you sick fuck."*

Where was the wall when you needed to bang your head against it? He sighed. "Okay. So, how did you say this thing goes on?"

Stephanie Vaughan

While always naturally artistic, Stephanie Vaughan did not pursue writing until she was challenged by a friend who thought herself 'too sarcastic and cynical to be a romance heroine.' Stephanie decided to prove her wrong. The floodgates opened and she found herself bombarded by characters demanding their stories be written.

A native southern Californian, Stephanie lists her influences as The Marx Brothers, Suzanne Brockmann, Woody Allen, Linda Howard, Dennis Miller, Angela Knight and Ella Fitzgerald. Stephanie still resides in southern California, where she lives with her husband and son, and indulges her passion for great coffee, "nature's perfect food."

Stephanie loves to hear from her fans. You can find her on the Web at www.stephanievaughan.com.

BLACK WIDOW

Lena Austin

Dedication

In fond memory of the real "Black Widow," who was more than a teacher. She was my friend. I miss you, Kelly.

Chapter One

The jangle of the ringing telephone disturbed Calder's peaceful contemplation of the words on his computer. Writing the Great American Novel didn't pay the bills, so Calder picked up the phone when the caller ID displayed his agent's number.

"Hey, Calder, my man! Glad I caught you. Got a job I know you're gonna love," Ruben Grimes proclaimed, as he always did.

With a purely internal sigh, Calder said, "Yeah, yeah, Ruben. That's what you said about the article I did for that parents' magazine where I ended up on a Greyhound bus full of thirty screaming kids going to a theme park. My ears still haven't recovered." The article might have brought him money, but the cost to his nerves had hardly made it worth his while.

Still, he couldn't help but like Ruben. The guy worked hard to find Calder steady jobs so he could pay the bills until his first novel sold. Calder had forgiven Ruben the day the check arrived.

"No, this time I'm positive it is right up your alley. That degree of yours is finally going to get some use. You hit the big time, my man! You may have hated that article in *Parents*

Weekly, but your take on how theme parks can be healthy experiences caught the eye of an editor who happens to have kids."

Ruben drew breath and launched into a spiel that actually had Calder grabbing a pen and notepad in a hurry. Calder couldn't believe his ears. It *was* the big time, with a correspondingly huge payoff, if he could deliver. No deadline, and that alone was impressive. There was only one catch.

"No wonder they aren't giving me a deadline date. Geez, Ruben, I don't have a clue how to get involved in a BDSM society, much less penetrate its secrets," Calder protested.

"That's the trick, buddy. Look, an ex-cop with psych and sociology degrees has the best hope of getting in and writing that article. I sold you to them on this, and they agree. You gotta try. What have you got to lose?"

"My skin?" Calder suggested. "I have dire visions of losing precious flaps of epidermis I'd rather keep intact."

"Tell you what, Calder. Do some research on the Net, read a couple of books on the subject, and get back to me." Ruben hung up the phone, probably because he was afraid Calder would refuse.

Calder sighed, and opened up his browser.

A few hours, and more cups of coffee than his stomach could handle, later, Calder pushed back from his keyboard with a groan. His eyes burned, and his hand hurt from all the notes he'd made. The legal pad was full, and it had only been half-used when he'd started.

"Geeee-zus!" He rubbed his eyes. "This is like learning a whole fucking new language. Safe words, releases, equipment, and that's just the start. Okay!" Calder pushed to his feet. "First things first. I'm going to make a monster sandwich, then I'm going to the library."

The pickles had just hit the plate to complete a sandwich worthy of the Tower of Pisa when the phone rang for a second time. Ruben again.

"Pushy, aren't you?" Calder said in lieu of a greeting. But he said it with a grin. "What, Mrs. Grimes wants another diamond or something that you call me twice in one day?" He bit into his sandwich.

Ruben chuckled. "I just figured you had enough time to log on and get intrigued. Was I right?"

Swallowing so he could laugh, Calder let loose a vulgar epithet. "Yeah, you got me. And I'm more than intrigued, you sneaky bastard. Though what the librarian is going to think when I ask for a book titled, *Screw the Roses, Give Me the Thorns,* I don't know." He contemplated the filthy looks he'd get as he swallowed another bite.

The snort over the phone was worthy of a thoroughbred. "You never can tell, bud. She might be a member of one of those clubs. It's the quiet ones you gotta watch out for."

"Ruben, you married a Broadway actress. You wouldn't know quiet if it bit you in the ass."

"So, can I say you accept?"

Calder finished his sandwich and let Ruben stew a minute. "Yeah, okay. Any way I can get an advance? This one may take some time."

"Not likely, but I'll see what I can do." Ruben sounded thoughtful. "Tell you what. If you think it can happen this way, write me up a proposal and I'll pitch it as a book as well as an article."

"Deal." Calder hung up the phone and headed to the library.

* * *

Surrounded by books was the way Calder liked to be. He'd lugged home a huge stack, topped by the *Screw the Roses* book that hadn't even gotten him a raised eyebrow from the librarian who'd checked his books out.

He now sat on the couch with stacks of books organized in piles. It had been easy enough to separate them into two main groups. He could tell which of the books had been written by tight-assed scientists, and which had been written with humor from actual participants.

"This is why you never got that doctorate," he muttered to himself. He was afraid he'd have ended up a dried-up old prune, writing about life instead of living it.

He'd lived that true-crime thriller Ruben had touring New York editor desks. Calder rubbed his right knee. The replacement surgery had worked, but his career as a cop had ended when the bullet did the initial damage. Maybe someday he'd make enough money off the book to make up for losing his career.

Calder put on his glasses and picked up a book from the "participant" stack. "Another day, another project. And at least this one is as far away from the halls of academia as you can get." He settled back on the sofa and began to read.

This was Monday. Wednesday, he had a call to make.

* * *

The nearly naked man in front of her offered her another cup of coffee, but Kelly didn't give any indication she noticed his bare state. She glanced up from her paperwork and took the delicate china cup and saucer. Sipping the hot brew, she nodded her approval.

The man departed silently. If he was disappointed, he didn't show it. He'd been trained well. Her blue-eyed gaze followed his sculpted ass without appearing to leave the stack of forms in front of her.

"That new thong looks good, Angie," she commented to the black-haired beauty sitting on the left side of her desk.

Angie saluted with her cola can. "It should. It cost the moon. But I saw those spangles and just had to decorate Troy in it."

"Yeah? You'll have to share the catalog. By the way, I appreciate your bringing Troy along while you help me with this crap." She gazed with hatred at the stack of receipts and tax forms in front of her.

"Hey, what's your accountant for, if not helping you sort through paperwork for your quarterly tithe to Uncle Sam?"

"I wish I didn't have to do it at all. It's getting to be too much for one person to handle." Kelly stared out the window and tried not to think about the past. A year had come and gone since Denny's death, and she should start living again.

"What you need is a partner, Kelly. Someone with the brains to handle the business end and won't choke over how you make your living. Ideally, someone who could be your partner in all things, but that may be asking the moon and stars. Denny was one-of-a-kind."

"What I need is a life." Kelly got up from her desk and moved around the room sipping her coffee. She knew it infuriated her best friend the way she could never keep still, but sitting in a chair for very long was more than she could bear. "I thought when I retired from the profession that a little volunteer work would be enough to keep me occupied, along with a few private clients. It's not working. I'm bored."

Angie kept right on working, her fingers busily tapping on the calculator or adding numbers to the computer that usually sat in lonely state behind Kelly's writing desk. "Yeah, well, it was getting too rough to continue being a professional mistress since that conservative bas— I mean, our beloved mayor, decided he was going to clean up the town. Idiot." Angie sneered at the thought of the self-righteous right-wing bureaucrat up for reelection at the end of the year. "Closing the bars around the military bases was dumb enough. Where did the soldiers end up? Causing trouble downtown, in the mayor's backyard. So, he reopened the bars and started trying to shut down all vice in this city. All he did was drive out legit business owners like you. I haven't seen any reduction in the hooker population."

"I'm not arguing with you!" Kelly threw up her hands in mock defense against Angie's vehemence. It was an old rant. "But you and I both know I was ready to retire anyway. When I wasn't running around with my kit to the airport hotels to beat on some fly-by-night business traveler, I was spending way too much time downstairs trying desperately to come up with something new for insatiable regular clients."

The silence lengthened, punctuated only by the occasional tapping of keys as Angie prepared Kelly's taxes for the quarter.

Kelly was considering turning on the stereo just for some background noise, when Angie finally turned around and laid her glasses on the desk. "Okay, so you're bored. Obviously the volunteer work isn't enough. You're used to a much faster-paced lifestyle. How about charity work?"

"Oh, I can see that now!" Kelly laughed mockingly. Then she went into a wicked imitation of a snobby matron having a mock heart attack, and said in a quavering voice, "The infamous Black Widow daring to want to give us her dirty whore's money?"

Angie chortled. "No, you're right. They would never understand that you have an unbroken rule never to have sex with your clients."

With a contemptuous sniff, Kelly fiddled with the curtains at the window. "Who would want to? And even if I did, that would put me into the legal realm of prostitution. No thank you. It's my business to perform BDSM acts for money, not sex. It would be the same as asking Picasso to paint a house," Kelly pronounced with some pride.

"Now that conjures up a visual," Angie drawled. "So, we've circled back around. You need a new occupation. Something besides working at the hospice. Okay, charity work is out. How about going back to school? Learn a new skill." She tapped a perfectly manicured fingernail on her chin.

"Oh, yippee-skippy. What would I take? Creative Basket Weaving? Somehow, I don't see myself back in college. Even if I did, what would I do with a degree? Soon as any employer found out about my past, my ass would be bouncing on the sidewalk." Kelly would have laughed, but it wasn't all that funny. She felt trapped by a profession she had loved for so long.

"Then you need to be self-employed. As your accountant, I recommend you think about it. Uncle Sam will take a huge bite out of you until you find somewhere to invest besides CDs and T-bonds," Angie warned.

Kelly snorted. "I could always find myself a gigolo to spend my money on. Some handsome guy to complicate my life, spend my money, and keep my name in the scandal sheets." The suggestion was amusing, but easily discarded.

"That's not a bad idea, pal. The getting a guy thing, anyway. Someone better than Michael."

Kelly groaned, and began to pace again. "Whatever possessed me to accept him as a subbie, I don't know. He's so pitiful."

"What's his latest trick to get your undivided attention?" Angie rested her chin in her hands.

"Does it matter anymore? He's tried hypochondria, failing to pay his bills until he had to file for bankruptcy, and beating on my door at two AM because he got locked out of his apartment." Her feet made no sound as she paced across the office, but the carpet felt good to her bare soles. Wearing heels was such a bitch that Kelly ran around barefoot at every opportunity.

"I remember that one," Angie chuckled. "He got one helluva shock when he found out you'd gone to Vegas with a client for the weekend."

Kelly snickered. "Yeah, that one backfired. After the neighbors called the cops on him and he spent a night in jail for disturbing the peace, he meekly paid his rent and hasn't tried that kind of idiocy again."

"When are you going to get rid of that twerp? He's more trouble than he's worth." Angie never made any secret that she disliked Michael in the extreme. And so did everyone else.

The feeling was mutual, unfortunately. Michael knew Angie saw through him, Kelly deduced. "What Michael needs is a full-time Mistress he can live with and cater to in abject servitude."

Angie stood up while the printer chattered in the background. "Well, honey, you're not that Mistress."

"Oh, hell no! If I wanted a man in my life, I'd rather have an independent, quiet soul. I like my life uncomplicated."

Angie brandished the total taxes due form. Kelly winced and wrote a check. As Angie stuffed forms and calculator into her briefcase, she had to have the last word. "That's the trouble, hon. If it has tires or testosterone, it will be trouble!"

Chapter Two

Calder rolled out of bed with the speed of summer lightning when his alarm sounded. It was a habit he couldn't break from all his years on the force. One efficient slap and the old Westclox wind-up ceased to be an annoyance. Why had he set his alarm? He couldn't remember until he was halfway to the coffee pot.

What would be unintelligible mumbles to anyone else was in actuality, "Oh, yeah. I've got to call Brad before he goes to work. Coffee. Need coffee. If God had wanted more people to see the sunrise, he would have made it later in the day. I hate mornings." At least the elixir of life he made from his own pot wasn't the sludge he'd drunk for years at the cop shop.

Cupping the mug of precious liquid, he stumbled to his desk and pulled his ubiquitous legal pad in front of him to go over his notes until he had more than two firing brain cells. Another mumble translated as, "Got to have all my ducks in a row before I call Brad. Who would have known dirt on my old college roomie would come in so handy?"

Despite the differences between a math major and a psychology major, he'd gotten along reasonably well with Brad in that dorm room. Calder had even been an usher at Brad's wedding. He hoped nostalgia would unlock a very tightly closed door. He'd known Brad indulged in the BDSM lifestyle, but had turned a blind eye to the occasional evidence. And he'd kept Brad's secret even after they graduated. He hoped that loyalty would buy him something now.

Half a pot later, he pulled up his contact list on the computer and dialed the phone. It was rude, in his personal rulebook, to pretend chitchat when he meant business, so after a few brief pleasantries, he got down to the true reason he'd called.

"You want to WHAT?" shouted Brad. "I know damn well you aren't coming to play. What's the game?"

Calder took the phone away from his ear and winced. "Yeah, I know, Brad. You have every right to yell at me and be suspicious. Hear me out, will you?"

Brad took a distinctive slurp of what was probably a cup of herbal tea. That's what he'd drunk in college, claiming caffeine gave him the shakes. "Okay, but don't skip a detail. I don't have a client for two hours."

"That's one thing we always had in common. We like to know every angle. Yours just happened to include a hypotenuse," Calder joked.

"You're still a smart-ass. I'm waiting."

"Okay, and I'll make it consecutive. I got a phone call from my agent. You did know I took a bullet in the knee and turned to writing, didn't you?"

"Yeah. Saw your byline a few times. Good stuff, Shrink."

"Thanks. Anyway, my agent has a new job available when he calls. Enough to pay off what's left of my medical bills and keep me in crackers for a couple months is what I figure."

"When will you let me be your accountant and manage all that crap for you?"

"When I can afford your expensive ass. But you can do my taxes at the beginning of next year." Calder grinned. It had been a standing joke between them since their college days. "Anyway, the assignment is to do a very clinical take on the psychology of BDSM." He heard the intake of breath, but plunged on. "Not a hate article, no moral judgments. You know damn well I'm sympathetic, Brad."

There was silence for a few moments, then a sigh. "Sympathetic, I don't know. But you kept your mouth shut. How much do you know, anyway?" The tone was cautious.

"Only what I've read in books. Good and bad opinions, some terms, and a fair idea of what goes on. That's it. I skipped the porn, figuring that wasn't real." Calder kept his voice cool and clinical.

"Man, you have a lot to learn, but no more than the average newbie. Only problem is you fall under the general and hated category of R.E.P.O.R.T.E.R. You have no idea how many of my friends cherish their privacy."

Calder had to chuckle at Brad spelling "reporter." But he got the point. "I can make some fair guesses. Look, I'll go incognito. I'm there to observe. Maybe ask some questions."

"Let's get something straight. You don't ask reporter-type questions. If you think you're treading on thin ice, you come to me." Brad's hard tone softened. "I know you. You're like a bulldog and you won't give up. You'll just find another source.

I'd rather have you under my own eye than worrying you're going to blow the lid off the community."

That was fair. Calder understood the need to keep a dangerous unknown under personal observation. "Okay, I can deal with that. Do I need lessons or special clothes? How long do I have to get ready?"

"I'm getting to that. Keep your shirt on. And that's the first rule. You come in street clothes, dress casual. Jeans and a tee shirt. I want it clear you're not there to play. We get casual observers who are just curious all the time, so that won't be remarkable. No recording devices, not even a notepad, got it? In exchange, I'll go over all your observations with you and answer any questions Sunday."

"Deal. When and where?" Calder breathed a sigh of relief. He didn't want to waste his precious savings on some weird-assed outfit just to fit in.

"Here at my place, Friday night. The party starts as early as seven PM, but there's no sense in showing up before eight. The ball doesn't start rolling until at least nine or ten. And don't expect a lot of sleep that night. We don't shut down until four AM at the earliest." Brad dictated the address, not knowing or caring that Calder had a cop's connections and could have found out on his own.

Calder let out a long, low whistle. "Nice neighborhood, pal. Maybe I should let you handle my royalties."

"It works for us. Angie is an accountant now, too. Nursing was killing her." Brad seemed to be relaxing, probably glad Calder hadn't argued.

"Yeah? You got time to tell me about your life since we graduated?" Calder leaned back in his desk chair and prepared to catch up on lost time.

* * *

Kelly rubbed the bridge of her nose and tried desperately to keep her mind on her appointment book. She had a monster headache brewing, and the worst was yet to come.

She still had to call Michael and remind him about the PEP meeting. "People Exchanging Power" was the best of the local BDSM clubs, and she'd be damned if she'd be late and miss seeing a few friends.

The German-accented voice on the phone gabbled in her ear, reminding her of what she was supposed to be doing. "Yes, Mr. von Stein. I have you down for Thursday evening at your usual hotel. I'll call you from the lobby. See you then. Good night." She put the phone on the desk.

Herman von Stein was a favorite client. He didn't ask for much, just the chance to have dinner with a woman, and a little bondage. Easy stuff. She had a new knot for him too. Angie's birthday gift of a Boy Scout handbook of knots was being put to good use.

Kelly stared balefully at the phone. "Better get this over with," she muttered. If she were very lucky, she'd leave a message on Michael's answering machine and be done with this unpleasant task.

No such luck. Michael answered on the second ring with an eager, "Yes, Mistress? How may I serve?" Kelly swore he stared at the phone like a vulture, and only read the caller ID to avoid bill collectors.

"Michael, I remind you that the PEP meeting is this weekend. You make me late again, and your punishment will be infinitely worse than kneeling on rice grains, bound and gagged for two hours. I don't care how much of a pain slut you think you are, you didn't last long, did you?"

A small catch of breath, then a subservient, "No, Mistress. I did not last long. I will be ready, Mistress." He'd probably been hoping she'd forgotten how he'd forgotten to take a bath and she'd been forced to order him to take a shower before she would take him to the last PEP meeting. What was it about males and bathing?

She'd threatened to leave him and go alone, but he'd whined and begged until she'd given in. He'd been sorry when she'd borrowed a handful of uncooked rice from Angie's kitchen and made him kneel in it while she played with others right in front of him.

Then she heard the telltale "blip" of a computer game. He was playing a game while, in theory, taking instructions from his Mistress. That was against the rules, and he knew it.

"Michael! I heard that." Her voice was low and dangerous, as was expected. He did it on purpose, the little bastard. He liked being punished so much he went out of his way to be a brat and force her to concoct more and more elaborate ways to discipline him.

Well, she wasn't falling for it this time. "You're not giving me the proper attention. I have nothing more to say to you. Your chastisement for tonight and the next twenty-four hours is…nothing. Do not call here, and do not show up. Goodbye." She slammed the phone down in his ear.

She looked up to see her housekeeper striding in the doorway with a fresh cup of coffee. Sadie's head was down, but she was grinning from ear to ear. "That's telling him, Mistress," Sadie murmured as she put the fresh cup down and removed the old one.

Kelly stared for a moment, and then began to laugh. "And so satisfying! Accept no calls from Michael tonight, Sadie. No messages, either."

On cue, the phone began to ring. A glance at the caller ID showed Michael had gotten over his shock, and was now disobediently dialing frantically. Sadie snickered.

"And I'll be sure to check the peephole before I answer the door. He won't bowl me over like he did last time."

Kelly closed her appointment book. It never left the desk surface, but every sub she had knew better than to touch it. All except Sadie, who acted as personal secretary if there was a need.

"You've got a meeting with the Dommes-in-training tonight, Mistress. Shall I arrange the drawing room suitably?"

"No, tonight we will be in the dungeon. There's to be a demonstration," Kelly said with a smile of pleasure.

"Oh, Mistress! How delightful! On whom? What shall we be doing?" Sadie's eyes shone with anticipation. It was part of her pay to be a demo model. Her swarthy skin was perfect for demonstrating certain skills to perfection.

Kelly grinned. "You and Devon, of course. Wax play tonight."

Sadie flashed that bright smile that had made her a model in her younger days. "Wonderful! I'll go get the warmer on and see to it Devon eats before I set it up. He's too skinny. Mistress Tawny will bring him, as usual?"

"Yes. Now, I'd better go finish braiding that new whip." Kelly got up and brushed eraser bits off her jeans.

Sadie looked with a jaundiced eye at Kelly's ripped jeans and bright red tee shirt that had "Bitch" emblazoned on the chest. "You'd better make it quick. You sure can't demo in that. You'd swelter."

Kelly laughed and snatched up her coffee before heading to the garage workshop where she created her equipment. "I'll be wearing the green corset and tap pants tonight, Sadie. And wait until you see the new bustier I'll pick up from Master Tim's tomorrow! But today, I'm comfy. Call me at five, would you?"

Kelly scooted through the kitchen, sniffing at the roast in the oven. Her secret depression grew worse, and with no one to see her, her shoulders slumped. She glanced with longing at the perfect kitchen she'd designed.

When Denny had been alive, all subs went home at five PM, sharp. Kelly spent many a late afternoon "making messes," as Denny called it. They'd eaten at the little bistro set sitting forlornly in the corner. Now, with no one to enjoy her cooking, she'd allowed the subs to take over and feed her as part of their duties.

"Someday, I'm going to bake a sinful chocolate cake, and have someone to eat it again," she vowed. Then she stormed into the garage to take her frustrations out on an innocent set of leather strips.

Chapter Three

The beatings had already commenced. She could hear the faint beat of rock music through the floors. "Damn!" Kelly muttered to herself. "I do not like being late to the PEP meeting!" The Saturday PEP events were her one night a month to relax.

"I'm so sorry, Mistress," whined her submissive, Michael. The short, skinny blond trotted after his Mistress, panting as he carried his own light gym bag and her much larger, heavier suitcase.

"Yes, you are!" Kelly snarled. "This is the third time you couldn't manage to get your shit together for a scheduled monthly party. What the fuck is your problem? You can't read a calendar, all of a sudden?"

"I got distracted, Mistress."

Kelly descended the stairs of the mansion, heading toward what might be loosely termed a basement. She'd come screaming up the drive in her PT Cruiser, parked, and had thrown the gear bags at Michael. Her feet, properly shod in high heels, already ached from that run up the steps and through the doors of her best friend's home in Cherry Hills. "Yeah, yeah, I know what distracted you. One of your idiot video games. Put a fucking alarm clock on your desk!"

"Yes, Mistress. Thank you, Mistress. That's a good idea. I promise!"

Michael was puffing like a freight train, Kelly noticed. What made her choose a skinny, brainless subbie like him, anyway? Well, maybe not brainless. To be fair, he was a computer geek who could do amazing things on anything that had a keyboard. But give him anything more complicated than a mechanical pencil, and he'd hurt himself.

And he didn't have one whit of common sense. None. She had to call him twice daily to remind him to eat, or he'd call her for the dumbest reasons. And he managed to find the most inconvenient moments to do so! Last night it had been how to cook himself a steak. A steak, for Chrissake.

Michael finally reached the bottom of the stairs and waited subserviently for Kelly to choose her spot. The dungeon was full tonight. The huge basement of her best friend's mansion was filled to capacity. Luxuriously paneled in dark woods, the main portion carpeted, the room gave the ambience of the most posh dungeon possible.

Every armchair and wingchair housed a Dominant with at least one submissive serving every need. Well, except sexual needs, of course. "Get a hotel room!" was a frequent cry if someone got too explicit in public.

To Kelly's annoyance, at first it appeared as if every booth was taken too. She shot Michael a look that should have flayed him worse than anything she'd ever given him. He wisely kept his gaze on the floor, but his whole demeanor was one of satisfaction. He thought he'd paid her back for ignoring him. He'd find out soon enough she played revenge games better than he.

Finally, Kelly found an open booth with a nice St. Andrew's cross. Bless her, Angie was sitting in the chair of that booth, waving. With a sigh of relief, Kelly made her way through the crowd, avoiding swinging floggers and hot-eyed Doms with a keen nose for self-preservation.

Michael, naturally, got stuck trying to carry his load, and would be a few more moments before he deposited the bags and began setting up her toys for the night's pleasures. Kelly rolled her eyes skyward as a yelp let her know he'd not been as adroit avoiding floggers.

Angie, understanding pal that she was, just shook her head. "You need to dump that loser. He's a leech, not a subbie."

"I know, Angie. You got any suggestions?" Kelly sighed as she took off her jacket. The usual whistles and catcalls at the sight of her new leather bustier got the usual response of one finger skyward, which was followed by a smattering of laughter.

One enterprising and brave fellow yelled, "When?" in response to the finger.

Kelly ignored him.

"Daaaaamn!" Angie exclaimed, admiring the vivid red hourglass shape symbolizing the black widow emblazoned on the bustier. "You weren't kidding when you said it would be special." Kelly did a slow turn to allow Angie, and not incidentally the crowd, a chance to admire. After all, she had a rep to keep. She smiled at Angie, who winked at her.

Michael finally made it through the crowd, and dumped the bags unceremoniously on the floor near the cross. Fortunately, he had this routine down pat and managed to get her toys laid out in good order. He snapped on his collar, and stood waiting by the cross for his Mistress.

"At least you never fucked the twerp," Angie consoled in a soft whisper. "Let me scope around and see if there's one of the Gorean Mistresses around. That would sort his ass out in a hurry."

Kelly laughed and shooed Angie out of the booth. "You know I don't have sex with my subs. I got a rep to maintain!"

"And when was the last time you did a horizontal tango with anyone?" was Angie's parting shot while Kelly threatened her best friend with a flogger.

Clamping Michael with his back outward, Kelly got to work. This wouldn't take long, and then the wuss could rest while she found a playmate to give her a real workout. Maybe that long, lean fellow in jeans watching her with blazing eyes.

* * *

Calder, his arms folded, leaned up against a convenient wall, and nudged his host. "Who's the brunette with long legs in the leather bustier?" The tiny black shorts and leather top left little to the imagination. Not that he blamed her for wearing as little as possible and arranging her hair into a short, sensible braid. It was hotter than the nine hells in this tightly packed place.

Brad waved at his wife Angie as she flitted about the room making sure all was safely played before answering. "Oh, that's the Black Widow. That's what they call her. Used to be a professional Mistress before she retired."

"Retired? She looks like she's maybe thirty."

Brad nodded. "Thirty on the nose. When you make $300K a year, you can retire in less time. I should know. I'm still her accountant. And her husband had a hefty insurance policy when he died. Left her with a paid-off house, two cars, and some nice municipal bonds. Poor bastard. Died of cancer."

"So, what does she do now that she's...retired?" Calder asked. His reporter's mind was taking in a thousand bits of data, but this one just didn't want to file itself. There wasn't a word to describe the Black Widow, except lush. Everything about her was almost too much to handle. He felt his jeans tighten just looking at that body poured into bits of leather and string.

Brad just chuckled. "Takes a few private clients left over from her pro days, mostly, if what you mean is work. She also volunteers at the hospice. Hard to imagine the most famous Mistress here in town running around emptying bedpans, but that's what keeps her happy."

"Think she'd let me interview her? It would mean a lot to my piece." Calder was intrigued. So, that was the infamous Black Widow, who was whispered about in every man's group when the subject of kinky sex came up?

Brad tipped back his head and guffawed. Not that it affected the swirling mass around him. The heavy metal rock music pounded so loudly, even his hearty laugh was drowned out. "Not bloody likely! Widow keeps to herself, talks when she pleases, and your profession alone is enough to scare off half the people here. I snuck you in here with the deal that you'd mention no names, and no pictures. Why don't you observe for awhile?"

Calder nodded his agreement, but wandered closer to the Black Widow's booth before taking up a position in one of the chairs scattered throughout the dungeon. Hard to believe his old college buddy was into this, but the evidence was all around him. He'd promised no paper, no recording devices, just his trained memory, and he'd stick to it.

The Widow was just picking up a large, heavy looking device that looked like a handle and a bunch of large soft leather strips. A flogger, Brad had called it. It was taken from the middle of a long line of devices of various ominous appearances. Obviously, the lady was methodical and organized. Judging by the thing she'd just put down that looked like a horse's tail on a handle, she'd start at one end of her tools and move toward the other. He identified a rabbit fur glove, a few clamps—some of which now dangled from the poor skinny little bastard's nipples—the horsehair thing, and the collection of floggers and whips. Damn. Even a riding crop. Calder's back hurt just looking at it.

Black Widow examined the flogger carefully, even tugging on a few of the strips before swinging the flogger in a figure eight pattern and walking closer to her victim. No, not victim, he corrected himself. Submissive was the correct term.

The submissive's back was pink from the horsehair thing. Calder supposed it was called a horsehair flogger, since it had the same basic shape as the leather flogger Widow now employed effortlessly. The tips of the leather strips fell in an orderly pattern on the man's rapidly reddening back. There was no blood or bruising, just an ever-increasing amount of color to the skin. Weren't there supposed to be strips of flesh hanging off and blood flowing?

Calder did a fast check of the rest of the dungeon. The party was in full swing, and so were many floggers, even a few short bullwhips. However, there was damn little blood, and no screaming that he could hear. Not that he could hear much. Was that supposed to be called music?

"So, how are you enjoying things?" a sultry voice shouted in his ear.

Calder turned and beheld Brad's wife, Angie. "Hey, kid. Can't say I'm enjoying this, but it is interesting. Why..."

He never got to finish his question. The skinny guy on the cross began to yell, "Mistress!! I'm coming! Please! Finish me!" Over the pounding music, the whole crowd turned and watched avidly.

Angie snorted. "Wuss! He never lasts long. Thinks he's such a pain slut. Poor BW!"

Incredibly, the Black Widow grabbed up a bottle and some cotton, and slathered the young man's back with what smelled like isopropyl alcohol, even from Calder's position just outside the booth. The kid screeched, but before he could draw the next breath, she'd set him on fire with a lighter! Just as quickly, the Widow patted out the flames with a towel from her left hand, even as she drew the lighter away with her right.

Calder had tensed in an automatic reflex, but Angie had slapped a hand on his sternum and shouted, "Wait!" It wasn't easy.

As the kid hung there, limp and panting, "Thank you, Mistress, thank you!" applause broke out. The Black Widow, barely even sweating, gave a short nod acknowledging thanks, and turned back to her beaten submissive.

"What's she doing now? Isn't she done?" Calder asked.

"No way, hotshot. What? You think we just leave them like that? Watch. This, you won't learn by reading books. This is the important part." Angie flipped her black hair over her shoulder and pointed.

Calder watched as The Black Widow snatched up a spray bottle full of a vile-looking green liquid and began liberally anointing the submissive's back.

"That's BW's own special blend of soothing agent," Angie supplied before he could ask. "Main ingredient is, believe it or not, chamomile tea. Works like a charm to soothe Michael's nerve endings. See? He's already coming out of subspace. She'll be able to take him down in a few minutes."

Angie was right. "Michael" was standing upright and breathing normally in a few moments. Calder was surprised to see "BW" hold the kid as gently as she could in a hugging embrace while she released the cuffs, and lead him to a position on the floor. The kid sat, nodding his thanks when a cold drink from a small cooler was given to him. BW murmured soothing things, and even cuddled the scrawny guy briefly in a hug.

Angie turned and faced Calder. "That cool down will take a few minutes. They are always a little shocky when they come down from a scene. You gotta treat your subs right. Even assholes like Michael. Any questions?"

"Only about a million of them!" Calder shouted back in her ear. "But I'll wait until I can hear myself think, much less the answers."

Only when Michael began to respond in what could have been full sentences did BW get up off the floor and begin cleaning. She wiped everything that could be cleaned with more of the alcohol, and used a disinfectant spray with a pungent smell on everything else, even the wooden cross.

He watched as Michael reached with shaking hands into a small blue gym bag and pulled out a large candy bar. His hands trembled so badly the kid couldn't even unwrap it. BW stopped her cleaning, knelt, and tenderly opened it for him. She even broke off a piece to hand feed her sub until he took the bar back and ate on his own. Only then did she return to her cleaning.

Fascinated didn't begin to describe Calder's emotions as he watched Black Widow give the booth a cleaning and sterilization a nurse would be proud to claim. Some tiny little snake squirmed jealously in the pit of his stomach, envious of the poor bastard that had just been beaten for getting such loving tenderness.

The dichotomy between the Hollywood image of the beautiful Dominatrix and the woman energetically cleaning had Calder staring and visibly clamping his jaw to keep it from hanging open like a yokel. He had to know more, and damn Brad's rules.

Chapter Four

Brad appeared just as BW gave Calder one helluva view of her spectacular ass while she bent down to get a diet cola from the tiny cooler. Calder barely managed to keep his tongue from hanging out like a wolf's.

Instead of coming up to Calder, he went straight in to BW with a concerned look on his face. "Kelly!" he shouted, loud enough for Calder to hear over the pulsing of Metallica. "Stay around here for about an hour, okay? There's going to be knife play in number three!"

"Aw, damn!" Angie exclaimed, as the infamous Black Widow shuddered and wrinkled her nose. "Brad! Brad! Are you going to be safety monitor on that? And turn that music down!"

"Yeah!" Brad shouted. "You stay with Kelly and Calder, okay?" At Angie's nod, he raced off.

Within moments, the music volume reduced to something below earsplitting, giving Calder's abused eardrums some welcome relief. Mozart was more his speed.

BW walked over, swigging long and deep from her can. "Ye gods, my feet are killing me. I'm losing the shoes for the rest of the night." Her voice was low, throaty, and cultured, with just a hint of the Deep South. She bent down to loosen the ankle straps that held on the skyscraper heels, and gave Calder a view that had him wondering why her tits didn't fall out. They sure threatened to do so at any moment. She lost a good four inches in height. "Ahhh!! How do you spell relief?" BW asked to the ceiling.

Angie just laughed. "Self-inflicted torture, pal."

BW eyed Calder speculatively. "Any luck?" she asked, apparently to Angie.

"Oh, no, Kelly. This guy wouldn't know Gorean from sensual. He's just observing tonight. No luck."

They were interrupted by the meek voice of Michael. "Mistress? May I please go watch the knife play?"

"Sure, babe. Go for it," BW answered without turning her head. Calder was positive now that her casual air of low-class was just an act. "Babe" hadn't come out naturally. Her whole posture and voice screamed "Lady." What a puzzle.

BW took another swig of her soda as Michael sped off without another word. "So, observer, huh? And your name is Calder?"

"Calder Burgess, at your service," Calder answered with a mocking half-bow.

"I doubt it." BW winked saucily.

Calder took a few moments to figure out that "service" around here took on a whole new meaning. "Just curiosity, tonight, Black Widow." He grinned, appreciative that the joke was on him. "Would you care to explain your implements to me?"

* * *

Kelly studied this Calder fellow for a few minutes. He was tall, at least a six-footer, and had that easy confidence of an "innocent," at least as far as BDSM was concerned. Intelligent green eyes, sun-streaked brown hair, and a hint he might wear glasses around the nose. She hoped not. Glasses were one thing that made her melt, big time.

You're so repressed, Kelly. Get over it.

Calder took her silence for consent and walked over to examine her large collection of toys with his hands wisely behind his back. She'd hate to have to break his fingers.

Geeezus! Get a load of that gravity-defying ass. Down, girl! Crap, I need to get laid before I burst.

Calder pointed without touching to her collection of clamps. A larger box with divided trays was on the floor nearby, but enough of each type was in the small pile. "What are those for?"

"Stimulating nerve endings in specific locations, Einstein." Rolling her eyes at such innocence, Kelly strolled over, getting into "BW mode" as she called it. She pointed toward a few plastic-coated alligator clamps with screws to make a perfect fit. "Those are the mildest. They do little more than restrict blood flow in the area involved, causing a certain amount of increased sensitivity. Of course, they are only good where skin is loose, such as nipples, scrotum, and occasionally ears or torso."

Calder had grinned at the mild insult, but shuddered at the mention of a guy's tender balls. "It doesn't hurt?"

Kelly snorted. "Not those! Even the clothespins and other stronger items do little more than pinch. They stimulate the erogenous zones, nothing more. Now these," she held up a rather wicked looking pair of tiny tong-like devices with sharp teeth in the prongs, "do a little more in the way of the pain department. But they are only good for pain sluts." She held them up to the vicinity of her own nipples. It was almost second nature to tease a man like Calder.

Calder looked thoughtful. "Pain sluts? Those who are in it for pure pain?"

Kelly nodded. "Got it in one, babe. There are those in this world who can't seem to enjoy what you and I would call normal stimuli for sexual pleasure. You have to bring them right up to the limit of stimulus, where the brain is almost overloaded." She picked up a small device that looked like a less-wicked pair of the alligator clamp things. "Stick out your thumb and forefinger, sweetie."

Long and Luscious Calder hesitated, delighting Kelly with his wariness. This one was a smart cookie. Whoever said the brain was the best sex organ was definitely right. Well, she knew how to engage the masculine mind. Kelly winged an eyebrow to her hairline. "Don't be scared, Calder," she coaxed. "This is merely a small demonstration of how the brain overrides the body. It won't do more than pinch."

Pride overrode his good sense, just as she planned. His eyes glittered, and he thrust out his right hand.

Kelly rewarded his bravery with a smile. "Thank you for trusting me, Calder. Now, pay attention." She clamped the little device on the loose skin between his thumb and forefinger, tightening it down until she felt his hand tense in hers. "Trust is a big part of BDSM, as you well know." She shot a look at Angie, who nodded and moved one step to stand behind Calder.

"Someday, you'll have to elaborate on that for me. Ouch!"

Kelly favored him with a deliberately worried expression. "Oh, is that too tight? Some people are so sensitive there." The initial pinch would fade in three seconds or so, if she could engage his attention that long.

Calder looked at his hand. The little clamp dangled there. "No, it's okay. It just hurt for a second."

"Good. Calder, look at me, not your hand." It was a low, soft command, deliberately enticing.

Calder's gaze snapped up and locked on hers.

Kelly gave him a sweet smile and said softly, "Pardon me." Without warning, she reached out to caress his crotch in a long, slow sweep.

"Whoa!" Calder exclaimed, and jumped back into Angie's waiting arms, panting.

That hard package had been difficult to resist. Its size gave a clear hint of the joys under the denim. Kelly returned to her usual impersonal mask. "My apologies, Calder. But if I'd warned you, the sensation would have been reduced. Did you not feel more than usual in that simple caress?" She moved forward to where Angie was making sure of his balance, and removed the clamp.

He was still stunned enough to answer honestly, "God, yes!" While still breathing somewhat heavily, he made a valiant attempt to regain aplomb, and jerked upright.

Kelly played with the clamp in her hand. "It's a simple psycho-physiological reaction to direct stimuli. The brain reacts to the tiny amount of pain by 'awakening' to where it feels everything more. Of course, there is a threshold. When the brain reaches a pain-pleasure combination of a certain level, it naturally chooses pleasure over pain. Orgasm often results from the overload."

Calder's fingers twitched, as if he were dying to take notes or something. She loved an intelligent, organized personality. "You can experiment on yourself later, but it doesn't work quite so well when the subject knows they are to be stimulated. That's the reason the tests fail in the lab." She handed him the clamp. "Something about you says that you'd be the type to try and repeat this at home. At the risk of being crude, I suggest using it the same way, but on your left hand. Then beat off. You should get a decent reaction enough using that method."

He blushed as he put the clamp in his pocket. Kelly hid her delight with difficulty.

"Moving on." She picked up the horsetail thing. "This is a horsehair flogger. Stick out your hand."

Let's see how you react, gorgeous. God, why can't I have this kind of a subbie? He's so innocent, it's cute.

Calder looked warily at the flogger. "Aw, what the hell. What can hair do to you?" He thrust his hand out. With a simple flick, she lashed out with the horsehair. The sting was incredible. "Ouch!" he pulled his arm back, and stared at his hand and forearm. No welts, and only a tiny amount of redness showed.

"Sorry about that. If I had warned you, you would have flinched. Stick it out again. This time, I promise, it won't hurt."

Calder slowly put his hand back into position. This time, the swing was obvious. The hair, instead of touching him with the ends, lay swiftly across his forearm. No sting. "That didn't hurt."

"No, but look at your forearm now." She folded the hairs against the handle neatly.

Calder looked at his forearm. It was now pink, and felt slightly warm. "But it doesn't hurt."

Angie gave him a nudge. "It's not supposed to, silly. A few strokes of the horsehair, and your nerve endings are stimulated and blood is flowing to the skin, warming it. It prepares the skin for the next step. And Kelly is being rough on you. She didn't do half of what she could to warm your skin and make this extremely pleasant for you. But this is just a demo. Nothing that would engage the psyche and make you hunger. And I assure you, she could make you very, very hungry for anything."

* * *

The Black Widow grinned, and turned back to Calder. He couldn't help but wonder what could possibly create a "hunger" in him, like addiction, perhaps? Well, it was possible to become addicted to sex.

A submissive, judging by the collar around his neck and the lack of clothing, slid bonelessly to the floor. No one in leather was in sight. Just two others in collars who tripped over the mess on the floor in their haste to get to the white-faced guy now seemingly unconscious next to a table.

Swifter than lightning, Kelly and Angie thrust whatever was in their hands at Calder and ran to the booth where the two rescuers cradled the downed man. One was taking his pulse while the other put a bottle of what looked like water to the victim's lips.

Calder followed, looking helplessly at the heavy flogger and soda in his hands. He was in time to hear the one in a red collar taking the pulse report in an authoritative tone, "He's going to be fine, Mistresses. Pulse is a little unsteady, but nothing to call an ambulance for. Keep dribbling in that liquid, Dave. Slowly."

"Who did this? Harry? Do you know?" Angie snarled.

"It was the new Mistress in white," Harry, the one in the red collar, answered.

The one called Dave cursed with a flair Calder could only envy. "Fucking idiot thing to do. Didn't anyone teach her safety cool-down procedures? She doesn't deserve a nice guy like Jim, here." While he talked he carefully continued to drip the liquid past the pale lips.

Angie stormed off, muttering dire threats.

"Get him on the table, guys. Facedown. How's the new practice, Harry?" BW was all authority. "I'll tend him. Calder, bring me my spray. And a towel. Should be fresh ones in my black bag."

Calder moved, dumping the cola and flogger onto the table in BW's booth. The spray was easy to find. The towels took only a few more seconds to locate in the organized and perfectly clean bag.

"Practice is doing fine. I love the new office. Ready, Dave? On three!" Harry expertly arranged his arms beneath the now semi-conscious man.

"Wait a sec! I'm a software geek, not a damn doctor. Okay, now!"

On the count of three, the victim was laid facedown on the table. BW began to repeat the ministrations she'd done on Michael. Within a few minutes the man was conscious and able to sit up. Harry and Dave volunteered to sit with him until he finished reviving. A meekly chastened Mistress in white leathers came back, and began to pack her equipment. She fled shortly thereafter. Her submissive was left to his own devices but did not seem concerned.

Calder and BW returned to their booth, and BW began to pack her things. She muttered imprecations, but didn't toss Calder out. When her temper calmed enough where he wasn't concerned she'd bite his head off, Calder asked, "What happened over there?" In a perverse way, he was grateful for the incident. It just wouldn't do to get a hard-on in this place, and that was sure to get him the wrong kind of attention. But damn! How could a guy not get stimulated when a beautiful woman in leather and little else shows him toys meant for kinky sex?

BW whirled to face him, her eyes still blazing. "Stupid cunt didn't know how to take care of her subbie, that's what. You don't play with someone and then walk off before you've performed a thorough cool-down treatment and made sure they are recovered from the subspace trance. People have died from being left like that. It's damn close to criminal negligence!" She took a deep breath and visibly calmed herself. "Sorry, I shouldn't yell at you."

Calder nodded calmly. He'd had a lot worse than a little bitty female spitting anger at him. Enraged junkies high on crack worried him a whole lot more. "It's okay, Black Widow. What would have happened to him?"

"You understand shock, don't you?"

He nodded.

"Good. What happens to a sub during a scene can be likened to a trance-like state, often referred to as subspace. If you've ever zoned out when something felt so good, your mind wandered a bit, subspace is like that. After they're done, they enter a form of mild shock, usually of short duration. It is the duty of a Dominant to see to their sub's health and well-being until they've recovered." Kelly's eyes softened. "In fact, you might say the whole reason a Dominant exists is for their sub's health and happiness."

Calder's face took on the confused and puzzled expression of one who has just been offered contradictory statements. "Huh? It's important to see to a sub's health, yet you set that guy on fire earlier. It doesn't add up."

Kelly couldn't help it. She laughed. "To explain would take some time and a less busy atmosphere." She stepped close to Calder and ran a finger up his shirt.

Calder suddenly felt as if a tiger was stalking him. A beautiful, dangerous tiger with big blue eyes.

Chapter Five

Calder could see Kelly wanted to say more, but just then someone wearing a very odd abbreviated costume came running up. BW backed off as if she'd been shot and began busily packing her suitcase. It gave Calder a certain amount of satisfaction to see her cheeks were pink.

The woman ran into the booth, dropped to her knees in front of BW, spread her knees wide in what looked like a very uncomfortable position, bent her head, and waited to be acknowledged. The odd costume had the one-shoulder draped effect of Grecian toga, but was cut very short. The thin material left nothing to the imagination. She wore a gold collar that looked almost like lace. A rope belt circled her waist several times. Calder had no trouble imagining what the rope was for.

BW ignored her for a moment while she stuffed another flogger deep into the large suitcase. Then she turned and said languidly, "Yes, slave?"

Calder raised one eyebrow. One minute BW was a tigress stalking prey, the next haughty and regal. It had to be a role. He glanced back at the slave on the floor. What about her had changed BW's attitude?

Without looking up, the slave-woman offered a packet to BW. "From my Mistress, the Lady Mina, with her compliments."

BW opened the packet. Inside was a gold coin. Craning his neck, Calder could see it was a standard Sacagawea dollar. What was it about a dollar that made BW smile? Whatever it was, BW thrust the coin in the suitcase and shut the lid.

"Convey my greetings to the Lady Mina, and tell her I accept. One moment." A few seconds later, a small blue gym bag was thrust into the girl's hands and she sped off.

"What the hell just happened?" Calder asked softly, more or less to himself.

"Oh, nothing much. I just sold Michael to Lady Mina. Whew!! Am I glad! Even if it means lugging all this stuff home myself, it's worth it." She nonchalantly put her suitcase near the entrance of the booth, and judging by the way her eyes scanned the room carefully, she was checking to make sure the place was clean.

Shock had Calder choking back a shout. "You just *sold* a guy for a fucking *dollar?"* he protested.

BW turned an impish smile on him, completely unperturbed. "Yup. It's not criminal assault or anything. It's not even a crime at all. And before you yell at me, two things. First, don't ever yell at me. You won't like the results. Second, there's more that went on than meets the eye. Oh, yeah. And do you like coffee?"

The complete non sequitur had Calder totally off stride and puzzled. "Uh, yeah." What was it about this woman that left him dazed and confused most of the time? Calder shook his head to clear it. The point was a man had just been sold for a stupid dollar. Calder wasn't about to get sidetracked by a beautiful, blue-eyed, classy broad in stilettos and a sexy bustier. No matter how disturbing she was, or how classy, she'd just done something despicable.

Folding her arms, BW looked prepared to hold a conversation despite the fact that a livid man stood towering over her. "Look, I'm ready to leave. There is very little good action tonight, and I've soured on play for now. If you want to hear an explanation that doesn't have to be shouted, you're welcome to come back to my place and have coffee."

Damn, the woman was good at keeping him off-balance. His mouth opened and closed a few times as he tried to work through the mental argument of whether to accept or not. Was she offering to take him home for a conversation? Or more? No matter. He couldn't refuse. The infamous Black Widow was offering him the equivalent of a one-on-one interview.

BW solved the issue by stepping close enough for him to inhale that perfume she was wearing. Had she been saying something about criminal assault earlier? That perfume was an assault on his libido, all in itself. His brain clicked completely offline.

She lifted a finger with a neatly trimmed, unpainted nail under his chin and closed his mouth. "You could catch flies in that thing. I won't hurt you. You can even have a chaperone in Angie, if we can spirit her out of this lousy party."

Blue. Her eyes are blue. Baby blue, was all his mind would think. *Snap out of it! Lust has no place right now, and you don't want to tangle with this kind of woman. She'll eat you alive, like a Black Widow spider.*

Those big blue eyes tilted to one side. "You aren't scared of me, are you?"

That pout had probably destroyed many men. It certainly was destroying his self-control. But that little insult to his ego could not be ignored. "You don't scare me, beautiful. Let's go. I've got a million questions, starting with selling a man after setting him on fire."

Black Widow hefted a small black gym bag he'd seen her load with the spray bottles and a few other bottles and jars. Okay, that made sense. The fragile stuff would be carried separately. "I promise to give you a full explanation and answer all your questions once we have some coffee. Fair enough?"

Automatically, he picked up the suitcase, and thought his arms would break under the strain. "My fucking God! What have you got in here? Chains?"

The grin she shot him over her shoulder was pure mischief. "Yes, of course! I'll show them to you later. If you're a good boy."

"I should have known," he muttered, and followed in her wake while she hunted up Angie to say goodbye.

Brad grabbed his arm in the kitchen, where they found Angie dispensing coffee out of a giant urn that looked like it belonged in a restaurant. BW dragged Angie away to another corner, and from the jumping up and down, giggling, and hugging, something good had happened.

"What the hell do you think you're doing, Calder?" Brad whispered urgently. "You promised!"

"I didn't ask for an interview, Brad. Honest. She's taking me home for coffee and to finish explaining her toys to me. She even asked if I'd like Angie to chaperone. I'm perfectly safe, and so is she." Calder pulled his arm from Brad's grip and winked as he followed the swinging set of black-clad hips out the door.

* * *

Brad leaned back against a kitchen counter. "Idiot. Why do you think they call her The Black Widow, old man? And from what Angie tells me, she's hungry."

He rubbed his forehead in indecision. Calder was treading on very thin ice. Kelly wouldn't harm him; Brad knew that more intimately than most. But Calder would walk away a changed man. Would he be able to live with it?

Angie came over and took his hand. "You look so upset. Is it because BW has picked a new man?"

Brad shook his head and caressed his wife's cheek. "No, baby. I subbed to BW a very long time ago. I graduated and moved on." His eyes flicked to the back door. "I'm worried about Calder."

It was the best he could do to warn his wife. He couldn't tell her what Calder was. There'd be mayhem, and everyone would know. Angie didn't know Calder like he did. She wouldn't trust him. He had to keep the secret, or their lives would come crashing down around them.

He could almost hear Angie's screech. "A reporter? You brought a fucking *reporter* into our midst? And you just let him go home with the most secretive one of us all? *Are you nuts?*" Brad shuddered.

Angie's tinkling laughter brought him back to reality. "So what? He looks like he can handle himself. Kelly just wants a nice horizontal tango with a guy who won't submit to her first."

"That's the problem, Angie. Calder won't submit. He's something new and different. And he's...innocent...to our ways."

Angie grinned. "So? She'll show him the ropes, literally and figuratively. He's going to have the ride of his life tonight."

Brad ran a hand through his hair and tried not to sweat visibly. "Baby, what sort of player would you call Calder?"

"A Dom," she answered instantly. "He's definitely got the potential. He's got that selfless quality and big heart. You should have seen him jump to help when that sub of Lady White's hit the floor." Angie smiled at the memory.

"Right. He's got a big heart. I agree there. But what happens when a new, untrained Dom appears on the scene? What happens to the best Doms before they put on the leather?"

She looked puzzled. "You know that as well as I do, since you went through it. They learn to submit first so they can appreciate fully what they ask of their subs and what it feels like to be one."

"Right. And how do you get an insufferably arrogant, Dominant personality to even consider doing something so contrary to their nature as to submit to another Dominant?"

Angie paced the length of the kitchen. "I'm a sub. I'm going to make some educated guesses. With an innocent like Calder, you'd engage their brain and their body. The kind of BDSM Kelly is capable of is addicting. Once you have what she can offer, vanilla sex is about as much fun as playing with wet cardboard." She looked at Brad for confirmation.

"That's close, but there's more baby. You said it yourself. The one thing that classifies almost all of the best Dominants is that big, caring heart. You have to be very selfless to take care of the mental and physical well-being of another person, sometimes trying to heal old hurts." He paused, and then plunged in. "Calder's major in college was psychology. Masters program."

"Whew! An untrained Dom with psych training just walked innocently into the world of BDSM. He's not just going to have issues. He's going to have whole subscriptions." Angie worried a fingernail with her teeth until Brad batted at her hand. "How Dom is he in real life?"

"Very. Works independently. Uh, in the entertainment industry."

"Shit. Independent, big caring heart, strong personality, and a creative streak all describe the strongest and best Doms I know." Her eyes opened to the size of saucers. "Your friend will hit his knees sometime soon. Oh, man. That's going to be hard on him."

Angie frowned and got herself a cup of coffee. "You may be right, darling. Kelly has always defined the relationship from the outset by collaring anyone who wants to play with her, sexually or not. Your friend wasn't wearing a collar when he left." Her coffee cup wobbled. "Oh, shit. She didn't collar him."

Brad nodded. "That's right. What does that say about Kelly?"

"She doesn't see it." Angie waited until a pretty brunette filled a coffee mug and ran back, probably presenting it to her Master. "Brad, she's just looking for a happy little fuck. Denny has been dead a year, and the cancer made him half-dead for two years before that. I thought she had a right to grab up the first guy that attracted her and turn him inside out. I would, after three years of celibacy."

"But she's picked the wrong guy this time," Brad commented while he refilled his own mug of tea. "For every skill she shows him, he's going to absorb it, understand it, and turn it back on her."

Angie quirked an eyebrow upward, and laughed. "They're either going to kill each other, or make the best team in the city." She shrugged. "Me, I'm going to shoot for the moon and hope for orange blossoms in Kelly's future."

Brad scooped her up. "Stop being a yenta. And don't you dare pester Calder when he comes over Sunday afternoon. Go grill Kelly, instead. I know you will anyway."

Angie widened her eyes in a patently false attempt at innocence. "Who? Me? Why I never!"

"Yes, you, wench. And I remind you that you started to chew your nails earlier. You've been naughty, my little sub." Brad leered at his wife.

"Rut-roh, Shaggy!" was all she got out before she was tossed over Brad's shoulder and hauled downstairs to her "punishment."

Chapter Six

After following BW home in his own car and being served a delicious cup of coffee—even if it was nuked and apparently from the morning—Calder followed her into her living room. She'd insisted he start calling her Kelly, "at least for now." Whatever that meant.

"So, let's see. I believe you wanted to know about the coin incident. Michael was always a submissive, not a pain slut and not into bondage. He prefers service. He thinks he's a pain slut, but he can't take much."

Kelly was pacing—no, stalking—around the living room like a caged panther in leather. That outfit was killing him. It ought to be against the law for leggy, sultry brunettes to wear such "fuck me" costumes.

"You see, there are three *main* types of BDSM. Bondage and discipline is one. Dominance and submission is the second. Sado-masochism is the third."

"Okay, let me get this straight. B&D is, like, tying people up and torturing them mildly, right?" At her careful nod, Calder continued. "D&s is like what Michael likes. Servitude, maybe sometimes humiliation. How am I doing?"

Kelly raised one eyebrow. "Simplified, but you're doing okay."

"Okay, the final one, S&M. That's the one I don't get. That sounds like there's more than mild pain involved."

"Very good. Yeah. Mild pain and the pleasure it derives can be involved, but some lines blur. For me, S&M means the hard-core stuff, like knife play and permanent physical damage. I don't do that, unless I am paid very, very well, and even then I have limits I don't cross."

"Well, I can agree to those definitions. So, what about Michael?"

"As I said, Michael is a submissive by preference. That's why he is such a wuss on the cross. He likes to be told to do everything. That's his thing, and it's understandable with the pressures of his life at work. He's IT. He likes to abdicate responsibility whenever he's away from the computers and not forced to make immediate decisions with million-dollar equipment. Anyway, he needs a full-time, live-in position with a Mistress. I'm not the kind who likes to have subbies underfoot, especially ones who can't or won't think for themselves."

"And his new Mistress is the kind who can give him that?" Calder asked dubiously.

"Yup. She's Gorean. Ever read the Gor books by John Norman? It's a whole slave society, and well thought out. Certain factions of BDSM enthusiasts have made a real-life version of that world. Lady Mina likes to live and play in that world, and for that you need subbies just like Michael. It's a win-win situation for Lady Mina. She'll get absolute service, and he will get the abdication of responsibility. He's going to be very happy. Mina is rare. There's maybe a handful of Gorean Mistresses in the US."

"So, the coin was a symbolic payment?"

"Yes, indeed! A dollar won't break her, and in her world, she's paid a good price for a slave boy of incomparable value." Kelly set down her coffee cup with a decisive click.

"I see. I'll have to mull that over. I know a few people that like to abdicate responsibility for their actions."

Kelly gave a short bark of laughter. "Don't we all?"

She sauntered over to a very impressive stereo system and hit a button. Chopin floated softly out of hidden speakers. Calder's abused eardrums blessed her.

"Now, let's get on to that fire play question." Kelly marched over to her bags and suitcase and rummaged in the "bottle bag" she'd carried in earlier. With a triumphant "Ah-ha! Here we are!" she pulled out the same bottle she'd used on Michael earlier, plus a zip-locked plastic bag with cotton balls in it, and a towel.

With an absolute disregard for the beauty and value of her coffee table, she sat on it and dumped her armload on the tabletop beside her. Calder tried to ignore the fact that she was practically sitting right on top of him and nearly nose-to-nose.

"I don't care much for this, myself, but in the interest of calming your nerves, it's worth the trouble." She wrinkled her nose at him and grinned mischievously. "Would you care to help?" She offered Calder a neatly folded white towel.

Calder took the white towel. "Sure. What are you going to do?" He couldn't quite keep the wary tone out of his voice.

"Set myself on fire." At Calder's inarticulate and half-strangled cry, she laughed. "Oh, sit back and calm down. It won't hurt, not even if you're slow with the towel." She opened the plastic bag and got out a few cotton balls. "I just don't happen to favor getting my arm hairs singed."

Using the bottle now in her hand, she slapped it in her palm to emphasize the steps. "Here's the plan, Calder, so listen up. Once I swipe my arm with the cotton, you get ready with the towel. I'll use the lighter, and you immediately pat the flames out with the towel. Got it?"

Calder nodded, not trusting himself to speak. He wanted desperately to stop her, and at the same time he was eaten up with curiosity. Curiosity was winning, by a bare margin. He clutched the towel fiercely, and tried to look as if he'd pounce at a moment's mishap.

Kelly, no, BW opened the bottle and the pungent smell of isopropyl alcohol filled the area. She looked up and saw Calder's intent expression. "Relax, Calder. All Dominants must be able to do this if they want to do it to their subs. It's only fair, isn't it, to know what the sub will feel?" She reached up to stroke his cheek. "Trust me, okay? I'm trusting you." She looked significantly at the towel.

Calder forced himself to at least stop clutching the towel. "Okay, babe. I'll try."

Kelly quickly loaded a cotton ball with alcohol and swiped her arm. A quick flick of the lighter, and her arm was on fire. After a second of fascination, Calder patted out the tiny flame with the towel.

He berated himself for morbidity, but when Kelly held out her arm for inspection, Calder couldn't help examining it with all the care he could give. Other than a few singed hairs, it wasn't even pink. The only discernable effect was slight warmth and the little crispy hairs.

"Isopropyl burns too rapidly to cause damage, as long as it is extinguished fairly quickly. The effect is all in the mind," BW reminded him in a soft voice.

Calder caught on. "I get it! The mind screams about being on fire and goes into the fight or flight reflex. Adrenaline is produced, heightening reactions and heartbeat. That's what put Michael over the edge. He got an adrenaline rush."

Kelly shook a finger at Calder. "And he was never in any danger. He knew it intellectually, but his emotions remain the same. Now, let's do you."

Calder winced and hesitated, but stuck out his arm with good grace. "Can't say I'm happy about it, but then again, I'm curious."

"Well, good!" Kelly responded cheerfully. "You'll get a better adrenaline rush for that healthy amount of fear. Think of it like a clinical experiment, Calder." She held out the lighter and a towel, one in each hand. "I'll let you pick which role you want to play. Lighter or patter?"

Calder looked indecisively at both for a moment. He couldn't bear the thought of giving control of the flames on his own flesh to anyone else, so he took the towel.

Kelly smiled and prepared the cotton ball. She held the lighter in her right hand and swabbed his arm with her left. With a quick glance to make sure Calder was ready with the towel, she flicked the lighter.

Calder watched the flames erupt on his arm, but felt only a little warmth. He completely forgot about the towel in his fascination. Kelly was ready for such a reaction, and snatched the towel from Calder. She efficiently put out the flame just as the warmth began to increase to something less pleasant.

"Well, you had a typical first reaction to the experience, same as I did," Kelly commented with satisfaction. "That is why I recommend that this always be done with another person. It should never be done on oneself while alone, so don't go home and experiment. BDSM is always practiced with safety first in mind. Never forget that."

Calder flushed with embarrassment. He hadn't done anything like that, just staring at an unsafe situation or emergency, since he'd been a rookie.

Kelly patted his cheek, arresting his attention. "How's your heartbeat? Do you think you got an adrenaline rush?"

"Unsteady, and yes."

"There you have it, then. That's the trick of fire play. See? I'm not such a monster, am I?" She smiled sweetly.

Personally, Calder wasn't sure if it was the fire play or Kelly herself that caused his unsteady heartbeat, but he acknowledged that tiny spurt of fear watching his own arm burn.

Kelly put aside the fire play implements and leaned forward earnestly. "BDSM is more about psychology and physiology than some aberration of the psyche. If you've ever played 'tie me up, baby' with a lover, used an ice cube, tickled, or had a role-play where you were the big, strong captor of a lovely maiden, you've tasted one of the milder flavors of BDSM."

Calder ignored the comment, because he had done those things now and then. He contented himself with a nod. His mind easily supplied the fantasy of tying Kelly up.

"Want to see some of the 'flavors' of BDSM in my dungeon?" Kelly picked up the fire play equipment and put it away. When she stood, her round ass was right in his face, and he had the irrational urge to take a bite.

"Yes, I would!" He put his empty coffee cup down. "Uh, shouldn't we put these back in the kitchen?"

Kelly favored him with a sardonic look. "Not necessary. I have a subbie who comes in every day to clean for me. She'll get it in the morning." She sauntered through the doorway and led him to an ornately carved door.

Following the lovely Black Widow was torture enough for Calder. There was more sway in those hips than in most back porch swings. The shorts left a pair of perfectly rounded ass cheeks in clear view, peeking from beneath the material.

Her descent down a flight of well-lit stairs hid those long legs from view enough for Calder concentrate on where they were going. Dark-paneled walls were smooth and well polished. This wasn't the cheap stuff. The rail was dark oak, if he had any knowledge of wood. In fact, the whole house was laden with subtle luxuries.

At the bottom of the stairs, Kelly waited and let him have a good look around. The main room was relatively small, but looked a little like a throne room, complete with a gas fireplace and carved mantel. One large, comfortable chair with ornate carvings took center stage on a thick oriental rug laid over the equally thick blue carpeting. Other chairs and floor pillows provided extra seating. A small kitchen gleamed white and perfect directly to his right.

Several doors led off the main room. Most were closed. One, nearest the kitchen, stood open. Calder stared at what looked like an oversized grade school desk visible in the room.

Kelly's eyes followed his gaze. "Curious, Calder? I can show you any room you desire."

"Yeah." Calder walked to the open door and stepped in. "Fuck me, it's a schoolroom." And it was. Complete with teacher's desk and chalkboard. But only two of those oversized desks.

"More often than not, I'm the schoolmarm, here." She chuckled. "Want to see?" Without waiting for his nod, she stepped into what looked like a closet.

Moments later, she stepped out again, completely transformed. She wore those same skyscraper heels, but she'd put her hair up in some simple twist on her head and had donned a pair of glasses. Instead of shorts, she now wore a tiny black skirt the width of a placemat. The bustier had been replaced with a skintight, white lace blouse, giving him an unimpeded look at the soft skin underneath. The whole outfit made his mouth water. Seeing those hard pink nipples peeking through the lace made his fingers itch to touch, to pinch.

Kelly looked severely at him. "Class is now in session. Sit down, Calder. You're late. Do you need to be switched?" She fingered a whip-like wooden switch.

Playing the game, Calder hastened to the nearest desk and sat down, grinning. "No, ma'am!"

"That's better." She turned to the chalkboard and lifted her arm to write, treating Calder to a spectacular view of her sweet, curvy ass barely covered by a tiny pair of virginal white panties. His mouth watered, and his cock rose up to the call. He barely could pay attention to the words, "Lesson Plan: Math" she wrote neatly on the board. Kelly then walked casually over to the corner of the teacher's desk and sat with legs spread, giving him an intimate view of those white panties. His mind blanked in pure lust. He wanted his face *right* there, *right now.*

"You see, Calder, I can play the teacher. I can also be the student—pigtails, teddy bear, and cute pout—but that is rare indeed. Shall we move on to the next room?" She wandered out the door, leaving the granny glasses on the desk, still clad in that outfit she was almost wearing.

Calder rolled his eyes skyward and pleaded for mercy, but got up and followed her out the door. Pink nipples winked like a beacon in the lit doorway she stood in front of, urging him onward.

Chapter Seven

Kelly laughed to herself silently as Calder stumbled out the door of the schoolroom and over to her side, his cock making a hard ridge in his jeans.

Come here, little fishy. Momma's got a treat for you. I'll have you soon enough. Even if no one else knew the pleasures of anticipation, The Black Widow certainly did.

She'd had to end that school session. It wasn't hard to read his face, nor the tongue that flickered out just long enough to wet dry lips. The naked lust in his eyes for her pussy was making her so wet, she'd get distracted.

So, you like to eat pussy, do you, gorgeous? Well, if you're a good boy, you might just get a feast later. Let's see how you do with a little easy stimulation.

Unable to resist, she patted his gravity-defying ass on the way in. To cover her lapse, she laughed. "Hurry along now. There's lots to see and do, you know."

Calder reacted like he'd been stung, propelling himself further into the room. His eyes were a tiny bit less glazed. She could hardly wait to get him on the cross.

He looked around the room, which she had decorated similarly to the booths in Angie's dungeon. A St. Andrew's cross was on the wall, like a giant X, with shearling-lined cuffs affixed to the four points. A table provided easy access to a long line of furs, clamps, floggers, and whips. Two spray bottles adorned a small shelving unit with a stack of neat white towels, and a small red box clearly marked "Medical." The armoire behind her contained other toys.

"Care to give the cross a try, handsome?" Kelly purred. When he shot her a look comprised of fear mixed with masculine ego, she almost chuckled. "No toys, Calder. I won't even lock you in. But you might want to take off your shirt to feel the wood."

Not ready for pain, huh? Well, that's okay, handsome. Next time. And there will be a next time. I guarantee it, just by the lust in your eyes. You want to explore this, don't you? And it's no longer just curiosity.

Calder stripped off his tee shirt. "Sure. I'll give it a go. Can't see the attraction, though." He stepped up to the cross and put his hands in the leather cuffs.

"Spread your legs, Calder. You won't be in line with the ankle cuffs if you don't." Kelly walked up behind him and pushed gently on his inner thighs until his ankles were aligned so that the cuffs wrapped around them. As promised, she didn't buckle them, but she did keep a hand on his inner thigh.

Standing near enough to brush the lace of her shirt on his bare back, she said calmly in his ear, "See how comfortable the cuffs are?" Calder's involuntary quiver as her lace-clad nipples brushed his shoulder blade was reward enough. "Would you like to feel how I warm up a client? I promise, no pain is involved." Her hand was still touching his thigh. She moved it up to place it with seeming casualness on one firm buttock.

Oh, man, I have got to see this naked sometime.

"Uh. Yeah, sure. I'm not locked in here. If I don't like it, I can just step away." His voice was thick, and he cleared his throat.

Good. She wasn't the only one barely in control of her lust. Kelly warned herself to be careful. Calder was no meek submissive. There was a small thrill that ran up her spine, knowing she was teasing a predator, just like herself.

Kelly reached for the spray bottle with the red cap on a warming tray. "I'm going to spray your back with something wet. I promise it doesn't hurt. Got it?"

"Got it."

Spritzing her warming solution on Calder's muscular back took more work than Michael's scrawny frame ever did. But time was on her side. The formula she used was made to slowly increase circulation and produce a mild tingling sensation. Who knew mint and capsaicin could do so much?

"Oh, man! What is that stuff?" Calder quivered slightly. "It smells pretty good, but my back is tingling."

"My special formula. Secret family recipe." And it was, too. But Granny never expected her famous cold tea recipe to have the use Kelly put it to. She picked up a rabbit fur mitt. "Next, I'm going to rub something on your back, Calder. It's soft and warm, but it's not me, I swear it."

* * *

"I'd say, do your worst, but I don't want to know what your worst is," he muttered into the wood. From his angle, he couldn't see what she was doing. The room's arrangement of furniture and lighting kept her movements just out of visual range.

Maybe that was good. He couldn't see her this way. But his memory supplied all the images necessary. Those tits were snowy globes with little pink peaks. He licked his lips and ached to taste them. Aw, hell, he ached to taste her from those slim toes all the way to her hairline. In small, greedy bites. Stopping at strategic points. Like her round ass. That sweet-looking white-clad pussy. On a fur.

Hey! Fur. Fur was rubbing his back. He slammed himself hard into the cross. "Geeeezus!" What the hell, rubbing up against anything hard seemed like a good idea right now. It wasn't going to ease his hard-on, but it might just allow him to save a little face in front of this spellbinding witch. He began to move in time with the fur that was softly moving all over his back.

Lace replaced fur. Warm lace. Oh, shit, those tits were back. Hard little nubs encased in a lace blouse. "Ready for a little light bondage?" came a whisper in his ear. Her hand snaked around to take his cock and hold on to it, denim and all. "You're ready for it, I see." Warm breath fluttered in his ear.

Calder moaned. "Lady, you're killing me."

The hand tightened, then rubbed his cock. "No, sweetheart. But I am going to make you scream."

"Scream?" Calder gasped. "No, I don't think so, babe. I draw the line at pain."

Kelly chuckled softly in his ear. "With pleasure, Calder, with pleasure. Are you ready for a little one-on-one?"

She hadn't stopped massaging his cock, and it was now hard enough to hammer railroad spikes. He pulled his hands out of the cuffs, then carefully stepped out of the unbuckled ankle cuffs and pulled away from the cross. Turning, he yanked her to him. "Equal terms?" he responded, his hands finding their way to that round backside of hers of their own volition.

"Almost. Are you ready to try a little bondage? I promise…"

"Yeah, yeah. It won't hurt. That, I've done before. But normally I'm the one in charge."

"We can try it your way another time. But you did ask about my toys. There's one last set, and they are in that room nearest the fireplace." She nibbled on his ear. "It's got a bed," she whispered.

"Fair enough, beautiful." He released her ass reluctantly. "Lead on."

Kelly took his hand with a playful grin and led him into a bedroom out of anyone's fantasies. A huge four-poster dominated—whoops, bad word choice, there—the room. Like some sort of a Victorian fantasy, the furnishings were all dark mahogany and lace. Even the bedspread was white and lacy looking. The fancy carved vanity had a big oval mirror, and various bottles, jars and creams completed the look of a woman's pleasure palace.

She dropped his hand and let him look, even allowing him to poke around in the armoire full of dressing gowns, lingerie, and fripperies. If she had "toys," none were in evidence.

"Calder."

Kelly's voice made his mouth water. He turned around and almost drooled on his shoes. Gloriously naked, Kelly stood next to the bed, holding a white rope.

"Good god, woman," Calder exclaimed reverently. "Voluptuous, that's what you are." A man would have to be dead to avoid crossing the room and filling his hands with her. "White skin, and no bones showing. I could die a happy man."

Kelly gasped softly when his fingers gently rubbed a pink nipple to hardness. "You like a woman with a bit of flesh on her, hmm? You're good with words, Calder." When one hand crept lower and touched her wet pussy, she rose on her toes and spread her thighs slightly to allow him entrance. Hot, slick flesh greeted his finger. To pleasure himself as much as her, he caressed her clit for a few moments while her arms wrapped around his neck. When her eyes glazed, he lifted his hand to his lips and sucked the juices off.

Calder bent down to enjoy a lingering kiss. Tongues tangled in a dance, each striving to outdo the other. When the kiss broke, Kelly stepped back, admiring and caressing his chest. "Mmmm...you work out." She bent to nibble on one brown nipple while her fingers played with a few stray chest hairs.

"Swimming," he muttered. But that brought him up short. Yeah, he swam. In the apartment complex pool where he lived, often taking his laptop to write. It was hard to remember he was researching an article for a magazine on the kinkier forms of sex. Not when a sultry brunette was bent over using tongue and teeth on his nipples and undoing his belt buckle with expert ease.

"Mmmmmm," she hummed again, moving over to repeat her treatment on his other nipple, leaving a damp trail between. That tiny vibration sent waves of pleasure to his cock, which warned him it would burst soon. He couldn't get any harder.

His jeans pooled at his feet. He stepped out of his loafers, then his jeans while Kelly was still latched on to his right nipple, but she let go almost as soon as he was done, and knelt to strip off his socks. Then big blue eyes gazed up at him, almost eye-level with his aching cock. "How fond of these blue briefs are you?" she asked.

"Uh, I like them," he answered, disconcerted.

"Then I'll remove them instead of ripping them off of you like I want to," she teased. They were down and off in a matter of seconds, leaving his cock free to stand at rigid attention.

Kelly stood and took up the rope again. "Okay, Calder. Last lesson tonight in BDSM. Then I'm going to have my way with you, and you with me. Fair enough?"

"Kelly, dammit," he began, but a gentle shove had him off-balance and on the bed.

"Bear with me a moment, Calder. Then, you'll have your reward. It will be worth the wait."

"Okay, okay." Calder made himself comfortable on the pillows, turning until he was in the correct position, with both hands raised above his head. Instead of tying him up, she simply gave him a piece of rope to hold in each hand.

"See, Calder? All you have to do is hold them. You can free yourself simply by letting go. This is just a demo, after all." Her voice deepened to a husky purr. .

"Better."

Kelly turned and picked up a small bottle and liberally anointed his cock with the contents. Before he could do more than gasp, Kelly grinned down at him. "Easy, big guy. It's just more of the same I put on your back, in a thicker formula." She gave the head of his cock a quick suckle. "Tastier, too."

Before his eyes, Kelly sat down on the vanity stool and anointed her own pussy with casual, lazy strokes. "I don't get to do this often," she admitted, her eyes half-closed. "Would you like a taste?" She spread her legs wide so he could see her pink, wet labia glistening at him in the low lighting.

"Come here, and I'll be happy to taste it. And you." Calder's cock was now throbbing and aware of the tiniest shift in the air currents. He could play this game for a little longer, but not much more before he exploded.

Like a cat on the stalk, Kelly approached the foot of the bed and began a slow crawl up to where he wanted her, right on his face. She lingered to lick and nibble at anything that pleased her, including a quick toe suck that made him writhe for a moment.

Fingers played with his balls while a soft mouth pleasured an inner thigh. With a soft "Growf!" she attacked the bottom of his shaft, following the strength of the underside all the way up with agonizing slowness. She paused and nibbled the head of his cock, teasing with her teeth until Calder wondered if he'd last. Her little pink tongue flicked the opening and drew out the pre-cum that glistened.

"I'm not going to be able to take much more of this, Kelly," he muttered.

"Neither am I. It's been way too long. But you're worth savoring," she murmured against his cock.

"You promised me a taste, and you've already got me on fire."

"And I never break a promise. You win, Calder."

Calder tested his ropes and how much room they gave him. Not much. He wouldn't be able to use his hands. Very well. No hands, just tongue. This wasn't so bad, this bondage thing.

Kelly positioned herself so that she could continue her work on his cock in a classic 69. Calder had no objections to this, as he planned to distract her as much as possible and focus on her pleasure. He was feeling increasingly guilty about not coming clean and admitting he was a journalist. But his lie of omission now had him tangled in a web of his own making.

Nibbling on a creamy thigh was just the ticket to get things turning his way. He went about his work with the hunger of a starving man. The writer part of him chuckled at the metaphor. Hunger—yeah, he was hungry all right. Good analogy. He'd have to remember that later.

The pink delicacy in front of him was more than any mortal could resist, and he wasn't above enjoying a temptation or two. First on his list was licking her labia like icing on a confection. Playful little tugs with his lips were second, just to listen and feel her moans through his cock. Good. She'd teased him all evening. Now it was *his* turn to make her writhe.

Soft brown hair tickled his nose until he burrowed past it. Whatever that goo was she'd spread on was tasty as hell and lit his tongue on fire. Mint and honey, his brain supplied. The herbal flavor added a whole new dimension, not to mention the way her clit popped from its hiding place at the first lap of his tongue. But the honey made it all sticky, so he took his time getting every last drop.

That same goo was probably what was slowing Kelly down too. She was taking her time with his cock, working from the base in slow, easy steps, licking and sucking like she had a candy cane to eat from the bottom up. It was keeping him just under the pinnacle, but her breathing was coming faster and faster. It wouldn't be long now.

Calder's tongue caressed her clit in hard pumping touches. Kelly sat up, panting and still, so Calder focused on her pleasure. One shudder was all the warning he got before she exploded. He lapped happily while she writhed and screamed, waiting for her orgasm to slow before plunging his tongue in again.

"BASTARD!" she screeched, but came harder. Literally propelled by the force of her climax, she crawled off and lay there, panting.

Calder didn't bother to answer. He'd had a small revenge in getting her to scream first.

"You bastard," Kelly repeated. "I'll get you for that. I make them scream first." Without warning, she leapt on top of his cock and began to ride hard and fast.

Watching her tits bounce in front of him, and thrusting with all his might, Calder knew it would be a short fuck unless he got her to calm down.

"Easy, babe," he warned. "You keep this up and I won't last long."

Panting, eyes glazed and her hair still up in that Victorian knot, she looked like a madwoman. But she listened. "Yeah? Okay, I'll slow down."

Calder was very sorry a few moments later. She slowly sank down on his cock, her muscles moving up and down every inch. It was worse than torture.

She laughed at his expression. "I call this the 'Incredible Munching Pussy.'" Having reached the bottom, she moved up the same way.

"I'm getting fucked by a madwoman," he muttered. "You're definitely trying to kill me."

For once, Kelly didn't answer. A feral smile crossed her face. She began to fuck him faster with every down stroke. Calder couldn't help himself any longer, and instinct took over. He met her down strokes with thrusts of his own, his face contorting with the effort not to release the ropes. A bargain was a bargain, but it was so hard.

His eyes flew open wide and he cried out, "Oh, God!" Without conscious thought, he let go of the ropes and grabbed her hips, finishing with deep penetrations until he felt himself turning inside out with the strength of his own orgasm. With one final movement, he shoved her hard down on himself until he felt his cock head literally hit her cervix. Her shrieks of renewed orgasm nicely covered his shouts.

Kelly, now released from his hands, fell panting on top of him. "If you move, I'll kill you," she warned.

"Not likely, beautiful. Right now, I'm concentrating on remaining alive. You're one dangerous woman." Calder took her threat as an empty one, considering she was kissing his shoulder at the same time.

It was the last thing he remembered.

Chapter Eight

Calder awoke to the new and strange sensation of softness and warmth, as well as a tickling sensation on his nose. The surface beneath him was soft, unlike his bed in his apartment. Something both pliable and warm was partially wrapped around him, not to mention a blanket that smelled of Kelly's perfume. His eyes shot open.

The morning light coming in from a basement egress window revealed the Victorian bedroom where he and Kelly had played and made love. And that warm silkiness wrapped around him was Kelly herself, asleep. The tickle had been provided by what was left of her schoolmarm hairdo.

Calder grinned. Man, what a night. He was chagrined to have fallen asleep on her, and would have to make it up to Kelly as soon as he recovered. He hoped that little bathroom door he'd seen led to a shower.

Gently easing his way to disentangling himself from Kelly, he was grateful when she made a mild protest and rolled over, taking the blanket with her. Smothering a chuckle at seeing this display of dominance even while she slept, he made his way quietly to the bathroom.

With a sigh of gratification, Calder found not only a sink and toilet, but also a shower stall worthy of kings. Fresh and fluffy towels hung conveniently nearby on a warming rack. The hot water felt like a waterfall compared to the stingy spray in his apartment, and he nearly groaned aloud. Even the soap smelled of luxury.

He dried off and carefully hung the towels back on the warmer, where he presumed they would dry. Then he tiptoed back in the bedroom and found his clothes. Kelly didn't stir.

Calder decided to sneak upstairs and find that coffee cup he'd left in the living room. Maybe Kelly wouldn't begrudge him a cup, and he'd be happy to make a fresh pot for the use of it.

Stepping carefully outside the bedroom door, he heard a small tinkle and a gasp. Turning around quickly, he saw a woman wearing a collar holding a tray with two cups and a carafe.

The dark-skinned woman stared for a moment, and then bent her head. "Good morning, Master," she uttered softly with one eye on the bedroom door. "Coffee is served, if Master wishes it."

Man, he could get used to this. "Thank you. Your Mistress is still asleep." He closed the bedroom door so Kelly wouldn't be disturbed. "But, who are you and why do you call me Master?"

The woman gave him a glittering smile. "My name is Sadie, Master, and I'm the housekeeper. And there are several clues. First and foremost, you aren't wearing a collar. Second of all, no one has ever slept overnight in that bed except the Mistress. Can't imagine anyone would who wasn't her equal." Sadie handed him a cup, black as sin and just as fragrant. "Third, I'm a sub. I recognize a Master when I see one."

Ah, so this was the housekeeper. "And I assume you guessed how I'd like my coffee from the cup left upstairs last night?"

"The car in the driveway was the first clue that someone was here. Second was the cup. Third was when I didn't find Mistress in her own bed upstairs when I went to, uh, clean." Sadie looked a bit uncomfortable, and it wasn't hard to guess why.

Calder snickered. "You mean you went to investigate and make sure your Mistress was all right. I don't blame you. That's why you brought down a tray. It was a good excuse to go find your Mistress."

Sadie relaxed visibly. She indicated a chair across from the throne dominating—there was that word again—the sitting area. "Why don't you sit down, Master...?"

"Calder. And yes, I think I will. Thank you."

Calder sat in a chair facing the room where Kelly slept, and Sadie knelt comfortably nearby, seemingly content to wait on his every need. He studied her for a few moments. Her khakis and polo shirt seemed normal. The only thing out of place was the black collar with a silver spider pendant hanging from it.

A glance at his watch had his eyes flying open. One o'clock. No wonder he was reasonably coherent. It wasn't technically morning anymore. He sipped his coffee and wondered what to do. Conversation seemed reasonable.

A clearing of the throat got Sadie's attention from her smiling contemplation of the patterns of the rug. "Sadie, I'm curious. Would you answer a few questions, if they aren't private information?"

The big brown eyes twinkled. "I'll answer what I can. When I can't, I'll tell you."

Calder foundered for a moment. "What do you think would be an appropriate gift for your Mistress to thank her for all she did for me last night?"

Sadie's lips twitched.

"Besides that, Sadie." He laughed softly. "I'll be happy to provide more if she wants it, but I mean a real gift."

Sadie chuckled, but sobered. "I'm going to doubt you'll collar yourself, so may I suggest the usual gifts you'd give a lady? Flowers, candy, stuffed animals, you know." At Calder's raised eyebrow, she looked stern. "Mistress is the same as any other woman, Master Calder. And don't you even begin to think different!"

Calder grinned, unperturbed. "No, Sadie, she's a helluva lot better than most women." He wasn't about to admit his raised eyebrow had been over the concept of collaring himself. Now that he had seen the painless and pleasurable side of BDSM, it still didn't make him want to do what Sadie was doing. Servitude just wasn't his thing.

"Why, thank you, Calder," drawled a voice from the door of the bedroom.

Kelly walked over, wrapped in an emerald green silk kimono he'd seen in the wardrobe, and picked up a coffee cup. Sadie leapt up to pour, and soon Kelly was seated on the throne-like chair near Calder. She toasted Calder with her mug and sipped appreciatively.

"Mistress, I need to remind you that you're scheduled to go to the hospice from three until six," Sadie reported.

"Yes, I remember." Kelly turned to smile at Sadie, and then returned her blue eyes to Calder. "I hope you'll forgive me, but I will need to see you out shortly."

Calder made to put down his coffee cup, understanding but somewhat disappointed. Well, he had more notes in his head than he thought possible to transcribe. Kelly raised her hand, and part of him dared hope she'd want to see him again. Something in him craved her company, and it was more than the great sex.

"I've got nothing on the books tonight, do I Sadie?" Sadie shook her head. "Good. Calder, I'm sure that, given a few hours, you're going to have a thousand questions. Why don't I pick you up on my way home, and we'll have dinner here together?"

The prospect of a meal that didn't come from the microwave or a can had vast appeal, even beyond having it with Kelly. He'd have killed for it. "I'd love it. I'm a lousy cook, but can I bring something?" Some irrational part of his mind screamed, *Flowers? Candy? Me?* He told it to shut up, and instead grinned cockily. "What's for dinner?"

Sadie answered, "Pot roast, potatoes, salad, and green beans, Master."

"And chocolate cake," added Kelly with a smile.

Calder tried hard not to melt. "Sounds great." He got up, kissed Kelly tenderly on the lips, and dug his keys out of his pocket. "I'll see you in a few hours."

"Give Sadie your address on your way out, Calder."

Kelly rose and walked languidly behind them as Sadie escorted Calder out. She waited to wave at the bottom of the stairs until the door shut on Calder's back.

Sadie turned in time to see her Mistress grin, whoop, and start to run up the stairs.

Kelly yelled as she hit the first landing, "Call the hospice and cancel my appointment today, Sadie! I have a cake to bake as soon as I'm dressed!"

Sadie put her hands on her hips as soon as Kelly was out of sight, and shook her head. "Good thing there're two ovens," she muttered, and bustled into the kitchen.

* * *

Calder sat at his desk, typing furiously, with one eye on the clock and one eye on the monitor. He couldn't get it all down in time. He knew that. Bits and pieces of data of how certain forms of BDSM worked on the psyche was all he had. He'd gotten the forms of BDSM organized into categories, and was cutting and pasting the notes as he remembered things into the appropriate category.

This article was almost getting out of hand. He would have to condense the hell out of it, focusing only on the psychological aspects that would sell. That burned him. It wouldn't be enough. Did he have enough to create a proposal for Ruben to sell as a book?

He glanced at the clock. Five PM. One hour. He would do what he could. He had the outline. He had some data. He got to work to create the rest.

* * *

Kelly tooled her 1982 Harley Wide-Glide down the street, following the directions to Calder's apartment. She admitted to herself that "Baby" as she called the Harley, was all for show and the double takes she got.

The cake was cooling on the counter with Sadie's sworn word she'd frost it while they ate dinner. After a frantic run to the store for ingredients, and making a mess of the kitchen that had Sadie in despair, Kelly had the cake. It was a personal triumph. It was like coming out of a dark room into the light.

It didn't matter if Calder was a permanent fixture in her life waiting to happen. That remained to be seen, and she wasn't about to make any predictions after a one-night stand. All that was Calder would be revealed, if he chose to continue. He had been the catalyst to make her want to live again, and right now, that was good enough.

She pulled into the apartment complex and rode around until she found the building number. It wasn't a bad complex; relatively clean, but also inexpensive. The amenities were just a pool and a shabby tennis court. There were eight apartments to a building. She looked up at all the windows and spotted Calder looking out a window on the right, waving her up.

Locking up Baby and her helmet was easy, and so was finding his apartment number on the mailboxes. "Burgess" was number 202. She hustled up the stairs and knocked on his door.

Calder opened the door immediately and dragged her inside. Her small squeak of surprise was muffled against his lips.

When Calder freed her lips to nibble her ear, she murmured, "Feeling in charge, hmm?" Kelly was inclined to let him, at least for now.

"If I weren't starving," Calder laughed and let the implied threat hang. "Let me grab my coat. Hope you have a spare helmet."

"I do." While Calder rummaged in an over-full closet, Kelly let curiosity take over. The whole apartment was neat as a pin, except for a desk where the dining nook would be. She spotted many BDSM research books from the library, and smiled. Calder took everything so seriously. He'd probably studied up using the Net, as well. That sleek little computer system was not one of the cheap models, and neither was the matching high-speed laser printer.

"Ready!" Calder said behind her, jiggling his keys. He closed the apartment door and locked it behind them before following Kelly down the stairs. His appreciative whistle was all for the Harley when he caught up. "Nice!"

Kelly tossed him a black helmet. "World's most expensive vibrator!" That elicited some chuckles from two admiring teen boys who happened to walk by. Kelly waited until they were out of earshot, for Calder's sake. "You get the bitch seat." Tugging on her helmet, she got on and waited for Calder to mount up behind her before firing up the engines. The last thing she heard was his appreciative chuckle.

Chapter Nine

Kelly ran into the kitchen, startling Sadie. "Okay! Okay! He's seated in the living room." She eyed the cake, searching for minute flaws and gave it a poke. It was cool.

Sadie shook a wooden spoon at Kelly. "Mistress, you just calm yourself. Someone is going to think you're acting like a subbie. Get hold of yourself, right now."

Kelly stopped, looked at Sadie, and threw back her shoulders. "You're right, Sadie. For gosh sake, Calder is just a man." She rolled her eyes. "But oh, what a man!"

Sadie's eyes softened. "You'd best be careful. Your heart is going to land at that man's feet unless you lock it up tight." She transferred the spoon to her other hand and poked her shorter Mistress playfully on the nose, causing them both to grin like cats about to share a saucer of cream. "Chocolate cake baked by your own two hands is bad enough for one night."

Kelly gave her infamous raised eyebrow. "You know what they say, Sadie. The way to a man's heart and all that."

Sadie turned to stir the gravy. "But do you want his heart?"

Kelly paused in digging through the drawer for a cake knife. Her hand trembled for a moment, and she willed it to steady. "I guess I do."

Sadie checked the roast before answering. "Then you'd better be willing to risk your own, Mistress."

"Oh, dump the Mistress thing for a minute. Let's be women. I think I have a problem."

Sadie closed the oven door on the savory smells inside and straightened. In the subtle ways of subs, she took off her collar without removing it. "Then you listen up, Missy. That man may be gorgeous, but he's a Dom waiting to happen. Hell, he makes me want to hit my knees, and I am not his by any stretch."

"Me, too," Kelly muttered.

"What are you going to do about it?"

"I don't know." For the first time ever, Kelly was indecisive about her role with a man. It was very disconcerting.

"Well, you better think about it quick," Sadie advised. "I'm pretty sure you're on tonight's menu as dessert. He's that kind."

Kelly smiled in anticipation. "You know, Sadie, I just might let him. After all, what better way to know if he really is Dom material? I can handle myself." Her mind made up, Kelly nodded, and then went back to her guest.

"Oh, you are sunk, honey," Sadie muttered as Kelly left the kitchen.

Kelly pretended not to hear Sadie's comment, but she purposely did not hurry as she made her way through the butler's pantry, the dining room, and across the foyer to the living room.

Maybe she was being an idiot. She hardly knew Calder, but something about him said she could trust him. And she knew what the possibilities were tonight. She was going in with her eyes wide open. Every safety precaution would be in place. The sensuality of food was sure to be a good indication of how Calder might play, if he were taught. In the meantime, it was worth it to her to eat at home, and get to mess about in a kitchen again. She was tired of restaurants.

Calder leaned back in the comfortable dining room chair with a satisfied smile. Pot roast, mashed potatoes and gravy, steamed veggies, and biscuits now comfortably lined his stomach.

Kelly was out of the room, having promised to see to dessert. He belched quietly in hopes of making room for the cake she'd promised.

What was more, he'd had more fun tonight with Kelly than he'd ever had at a dinner table. They'd talked about everything under the sun from the latest movies to world politics. Mostly they'd agreed, but even when they hadn't, they had discussed their differences with companionable humor.

Why couldn't he have met Kelly in any other situation? He could take her out on a "real date," even if it meant dipping into his precious savings. Maybe he'd splurge and spend some of his pay from the magazine article. It would be worth eating beans for a week.

The dining room doors slid open, and Calder's eyes were riveted on the big chocolate cake atop a fancy glass pedestal Kelly carried. Behind her, Sadie followed with a silver coffee service on a tray.

"Chocolate cake and coffee? My stomach is going to think I died and went to paradise," he commented with reverence.

Kelly smiled, but the gleam in Sadie's eyes caught his attention. She winked at him behind Kelly's back, and then departed silently. *What was that all about?*

Calder's eyes lit up at the size of the cake slice delivered to him by Kelly herself. Then the significance hit him. Kelly was serving him. Was this a hint?

He was learning how subtle the art of Dominance and submission was. Even the spelling. Dominance was always capitalized, submission always lower-case. Maybe he needed to ask Kelly if he was right.

Calder forked a large bite to his lips and thought he'd die. The chocolate melted on his tongue and made his taste buds dance in ecstasy. He moaned aloud.

Kelly, looking relieved, began to eat her much smaller slice.

Calder cleared his throat. "Mind if I ask some of those million questions you predicted I'd have?" He grinned and nodded at her smaller slice. "Then I have an excuse to make a pig of myself while you take your time eating that little sliver and answering my questions."

With a small chuckle, Kelly gestured with her fork. "Go ahead, gorgeous."

"That's my line." Calder speared another piece. "I've noticed that Dominance and submission have a lot of subtle cues. Am I reading it right?"

One of his professors had lit up the same way once that Kelly did now. The professor had given him an "A." Kelly leapt up and planted a kiss on him that rocked him backwards. Whatever he'd done right, he hoped he could do it again.

"Calder, you're so fucking brilliant, it amazes me." Kelly regained her composure and sat back down. "Yes, the cues are subtle. They are part convention, and part long-term relationship. For instance, many of the same gestures you might associate with animal training can be used to convey a silent command." She made a motion with her hand, palm to the floor. Calder had seen it many times with the canine teams. "Only in this case, instead of the command for 'sit,' it means 'kneel and await further instruction.'"

"I can see that, Kelly, but it goes deeper than that. Sadie told me she could tell I was a Dom. And I knew, without knowing how I knew, she was a sub even before I saw the collar." Calder pondered while he stuffed another forkful of cake in his mouth.

"Very true, Calder. That's body language. Even were you to be naked in a room full of subs, your body language says, 'I am a Dom.' You hold your head high, you stride confidently when you walk, and you look people in the eye and assess them. Subs tell you they are submissive." She gave a wry smile. "Rapists and other criminals use the same subtle cues to choose their victims. Surely you've read that."

He'd more than read it; he'd seen the awful reality. And he'd seen what happened when the downtrodden snapped like dry twigs. He cleared his throat. "I see. Do subs ever turn Dominant, or vice-versa?"

Kelly laughed. "Damn, you're good! Yes. Those who can vacillate depending on circumstance and mood are called switches. And every good Dominant has learned to submit, so that they might intimately know what it is like."

The implications hit Calder like a club. His jaw dropped. "You mean you, at one time, submitted?"

The gaiety of Kelly's laughter was infectious. "Of course I did, silly. And I was very good at it, too. Denny was a good master and a good trainer of subs. He even trained male subs well, and that's rare."

Her husband. Right…wait. "Males? He trained males?"

Now Kelly looked disappointed. "Oh, Calder! Don't tell me you fell for that stereotype that Dominants must have sex with their subs? It's about trust, not sex." She shook her fork at him. "Denny didn't touch me until after I graduated to Dominant. And then he had to convince me to marry him." She sobered. "And I'll spare you the math. I started subbing at twenty-one, and married Denny at twenty-four. We were married slightly less than five years."

Instantly, Calder felt guilty. "Hey, I'm sorry to have brought up old hurts. Tell me some more about subbing."

"It's okay, gorgeous. Um…let's see. How about I tell you a Dominant's game that's done with subs? It might amuse you."

"Like chess with live pieces?" Calder ventured.

"No, though that's done. This is done in a restaurant, one with tablecloths. Or, it might be done in a private home if the table is large enough, like this one." She gestured to the large dining table they were seated at. It looked like it could hold eight people without the leaves.

Calder nodded. He could almost imagine the leather-clad people sitting at the table.

"Imagine all the elegant diners, enjoying wine and good food, with their own naked submissive each seeing to the needs of Master or Mistress. In case you're wondering, the subs have already been fed in the kitchen."

Kelly's voice lowered. Calder shut his eyes to envision it all. "The game begins. Each sub crawls under the table, to kneel at the feet of their Dominant. This is a game of sex, and all the subs are also the lovers of their Dominant, by the way."

"Isn't that against the rules you just said?"

"It happens. You can't exchange trust with someone over a long period of time without great affection developing, even love. It is not advisable, in many cases, but it happens. Sometimes lifelong bonds are formed."

"Okay, sorry. Just seemed like a contradiction."

"Yes, it does. Having been professional, I personally would have stepped from a quasi-legal service into the ugly world of prostitution. That's a line I never crossed. And it is inadvisable for any Dominant to cross that line. What if you and your lover have a fight right after a scene?"

"Oh, ouch." He could see that all too clearly. Assault and battery, sexual assault, and a very unsympathetic legal system would be just the beginning. Not a pleasant subject. "Okay, back to the game."

"Close your eyes and imagine, Calder." Calder shut his eyes, but not before he caught a glimpse of Kelly picking up the knife and cutting a generous slice of cake. What was she going to do with that?

Kelly's soft voice, with that hint of Southern drawl, continued. "The subs are under the table. This game works best when it is all male Masters, so let's assume all are male at the table. All the subs are female. The conversation centers on commonplace, non-sexual topics. The game is simple. The first to show what is happening under the table loses. This is a game of self-control."

Calder heard a small scrape, and ventured a peek. Kelly had pushed back her chair, and was disappearing under the table. He had a feeling what that evil smile and the plate of cake in her hand were about. He grinned, and shut his eyes, ignoring the fact that Kelly's voice now came from under the table.

"Pants are unzipped, cocks are freed. The Masters continue their conversation."

Calder felt his fly being unzipped, carefully and slowly. He pretended not to notice. Just like the game. He would be Master, tonight. He stabbed another piece of cake, and pretended not to notice Kelly freeing his cock from his pants.

Something cool was smeared on his semi-hard penis. Ah, so that's what the cake was for—the icing.

Amusement now tinged Kelly's voice. "Remember the rules. No Master may indicate what is happening, and the subs must try their hardest to earn their reward."

Calder felt warm lips encase the head of his cock. He would have a hard time without the benefit of conversation. On cue, it seemed, Sadie stepped into the dining room to clean up.

Sadie took one look at Kelly's empty chair, and raised an eyebrow at Calder. He pretended bland innocence and gave her a cheerful, "Thank you, Sadie. Delicious meal."

Sadie's lips twitched. "Why, thank you, Master." With twinkling eyes, she gathered up a few dishes. With her free hand, she pointed beneath the table with a questioning look.

Calder nodded. It was getting difficult to maintain a casual air, with Kelly enthusiastically cleaning all the icing off his now rock-hard cock.

Sadie gathered up the remaining dishes, leaving just the coffee carafe and cake. Winking at Calder, she sauntered back the way she'd come.

Relaxing, Calder took his coffee cup and sipped. He spread his legs a little wider, and fisted his free hand in Kelly's hair. "Continue, lovely one," he murmured.

"Yes, Master."

Chapter Ten

Calder couldn't believe what was happening. Kelly, the infamous Black Widow, had "switched." Was that the term? He would Dominate tonight, and he hadn't a clue what to do other than enjoy.

Then it hit him. Yes, he did. She'd shown him. The song "Life's a Dance" ran through his head. How appropriate to hear someone singing about leading and following, and learning as you go. He'd do everything she had done to him, plus a few of his own ideas. Whatever he could manage.

And hadn't she said the subs tell you what works for them? If he didn't know, he could test it on himself first.

In the meantime, Kelly's little mouth was driving him wild. She'd gotten through the smear of frosting and was now very busily proving she could suck the chrome from her motorcycle. He ordered his mind to concentrate on anything but the way her tongue lavished the underside of his cock and its head at the top of a stroke before plunging back down. Ordinarily, Calder might have stopped her before he came. But the time it would take him to recover afterward would be the perfect opportunity to try out some of her techniques on her very willing person.

Kelly tugged on his pants. "Please, Master?" she begged.

Calder felt like obliging, and stood long enough to drop his pants, revealing he had gone commando in hopes of an evening of mutual enjoyment. Kelly crawled out from the table and attacked his cock with an enthusiasm unmatched by any previous woman he'd ever had.

The braid she wore made a perfect handle. Calder reached down and grabbed it, using it instead of her bangs as he had earlier. He began to thrust, fucking her mouth as a prelude of what was in store later.

His balls tightened, signaling impending release. Calder closed his eyes to let it happen. Kelly's fingers found the spot at the base of his balls and began to stroke in time with his thrusts. It was too much, and he growled softly as he shot into her receptive mouth.

Calder felt like he was emptying his soul. Something primal was coming to the forefront, while Kelly licked and sucked every drop from his willing body. Now he understood, if perhaps dimly, the full concept of the power exchange. Each gave and each took, trusting in their partner not to do damage.

When the orgasm edged close to pain, he tugged gently on Kelly's braid. "Stop."

Kelly released his overspent penis and it fell, nearly flaccid, like a marathon runner too exhausted to move. Her big blue eyes lifted with a satisfied twinkle, and she licked her lips and smiled. "Yes, Master."

That smile was an invitation to further improprieties, if ever Calder saw one. "I'd throw you on the table and have you right here, but I don't want to upset Sadie."

"Sadie has gone home, Master. She was to bring in the coffee, remove the dishes and load the dishwasher, and leave out the back door."

"Now that you mention it, I hear the dishwasher running. Good!" Calder reached down and picked Kelly up by her arms. He let her toes dangle just off the floor for a moment before planting her butt on the edge of the table away from the end where they had eaten. "Down!" he commanded.

Kelly obediently laid back, her grin never wavering. Calder stripped off her jeans with expert ease, and found her commando, too. "Delightful!" In a flash of inspiration, he flipped up her tee shirt, exposing her breasts, yet covering her face. Kelly giggled, so he knew he was okay.

Improvise, improvise. Calder looked around the dining room and spotted one of the unused napkins conveniently near Kelly's head. He snatched it up, and looped it around her palms so that both hands held it in an improvised bond, just as he'd held the ropes the night before.

"By the rules of the game, beautiful," he told his lovely captive.

"Oh, yes, Master!" she breathed.

Calder scooped up a large finger full of cake icing. He regretted ruining the symmetry of the frosting job but counted it a small cost. If Kelly let him take it home later, he'd make sure he destroyed the evidence.

He liberally anointed each pebbled nipple with a generous amount of frosting, eliciting a gasp and squirm. The squirm worried him, so he whispered, "Drop the napkin if I do something you don't like."

"Not bloody likely, gorgeous!" came the muffled reply from under the shirt.

Chuckling, he kissed the bump that probably was her pert little nose before feasting on frosting and the nipple beneath. His left hand lifted the breast to a soft mound in his palm while his right crept down to tickle her navel.

Kelly alternated between giggles and gasps of what he hoped were pleasure while his tongue made sure to get every molecule of frosting. Only when he switched to clean the other chocolate covered nipple did the gasps become more frequent, probably because his right hand had moved lower to find a ripe clit to tickle.

By the time the second nipple was clean, his cock stood at rigid attention again. He silently admonished it for its impatience, but didn't resist the need. Calder pulled Kelly's squirming and ready body to the edge of the table, and put the head of his cock right at her drenched opening.

Kelly spread her legs widely, and begged, "Oh, please! Please!"

Calder was more than happy to oblige the request, and slid home with a groan. Without further ado, he began to pound her soft flesh, taking all he wanted, all she begged for.

Kelly was in heaven. Calder had made the switch like an old pro, catching on to her game plan with perfect aplomb. Not even Sadie's sudden appearance had thrown him.

And what a Dom he was! He'd improvised beautifully, with imagination many couldn't match. Most men would have stopped her before she was done sucking him blind, thrown her over their shoulder, and headed downstairs, without creativity.

Instead, Calder had used what was available in the room. He had even remembered to create a safe word, or in this case, a safe symbol. Now he was fucking her like he didn't plan to stop until the sun rose or she screamed, whichever came first.

Unable to see his face, Kelly resorted to the most common of tricks—her voice. "Yes, Master! Fuck me! Fuck me hard!" she begged. It was a rare man who wouldn't redouble his efforts to hammer her silly, and she intended to be so weak when he was done that she'd get carried to the bedroom.

Calder was no exception. His thrusts became the subject of legend women bragged about when men weren't around to hear. Kelly just hoped the solid oak table could handle the strain. She allowed herself to lose control completely, as any good sub would. Nothing mattered but that Calder was hammering her like a man possessed, and her whole body was responding.

He had a good grip on her ankles, but she managed to get them on his shoulders, and his grunting moan was all the thanks she needed.

Every inch of her concentration was focused on what her pussy said felt wonderful. She could feel his balls slapping her ass, his cock ramming home to the hilt, and even how the pounding was stimulating her clit. It was all coming together as one giant nova of pleasure.

Calder's harsh breathing told her he wasn't that far from explosion, either. Kelly urged him on. "Come for me again, please! Come again!"

"You first," came a growling response.

No problem! "Yes, Master!" she screeched, and released. It was secondary from her point of view that Calder learned subs could be trained to orgasm on command.

Calder followed, with a moaning roar that made her glad the house was empty. The tiny little jerks of his hips kept her in aftershocks until both were spent enough to just stay where they were and pant.

Only when Kelly's hand fell away from the green napkin, to crash against the candelabra did both jerk back to reality. "Oops!" Kelly giggled.

"You dropped the napkin," Calder reminded her. "That's naughty, right?" he added with an insinuating tone.

"Uh-oh! Does this mean you're going to take me down stairs and spank me?" She could insinuate, too. Would he pick up on it?

"Since you suggested it, yes." Calder picked her up without removing the tee shirt and slung her over his shoulder.

"Eep! Me and my big mouth."

"I have other uses for your mouth later." Calder swung her toward the main hall, if her sense of direction wasn't totally screwed by not being able to see. Well, if he found his way without her, all the better.

Kelly caught a whiff of the hot wax warmer and knew he'd found the door to the stairs leading down to the basement. He fumbled briefly with the light switch, and almost dropped her.

"Hey, this isn't very romantic," Kelly teased. Actually, it was. She was thoroughly enjoying being hauled around like a sack of potatoes by a guy who showed little effort.

"It isn't supposed to be. It's supposed to be kinky." He adjusted her more securely, even patting her butt before beginning his descent.

The light illuminating the room was too bright, but at the bottom of the stairs, Calder found the dimmer switch and dialed for softer lighting. That much Kelly could tell through the fabric of her tee shirt.

He paused at the base of the stairs, as if contemplating his choices. Kelly wondered what he would choose. She opened her mouth to tell him the spanking horse was behind the third door to the right, on the same side as the kitchen, and then shut her mouth with a snap. It was much more fun to let Calder use his imagination. What would he do?

"That would be interesting," Calder commented.

That had to be rhetorical. She felt Calder stride forward a few steps, and then he swung her around a few times to make her lose her sense of direction. Her low squeal of surprise was automatic, but not without a certain amount of pleasure. "So, you've found a way to confound me, have you, Master?" She put all the rich good humor in the compliment she could manage.

Calder strode a few steps more. "This is a little feminine for my taste, but it will work." Sitting down, Calder put Kelly over his knees. Kelly caught a glimpse of her oriental carpet and knew Calder sat upon her own "throne," as he called her favorite chair in the dungeon. What a lovely subtle symbol of who was in charge tonight!

With her bare bottom up, Kelly was reminded of the vulnerability of her position. She squirmed to get comfortable, knowing what was coming and relishing the thought.

Calder played with her already well-used and excited pussy for a few moments. Then he caressed her bottom in warning, and administered one good smack to one cheek while continuing to finger fuck her with the other hand.

Kelly gasped. He knew how to spank! Her mind couldn't focus on both pleasure and pain, so her brain chose pleasure. Alternating cheeks, he spanked her until she was within inches of an orgasm, and her butt was surely pink. She hung limply and trembled, ready to beg to be fucked again. "Master," she began, hearing the plea in her voice.

"Hush. I've one more little punishment in mind. You teased me last night, and I've a little revenge planned." His voice held a hearty chuckle. "But this time, I'm going to let you see what is going to happen."

Calder put Kelly on the floor on her knees and stripped away the tee shirt. She blinked in the light and squirmed in her need. But Calder had ordered her to silence.

Now he stood and stripped off his own shirt, standing naked and hard before her. Where did he get the strength? She eyed his hard-on hungrily.

Calder grabbed her and picked her up, this time using the classic in-the-arms carry Scarlett and Rhett had made famous.

Kelly followed his gaze to the schoolroom door. She sucked in her breath as Calder kicked open the door then put her face first on the huge teacher's desk, bent over and ready, her sweet pussy exposed and ready for plundering. She thought she'd die if he didn't fuck her.

"Never tease a man with your virginal white panties and pretty round ass. He might take you up on the invitation," Calder murmured before plunging home.

"No man has dared, before you!" she cried for the sheer joy of it.

It was a long time before he carried her to the Victorian bedroom and fell in bed next to her. Kelly sighed and snuggled close, fairly certain she'd found her perfect partner.

Chapter Eleven

"You—you—what?" Brad sputtered and sat down heavily. He rubbed a hand across his sweating forehead and reached for a cigarette. His fears redoubled like some logarithmic formula with each passing moment.

Calder choked on a laugh, leaned forward to take the lighter from Brad's trembling hands and lit the smoke for his old pal. "You know, you say that a lot to me," he commented, his tone soothing.

Brad took a long, sucking drag on his cigarette and swore to himself for the umpteenth time he would quit someday. Even he, "Mr. Numbers" as his clients called him, had lost track. He regarded his latest irritation with narrowed eyes. "Then stop doing the unexpected, Shrink," he muttered. "Geezus Christ, Calder! What do you think you're doing? One good fuck with BW and I figured you'd have enough for your article. Aren't you supposed to be disappearing into your hole to type by now?" He tapped his ashes into the little glass ashtray Angie kept for him on his desk.

Calder returned to lounge in the large brown leather armchair and didn't bother to smother his chuckles this time. "Never figured I'd have the stamina to keep up with Kelly?"

Calder's arms were folded across his chest, betraying to his old buddy that he was hiding more, much more.

"Quit trying to distract me. I know damn well you're capable of a week in Vegas with a dozen women if it pleased you." Brad took note of the fact that Calder used BW's name with the casual air of long use. He shouldered aside the image of Angie's face saying she hoped for orange blossoms. Brad refused to believe it.

Calder stared at the coffered ceiling of Brad's well-appointed home office. "Then what's your issue, Brad? So Kelly and I are enjoying each other's company. We share a lot of the same interests." He caught sight of Brad's worried face and winged an eyebrow up. "I'm not using her, old man. I'm really liking this BDSM stuff, even if Kelly is keeping it light."

Brad stifled a groan. So Kelly was hooking Calder and reeling him in to be a sub. It was what Calder deserved, in a way, but the results could be disastrous. He decided to play it cool until he wormed more out of Calder. This would take the patience of a full corporate audit. He took another drag. "Okay, I admit that was a concern. I should have thought better of you. Tell me how your research is going."

Calder accepted the apology with a nod, but his green eyes lit up like yacht lanterns. He planted his feet on the floor, and leaned forward. "I'm getting all I need, Brad. There's a huge amount of psychological factors, as well as physiological responses, to BDSM that bears something even bigger than one little magazine article." He gestured expansively. "Why, there's a whole book of shit I could write, and more sympathetically than some old prude's guesses based on lab results of pain studies."

"Shit is right," Brad agreed. The reasons behind what worked for players didn't matter to him, but he had to grin at Calder's enthusiasm.

Calder ignored the comment and smiled back. "Yeah, yeah, I know you don't care. But I do. Damn, Brad, do you realize the stereotype of BDSM as all pain and nothing more is so inaccurate as to boggle the mind?"

Brad let irony weigh his voice down, and his smile turned sardonic. "Yeah, I do." He flicked another ash and waited for Calder's brain to catch up.

Calder jerked back a moment, and then began to laugh heartily. "Okay, I deserved that." Calder returned to sprawling in the armchair. "Fact is, there's a book screaming to be written on this. And I'm going to write it." He returned to staring at the ceiling, and clamped his lips shut, as if he wanted to say more, but wouldn't.

Brad tried to make his mind function, and couldn't. Calder was talking long-term commitment without realizing it, and Brad would be damned if he'd point that out. "But what about your magazine article?"

Calder put his arms behind his head and favored Brad with a look full of wry good humor. "Oh, they'll get it. I sent off an outline to my agent yesterday just before Kelly came to pick me up for dinner. Ruben called my cell this morning, practically crying with joy. He can't wait to present it tomorrow morning."

Brad felt his jaw drop and couldn't have halted it if he tried. No more than he could stop the next question that fell out of his mouth, one syllable at a time. "Kelly picked you up for dinner?"

he repeated. His cigarette was ash, so he stubbed it out and grabbed another.

Rubbing his stomach, Calder smirked with satisfaction. "Oh, yeah. Pot roast, mashed potatoes oozing with butter, and a chocolate cake." The smirk turned sensual. "Great cake. I wheedled the rest of it from Sadie this morning. It's a little worse for wear, but I'll destroy the evidence."

Brad had no trouble envisioning why the cake was slightly damaged. Denny had confided to him how Kelly's cake could be used. "So, Kelly made you a cake?" he asked with a casual air. Maybe Angie had been right after all.

"Yeah," Calder confirmed. "The rest of the dinner was made by Sadie. I could get to like having subs do the work. Sadie's a treasure. So is Kelly." Calder looked at his watch. "Whup, gotta run. Kelly's got some pain sluts coming tonight, and we're having a light supper beforehand. Sorry I don't have any questions for you, Brad, but Kelly's great at explanations."

Calder stood and grabbed up his jacket. He paused at the door, and turned back to face Brad, looking thoughtful. "Y'know, Brad, I can see why you're into this now." In an instant, his gaze was piercing. "It's more than pain, more than kink and more than a simple exchange of trust. You can trust anyone, until that trust is betrayed. You give love, and get love in return. It's wonderful, really." Then he turned and whisked out the door as if running from something he knew would catch him eventually, and not sure if he wanted to be caught.

Brad tapped out the inch-long ash on his cigarette and drew on the cigarette thoughtfully. He'd just seen the emergence of a Dom. "But what are you going to do when BW finds out you've betrayed her trust?" he whispered.

* * *

There was nothing guaranteed to gladden Kelly's heart more than "Girl Day" with her pal Angie. Once a month, Kelly and Angie got together to give each other the full spa treatment. Sometimes they used submissives to provide massage, but today they had elected to be alone. Even Sadie was not in evidence, having been sent out with a long grocery list.

"I am so glad that no subbie can see us look this silly." Angie put the finishing touches of the thick clay mask on Kelly's upturned face and giggled.

Kelly pulled her foot from the hot water in the foot tub and flicked a tiny spray of water in Angie's direction. "I don't want to be a Dominatrix for the next few hours. I want to luxuriate in just being Kelly." Her voice was just a little muffled from trying not to move too many facial muscles, but the good humor came through anyway.

Angie put her own feet into her tub of hot soapy water and pushed her face forward so Kelly could slather it with the thick blue goo. "Why not? You've always enjoyed being the infamous Black Widow, with as many subs as you could get up until now. Is it because of Calder?"

"Shaddup, or I'll accidentally on purpose shove some of this mask into your mouth, Nosy." Kelly mock-threatened Angie with a ladle full of the stuff. "Of course it's Calder. He treats me like a woman, not a goddess or his mommy." Her voice held an edge of pure contempt. The memory of Michael was still too fresh.

Angie nodded in between pats as the mask was applied. "I can see that. Gosh knows you've had enough subs treat you like that to appreciate a refreshing change." Her voice turned sly and insinuating. "Is he as good in the sack as he looks?"

Casting her gaze skyward, Kelly moaned, "Oh, God, yes." She could admit to herself she was just a tiny bit "saddle sore," and not just from the spanking.

Angie smirked and part of her mask cracked. "You're walking just a tad more carefully than usual, hon," she observed. "You'd better take a hot bubble bath after I leave to ease the ache."

Kelly was suddenly very grateful that the mask hid her blush. "Guess so," she agreed in the most noncommittal tone she could manage.

They listened to the stereo, meditating to Brahms in companionable silence until the bell timer announced their masks were dry.

"Okay, I'm going to pry now," Angie began, no longer caring if she cracked her mask.

"You mean you weren't before?" Kelly laughed mockingly through tight lips as she got up to go wash the dried mask off her face.

"Get a grip." Angie stood and followed Kelly to the sink, trailing water all over Sadie's floor. "Okay, blunt then. How's the status of your heart? Calder is definitely a sex crime waiting for a spot marked X, but you look like there's more involved than your puss."

Kelly gave Angie one baleful glare and stalled, washing the mask off with perhaps more vigor than usual. Angie folded her arms and leaned casually against the granite counter. That stubborn look on her face told Kelly she wasn't going to give up prying, but the twinkle of good humor remained in her eyes.

Kelly gave up, patted her face dry with a towel, and sighed. "Okay, okay. Yeah, I think my heart has a few strings on it.

Besides the obvious bedtime skills, Calder is intelligent, and more than accepting of my profession. He likes classical music and old Bogart movies."

Angie rolled her eyes. "You and he are peas in a pod, then. I swear you were born fifty years too late."

Kelly sniffed and pointed Angie to the sink. "You know darn well that old black and whites are all that's on at three AM when I've finally finished with clients and the dungeon is clean."

"That's why I go to bed." Angie splashed water on her face. "Geez, did you have to put this shit on so thick?"

"Yeah, I did." Kelly shook her head. "Ever hear of a good book, Angie?"

"Of course. But I like slasher movies and potboiler thriller books." Angie snatched up the towel Sadie had left for her and rubbed. Her strawberry pink tee shirt was soaked in front, so she yanked it off and sat down at the bistro set in her bra. "You know me, the ex-nurse. I like flying body parts and forensics."

"That is so sick!" Kelly teased. She opened the doors to the laundry pair in the kitchen and tossed the shirt in the dryer. "Aren't you supposed to be a staid and stuffy accountant now?"

"Why do you think I need a little excitement in my life?" Angie's tone was again wry. "And you're a fine one to talk, since you get excitement from beating on people."

Kelly threw up her hands, laughing. *"Mea culpa!* Okay, you win. But Calder has introduced me to science fiction. This is cool stuff! Hang on a sec!" She ran to the living room and pulled a well-thumbed book from off the sofa where she'd been reading when Angie arrived.

When she came back, Angie was already painting her toenails some incredible shade of pink that did not appear in nature.

Kelly brandished the fat paperback. "This is funny stuff! It's Heinlein, about some guy who's over a thousand years old named Lazarus." She read a passage that had them both roaring with laughter, quoting the cynical immortal character. They took turns reading in between coats of toenail polish.

When both had wiped their eyes and both sets of feet now sparkled with eye-blinding pink, Kelly clutched the book to her chest. "He gave me this book and promised to find me more."

It wasn't until she saw Angie's face that she realized how idiotic she must look. Kelly cleared her throat and carefully put the book aside. It hit her harder than any paddle from the dungeon below. "I've got it bad, don't I?" she muttered, averting her eyes from the amusement on Angie's face.

"Let's see. One, you have a sore butt and don't care. Two, you're opening up to new things. Three, you haven't collared Calder…"

"All right! Your point is made. I'm sunk. Now what?" Kelly couldn't keep the dread from her voice. "What if he doesn't feel the same?" She closed her eyes.

"Girlfriend, are you or are you not the Black Widow?" Angie barked.

Kelly nodded.

"Are you going to change who you are to please any man?"

Shock had Kelly's eyes flying open. "Fuck no!"

"Then he'll either like what you are, or he'll go away and you'll know he wasn't Prince Charming after all, now won't you?" Angie put her hands on her hips. "Now you just listen to

Mama. Think like Black Widow. He should see all sides of you, shouldn't he?"

Calder had only seen Kelly's softer side. The kind that baked cakes and loved to fuck until both collapsed in a heap. Angie was right. Calder needed to see the bitch that Black Widow was.

"Uh, yes. Yes, he should!" Kelly got up to pace, trailing cotton balls from between her toes. "He's going to see the hard side of BDSM tonight. And I must be all Black Widow for the client's sake. Calder's only had a glimpse of that."

"If he doesn't run screaming out the door, then maybe there's a chance for him, right?" Angie steepled her fingers together in front of her lips in a gesture of supreme confidence.

"Right! This evening, he sees the bad girl." Kelly got a dreamy look of anticipation on her face. "I wonder how he's going to react to that?"

Chapter Twelve

Kelly looked up at the clock on the microwave, gasped, and snatched up the remains of their dinner. "Shit! We only have an hour until they arrive. I lost track!"

Startled, Calder grabbed the last piece of garlic bread, well-softened with spaghetti sauce, from his plate. He watched, amazed, as Kelly efficiently loaded the dishwasher and turned off the burners on the stove. "Where's Sadie?" he asked.

Kelly glanced up with an amused grin as she wiped the countertop. "Downstairs. She and Devon will be the demo models tonight."

Gulping, Calder assimilated the implications in a nanosecond. "Sadie's into pain?" He tried very hard to keep his tone casual. He wasn't sure if he could help cause pain to a friend, and he did count Sadie in that category.

Kelly came around the island and poured Calder more sweet tea from the pitcher before starting to strip off her jeans. "Yup! It's part of her pay. She's not into hardcore S&M, but she likes the release of a beating now and then." She grunted, and stepped out of the jeans before yanking off her tee shirt. She now stood in a patent leather singlet held up by a jeweled chain that left little to the imagination.

Calder didn't need his imagination. He barely kept his tongue from lolling out and howling like a werewolf at the full moon.

She took one look at his face and shook a finger at Calder. "Nuh-uh, gorgeous." Folding her clothes, she laid them carefully next to her chair. "I'm Black Widow tonight, and therefore untouchable. You keep your hands to yourself until after the party. If you still want to rumba then, we'll see if I'm not too tired."

Calder noted an aura of reserve, dignity, and...his mind searched for the appropriate word—well, authority was as close as he came...fall over Kelly.

"Is it okay if I ask why you wear that little number," he gestured to the outfit, "if you're untouchable?"

"Simple. Heat. I'm going to work up a sweat very soon. You'll see." She sauntered out of the room barefoot and padded to the front door. While she checked to make sure the door was unlocked, by simply opening and shutting the door, she continued. "But first, I need to teach you about wax play and send Devon up to act as doorman. Come on. We don't have much time."

Calder followed BW down the stairs, musing to himself. He noticed even his appellation for Kelly had shifted in his own mind to BW. That alone was an art form.

"I can appreciate the psychological value of that outfit, as well," he commented as they made their way down the stairs. "It screams sex, wealth, and power."

BW's hands were busy, pulling her shoulder-length hair into a ponytail and then twisting it into a bun, but she nodded. She barely acknowledged Sadie and the handsome male sub Calder assumed was Devon when they fell to their knees in the main "parlor." But Sadie was cheeky enough to give Calder a wink.

Calder followed BW to a room he'd never seen opened before. When she sailed into the brightly lit room, Calder caught the strong scent of candles, that warm, waxy smell with an undertone of herbs. The generously sized room contained a large, long, padded table reminiscent of a doctor's examination room, a rolling cart, and a table with a candle arrangement.

"Come here, Calder." BW's tone was brisk, just a hair's breadth below a command.

"Am I to be your subordinate tonight, BW?" he asked quietly.

"Actually, your official title will be bodyguard, and that will be your primary duty. The client coming later tonight is a stranger. He has already signed the release papers and they are filed, but a smart Domme never works alone with an unknown male sub. It's for his protection as much as mine." BW's tone was as coldly businesslike as he'd ever heard, and her eyes were imperious.

"I get it. No chance of any accusations of assault, sexual or otherwise, as long as there's a witness." Calder decided to stand a respectful distance away, and assumed a position similar to "parade rest."

BW gave him a tight smile and a nod. "Nice, but I need you to experience this." She waved a hand to a small display of three pillar candles, and then lit them as Calder approached.

"Calder, which of these candle waxes is safe to use on human skin?"

Calder examined each pillar minutely. One smelled of beeswax and looked expensive. One was pink and gave off a floral bouquet. The final candle was a cheap white pillar you could buy anywhere.

"I'm going to eliminate the pink, scented one immediately. It could contain volatile oils that could cause allergic reaction and might make it hotter," he mused aloud.

"Correct." BW picked up the pink pillar and blew the candle out.

Then a thought struck Calder, just as he was about to choose the expensive beeswax candle. His physical therapist had used paraffin on his right hand after he'd broken his wrist a few years before. Paraffin was cheap. On impulse, Calder pointed to the cheap white candle. "That one, if it's made of paraffin."

If he'd thought BW was icy, then he was wrong. Her whole face lit up and her eyes warmed. "Very good, Calder. You're right. Stick out a hand." She picked up the beeswax candle and blew it out.

Calder trusted her enough now to present his hand, palm down, without a second thought. Kelly dribbled a tiny amount of wax from the white candle on the back of his hand.

Calder gave his lover a smile as full of promise as he could manage. "It's warm, and doesn't hurt at all. And I can well imagine how this would feel on more sensitive areas of someone's anatomy." He leered suggestively at the creamy white mounds barely restrained by her bra-like cups.

Kelly giggled and colored like a schoolgirl. Then her eyes lit with mischief. She reached under the table where the candles had been and pulled out a hollow wax form in the shape of a long mound, with a used wick sticking out the top. Calder stared for a moment, then looked inside and choked back a laugh. There was a clear definition of a penis inside. "Michael?" he asked. He could clearly imagine his own hardened cock getting dribbled with wax until the "candle" was formed. Michael would have had his lit, for the adrenaline rush.

At BW's nod, Calder couldn't contain his laughter any longer. He roared with it until a small "Ahem!" from the door interrupted.

Sadie held out a bundle of black leather and chains, with a pair of black high heels on top, to BW. Calder nearly slapped himself to keep his jaw from dropping. Sadie, who had always dressed in a simple pair of khakis and polo shirt, now wore a plain red thong and nothing else. Her smooth café-au-lait complexion was now rosy, and her nipples crinkled in what Calder assumed was high sexual excitement.

Before Calder could say a word, BW dismissed Sadie with a "Go." He put the odd "candle" back under the table as Sadie fled the room. Out of the corner of his eye, he saw BW return to that cool icicle that was her public persona by stepping into the shoes Sadie had brought. The shoes added so much height; they would have been nose to nose if they stood facing each other.

"Calder, I know this is asking a lot, but I'd like you to wear this while you're my bodyguard. If you like it, consider it a gift." BW thrust the leather bundle at him, looking serious, even slightly worried.

Calder took the bundle and unfolded a pair of leather pants with a matching belt. A chain contraption fell to the floor, but Calder was too stunned to care. "BW, this is a very expensive gift." He held them up to himself, and was surprised to see even the inseam length might actually be long enough. He'd never thought he'd be able to own leather, though he'd looked at the displays in stores plenty of times.

"I need you to look the part." BW shrugged, but he could read she was pleased.

Calder immediately stripped out of his jeans and pulled the pants on. They fit like a second skin, and required some undignified wiggling, but Calder was impressed with the buttery feel. "How did you know my size?"

Impishly, BW grinned. "You left your jeans on the floor when you showered this morning. The size tag was legible enough. Sadie and I took some educated guesses on the rest of the measurements. The ones used to create this." She picked up the chain contraption on the floor. "It's a chain bandolier. Would you mind?"

He eyed the bandolier dubiously. "Doesn't wearing chains make me a sub?" He couldn't even figure out how to put the thing on.

"Suspicious, suspicious!" BW snickered. "No, Calder. Not necessarily. It is just part of the costume. It will make you look mean." She made a vicious face. "If I were going to make you look like a sub, I'd put a collar on you. But that would be stupid. You couldn't act submissive if you tried, right now." She held the contraption up where two large holes in the chains were revealed. "Here, try it on, at least. I'll clip the back. If you don't like it, I won't make you wear it."

Relieved, Calder put his arms through the holes and BW moved behind him. He felt the chains tighten, and then heard a click. He shivered as the weight of the cold chains settled on his skin. "Shit! That's cold!" he complained.

"It will warm up in a minute, I promise." BW moved in front and gave him an assessing look from head to toe. "Yum, yum, Calder. You look good, especially with your nipples all crinkled." She flicked a nail over one brown nipple.

"Tease! I'll get you later for this," he growled, feeling his crotch tighten.

"Later," she promised, and stepped closer, her eyes hot.

"Mistress," came a voice from the door. "Whoa!"

Sadie stood in the open doorway with her mouth hanging open, staring at Calder. She choked for a moment before continuing, "Master Calder, don't you look fine!"

She blew out a breath and visibly got hold of herself, much to Calder's amusement. Maybe this costume wasn't so bad, especially now that the chains weren't feeling like they'd just come from the inside of the refrigerator.

Sadie turned to BW and was immediately deferential. "Mistress, your guests are arriving. Oh, and the gentleman client called. The flight was delayed, so he'll be a bit late, about an hour."

BW looked relieved. "Oh, good. That frees up a little more time for the demo." She smiled indulgently. "I assume Devon is getting petted as usual upstairs?" At Sadie's nod, Kelly tapped her chin with one finger. "Okay. Have Calder tie you to the table, then. I'll greet the ladies and do the hostess thing. Calder can come get me when you're prepared. Make sure he powders you well." She swept out the door without another word.

Calder stared at the empty doorway. What the hell was he supposed to do now?

Sadie eyed Calder, and then smiled. "Don't be scared, sugar. This is easy stuff." She walked over to the table and boosted herself up. Pointing to some ropes dangling from the legs near the head of the table, she urged, "Grab those and put them on my wrists once I'm laying down." She suited words to action and rested her head on the little pillow.

Shrugging, Calder picked up the rope nearest him and slipped the loop around Sadie's outstretched wrist, securing one arm above her head. Cinching the loop tighter around her wrist, he asked, "How's that?"

"A little looser. Don't want to cut off my circulation. Good. Right there."

Calder moved around the table and performed the same service to her other wrist and checked the fit. "Now what?"

Sadie nodded toward the table where the candle set BW had lit earlier resided. The white candle was still lit. "See the baby powder? Sprinkle it generously all over me, from neck to knees, please."

Calder spotted the distinctive white plastic bottle and did as he was directed. The room filled with the sweet scent, mixing with the smells of the candles. When Sadie's dark skin was liberally covered, he put the bottle back. "Now what?"

"Spread it all out. Make sure I'm covered as evenly as possible, especially my tits, and dump the extra into my bellybutton. Don't want wax collecting there."

Feeling distinctly uncomfortable, Calder began rubbing the baby powder all over Sadie's body, saving her breasts for last. He was having a hard time with this concept, even while his new pants tightened once more. "What's the powder for?" he asked, trying to sound like he rubbed baby powder all over a woman's body every day of his life. He told his hardening cock to shut up. It didn't have a clue what it wanted.

Sadie looked at Calder full in the face for the first time since she'd lain on the table. "The powder makes it so the wax doesn't stick too much. When BW scrapes it off me with those knives over there, it will come off cleanly."

"Oh," was all Calder could think to say. He glanced at the set of knives lying on a tray where a right-handed person could easily reach. Some were standard kitchen knives, and some were incredibly detailed knives with decorated handles. One looked particularly sharp and vicious.

He scraped the small pile of excess powder toward Sadie's navel and packed it in. "And the powder here prevents it from collecting in your navel where it can't be scraped out easily?"

"Right. I hate picking wax out of my 'innie' for days." She lifted her head and checked his work. "Decent job. A little more on the right nipple, and then you can go call the Mistresses down to play with me."

Calder tweaked the right nipple with his powdered hands and watched Sadie's eyes burn. How odd to touch a woman like this and know she'd get her jollies from something other than him. It was humbling, in a way. "What should I say?"

"You're a Dom, sugar." Her voice was throaty. "Just say, 'Black Widow, your sub is prepared' or something. They won't care. They are all going to be drooling over you and not hearing a word you say anyway." She lay back on the table and shut her eyes.

"Well, that's flattering. I think." Calder didn't know what to say about being told so blatantly he was a mere sex object.

"That's what you get for being so damn gorgeous. Now go enhance the Mistress's reputation. I promise they won't bite." She paused and her gaze roamed admiringly up and down his leather-clad form. "Well, maybe they will, the way you look."

Chapter Thirteen

Calder was definitely not used to being eye candy. He'd wedged himself into the waxing room, as he'd termed it, choosing a spot near the door. It didn't have the best view of BW's lesson, but he was invisible to most of the women. One of them had had the nerve to pat his butt when they'd all crowded down the stairs! He swore he'd never pat a barmaid's ass ever again.

The sub Devon wove his way in deftly and positioned himself next to Calder. The generous room was now somewhat more crowded than Calder was comfortable with, but he and Devon were several feet away from the students.

Kelly started off her lecture in the same vein as what she'd done with him. It amused him that most of the students picked the beeswax candle and paid for it with a minor first-degree burn spot on their skin.

Devon sniggered quietly, and leaned toward Calder. "Best they learn that now, before they are allowed subs of their own."

Calder glanced down at the slightly shorter man. "You mean they are all so new they don't have subs yet?" He kept his voice low.

Rolling his eyes, Devon whispered, "Hell, no! They'd hurt someone in their ignorance. Most of them are just practicing on their significant others right now."

Sadie seemed to have almost gone to sleep, she was so still. Kelly explained. "As you can see, Sadie has gone into subspace just in anticipation." BW's gaze flickered to Calder for a moment before returning to pin her students. "Your subs may not be as experienced. It may be wise to perform the preliminary techniques we discussed in our last lesson to ensure the correct trance state."

Calder nodded his head a fraction of an inch. He got it. Kelly, er, BW had defined the term "subspace" to him.

BW now picked up the white candle and began to dribble wax on Sadie's sternum, then her belly. BW never paused in her lecture. "As you can see, I started with the less sensitive areas before moving inexorably to more and more sensitive areas. This builds tolerance in the skin up until the wax hits the nipples," she looked up to grin impartially, "or other temperature-sensitive portions of the anatomy."

Calder felt his penis do its best to crawl into his belly with the visual. It was one thing to laugh at Michael's "candle," but BW was making it clear it could be done on any male. He wished with all his heart his leather pants were camouflaged to match the walls.

By the sly glances some of the students shot him over their shoulders, they got the visual, too. Calder stood up straight and returned their eager stares impassively. He was doing his best to say with his body, "Don't even think about it." By the sighs and disappointed looks, they got the message loud and clear.

Behind their backs, BW's lips twitched and she winked. The witch. She knew they'd react like that. She'd pay later. She cleared her throat, and got their attention back.

Devon was shaking with laughter. "That's telling them, Master Calder. You let me handle their little evils," he whispered. His bright brown eyes twinkled.

When Sadie was wearing a wax breastplate that nearly covered her from neck to the top of her thong, BW put the candle away.

Now BW pulled the rolling cart forward with the tray on top that held the knives. Sadie's eyes opened at the first rattle. Even slightly unfocused, her eyes held the sharp spurt of fear, and her breath rate increased.

Calder couldn't help the protective instinct that rose in him. Only BW's sharp flicker of a glance reined him in.

"Now, ladies, please note that this knife is a standard kitchen knife." She held up a normal chef's knife so everyone could see. "Sadie is familiar with this knife, and it is the twin to the one she uses every day. But her fear of knives is known."

Calder, forewarned by Sadie, knew BW would merely scrape away the layer of wax from Sadie's prepared skin. But there was a moment when he did wonder if Sadie would be cut before logic took over. If BW weren't an expert, she wouldn't be teaching. He forced himself to stillness.

"How long has Sadie been taking these wax scenes?" he muttered to Devon.

BW's lecture had given him a vital clue. Sadie was afraid of knives. Therefore, this was a form of aversion therapy. His psych training took over.

Devon leaned close again. "Only a couple of months. She's learning to love it. It's sort of like a roller coaster ride. You're scared silly, but you get addicted." His smiled turned sensual. "And she loves the reward at the end." He paused. "So do I."

Fascinated, he watched BW scrape away the wax, using evermore sharp and dangerous looking blades. The scrapings were frugally put into a bowl, presumably for reuse.

Sadie's "fight or flight" reflexes took over. Her swarthy skin turned white as her body sent blood to vital organs, and the pupils in her whiskey-brown eyes dilated. The rush of adrenaline must have been incredible, Calder thought clinically.

When every last bit of wax was gone, Calder could barely keep himself from at least going to hold Sadie's hand, which was clenched so tightly in its restraints, it was a wonder her nails weren't cutting into her palms.

Devon laid a restraining hand on Calder's arm, imploring him to be still. "Stop fidgeting. Everything is fine. You'll see." Devon cocked his head, listening to BW wrapping up the lecture as she cleaned up the remains of the powder and wax from Sadie's trembling body. "When they leave, go with the Mistress. Try to remain unobtrusive."

Calder would have asked more questions, but BW ushered her students out the door and jerked her head at Calder. Then she looked at Devon and nodded. Calder followed the students out, and BW shut the door, leaving Devon and Sadie inside.

The ladies trooped back upstairs, chattering like magpies. BW, ever the gracious hostess, offered everyone refreshments and followed. Calder put his foot on the bottom stair just as happy shrieks began to ring out from behind the closed door. When Calder hesitated, BW turned and winked. Crooking her finger, she whispered, "Let them enjoy themselves in peace. They'll be up soon."

Calder glanced back once before nodding. No wonder Devon said he enjoyed this.

* * *

Calder was beginning to wonder if he'd fly into a million pieces in his desire to ask Kelly all the questions beating on the inside of his skull. The students had finally been ushered out the front door. Calder was so grateful he could have cried. The questions and heated looks from the students had reached ridiculous levels.

One horny little blonde had made her fantasies perfectly clear. She'd rubbed his bicep and whispered, "I'd love to borrow you from BW for the weekend." Calder had simply pointed to his unencumbered neck and she'd walked away pouting. Maybe it would be funny, someday.

Devon and Sadie had reappeared, and served drinks and canapés. Now they took the depleted trays back to the kitchen, leaving Calder and BW alone.

BW dropped the persona of the Dominatrix and flopped down into an overstuffed armchair with a "whew!" She wrinkled her nose at Calder. "You looked great!"

Calder relaxed slightly. "I'm not used to being eye candy."

Kelly chuckled. "You'd look good in a potato sack and no help for it. I noticed Linda trying to get her mitts on you. Good thing you handled it." Her eyes narrowed. "I'd hate to have to kill her."

Calder laughed at that small sign of jealousy. He walked over and leaned down to kiss Kelly. "She never had a chance, beautiful."

Devon walked quickly into the room. "Limo just pulled up." He pulled at his abbreviated briefs and adjusted his collar.

Kelly nodded her approval, and he ran for the front door. She stood and whispered urgently to Calder. "Be silent, and be still. This is the hardcore tonight."

Calder reached out and grabbed her hand. He kissed her knuckles in the courtliest gesture he knew. "I'll be waiting for the return of Kelly." He wanted to say more, but he heard Devon greeting the client, so he returned to the wall and stood at parade rest.

Kelly stayed right where he left her, and he would have sworn he saw the sparkle of tears before Black Widow was back. Her chin went up. Devon brought the client for introductions, and then they all silently went downstairs.

Devon took the client into the room where the big wooden X, a St. Andrew's cross, was. Calder remembered the room. He now understood more of what that room was for: Pain. It was the largest room, save for the "throne room," with high ceilings and open floor space. Calder steeled himself. He'd seen this before, in Brad's dungeon. This was nothing new, he told himself.

Kelly waited a few minutes until Devon reopened the door, then walked languidly into the pain room. The man, who'd introduced himself as Earnest, was already naked and cuffed to the cross.

Calder stationed himself beside the door, and so did Devon.

BW's voice was cruel when she asked, "Have you been bad, Earnest?" Out of Earnest's line of sight, she was picking up the horsehair flogger.

Over Earnest's whimper of, "Yes, Mistress! Please punish me!" Calder leaned toward Devon.

"Isn't she going to spray his back?" Calder whispered, and then winced as the horsehair lashed out on the middle-aged man's back.

"Already done," Devon whispered back. "By me. Right after I cuffed him in. His preferences were sent by email from his usual Mistress a week ago. Standard beating. Nothing special." Devon shrugged with an indifference Calder couldn't hope to match. "Oh, and by the way, Earnest is not his real name. He specified the use of a pseudonym. Can't blame him. He doesn't know us well enough for that."

Calder watched, and kept his face as impassive as possible while Earnest's back bloomed a rosy pink from the attention of the horsehair. Having felt the flogger, he knew what BW was doing didn't hurt, and was just a warm-up.

That is, until the last lash. Calder jerked and winced as the flogger sang out with one of the stinging blows.

Earnest just gasped. "Thank you, Mistress!"

BW, not yet sweating or breathing hard, picked up a leather flogger. Calder gave himself a pat on the back for knowing the terms now. She marched up and checked Earnest's back. Apparently satisfied with what she saw, she showed Earnest her flogger. "Your mistress tells me how naughty you've been, Earnest."

Earnest nodded eagerly. "Yes, Mistress! I have been! Punish me as you see fit." He was looking at the flogger with what Calder could only describe as lust.

"Very well," she replied coldly. BW stepped back a few paces out of reach of the man's back, and began to swing the flogger in the figure eight pattern he'd seen her use the first night. Then she walked forward until the flogger's strips fell on the man's back flatly.

Earnest was soon writhing, but in a pattern, like a slow dance to music only he could hear. Still, there was no blood, no strips of flesh hanging.

Without warning, BW stopped and barked, "Give me a color, Earnest!"

"Green, Mistress! Green!" the man whimpered.

"Color?" Calder murmured to Devon. The beating recommenced with what looked like a dowel from the hardware store.

"Standard stoplight system," Devon whispered back. "Green means continue, yellow means I'm done, red means stop and end all playing now."

Calder berated himself for not remembering what he'd read in his research. "And the dowel?" He didn't remember a dowel.

"Deep bruising effect. Earnest will leave her with barely a mark on him, but by the time he flies home to his regular Mistress, he'll have a lovely set of bruises to show her that he was properly beaten." Devon sighed, longingly. "He'll have bragging rights among other subs for a good week or two with the pattern the Mistress is using."

BW again demanded a color. She was now sweating, but not breathing heavily. In fact, she looked no more mussed than if she had taken a brisk walk.

Earnest writhed a moment longer, then, his voice slurred, he answered, "Green." Another moment of mindless movement. "Finish me, please. I beg it."

"Very well!" She picked up a short bullwhip.

Calder shut his eyes, but heard the crack.

A grunt.

Another stroke of the whip hissed.

A gasping moan.

Calder felt a comforting pat on his arm, and knew it was Devon. He ventured to open one eye. As another strike caused Earnest to moan louder, Calder shuddered. Then the thought hit Calder with the same force as the whip hit Earnest. Kelly's voice saying, "All Dommes must learn to feel what their subs do."

He jerked upright. Some whip had touched Kelly's skin. Someone had done this to her. His eyes flew open wide with irrational urge to go kill that long ago Dominant.

The whip sang once more while Calder's imagination went wild, imagining it chewing into her soft, smooth skin.

The skin wrapped around the woman he loved.

Nothing in BW's arsenal could have hit him harder. He was in love with the woman wielding that whip.

The shrill scream of "Yellow!" rang out, yanking Calder back to reality. Earnest was done.

Chapter Fourteen

Calder leaned back in his chair and winced. "Ruben, will you please calm down and stop making my ears ring? I can't understand a word you're saying, for Chrissake."

He slugged another mouthful of the blackest coffee he could make and tried not to choke on the bitterness. The gourmet brew Kelly chugged had spoiled him.

"Okay, okay! I'll go slow. Sorry. I liked your proposal and the sample chapter you sent in, and got the usual power lunch with Eddie and Theresa," Ruben repeated.

The names meant nothing to Calder, but that wasn't unusual. Ruben was constantly forgetting that Calder never could keep straight what editor worked for what publishing house. "And?" He sipped again.

"You're on the auction block, buddy boy, that's what! Alpha Books and Pantheon Publishing are now in a bidding war for your book on BDSM!"

The coffee made an impressive spatter on his monitor. Calder ran for paper towels to clean up and blessed technology for a cordless phone. "How much?"

Ruben named a figure that had Calder tripping over his own feet. "Now, don't get excited, Calder. The bidding has just started, and you're an unknown," Ruben cautioned.

Calder's hands shook as he used window cleaner and paper towels to clean his monitor. "Hey, I'm happy right now."

"Yeah, well, keep your shirt on. This may take a week or more. I gotta ask you about terms. What are you willing to give up to get the higher numbers, how fast can you churn this puppy out, you know."

"No, I don't know. Explain it to me slowly in small words a cop can understand." Calder wiped his forehead with the same towels he'd just cleaned the monitor with.

By the time Ruben hung up, Calder had a headache and a grin that threatened to split his face in two. He started to dial the phone to tell Kelly when it dawned on him he couldn't. He hung up and stared at the phone. There was no one he could call. Brad was already eating antacids like candy, now that Calder and Kelly had been together over two weeks.

Calder walked over to his desk. In prominent view was a small, careworn burgundy velvet box. He opened it and looked at the tiny solitaire diamond his mother had worn right up until the day of her death. The two matching wedding bands lay in his jewelry box.

He closed the box with a snap and put it by his keys. It was time to come clean with Kelly and ask her if she'd accept the ring. He turned and marched to the shower.

* * *

"Mistress, your tail is on fire!" Sadie exclaimed.

Kelly peeked from behind the living room curtains to see Sadie, dust rag in hand, shaking her finger.

Pouting, Kelly emerged from the curtains. "Aw, c'mon Sadie! I was just peeking to see if Calder was here yet."

"Worse than a ten-year-old on her birthday! Girlfriend, that man's dick ain't that much better than any other's." Sadie shook her head, grinning.

Rolling her eyes, Kelly gave a roguish smile. "It's not the size of the boat…"

"It's the motion in the ocean. Yeah, I know. It's only been a week since Master Calder was last here. You're acting like you're starved." Sadie sucked in her cheeks to imitate hunger, and made her brown eyes huge and pitiful.

"Oh, but I *am* starved. That's the point. It's been a whole week since Calder kissed me at the door and said he had to go to work." Kelly sighed and peeped out the curtains again. "In the meantime, I've had to deal with being Black Widow all week, or going to the hospice. I want to be touched, made love to, and treated like just another woman."

"Least he comes around on weekends. And how many hours are you spending on the phone with one another?" Sadie asked indulgently.

Kelly colored as if she were the schoolgirl Sadie accused her of acting like. "Okay, you got me. At least an hour every night."

Sadie snickered. "And that doesn't include the fistful of posies he left on the doorstep Wednesday morning."

Kelly's blush heated up until she felt like she'd acquired a fever. The note had said he'd been out walking and couldn't resist a street vendor. The cheap bundle of daisies and carnations meant more to her than a dozen of the finest roses.

Sadie laughed and gave her Mistress a hug. "I'll stop teasing you now." Her eyes lifted and looked out the window. "Especially since Master Calder just pulled up. Go put a cold cloth on your cheeks."

Kelly fled to the powder room in the foyer and listened while Sadie greeted Calder at the door. As she pressed a cool, wet washcloth to her face, she muttered to the woman in the mirror, "Okay, so you've been lonely. And you're hornier than a three-peckered billy goat. And Calder is everything you like." The blushing woman in the mirror looked back at her mockingly. "Okay, okay, I'm in love. I'll deal. I always have."

The image in the mirror quirked a half-smile.

Kelly put down the cloth. "But first, I'm going to go get laid. And I'm opening the final door. If he walks through on his own, he's mine."

She heard Calder ask, "Where's Kelly?"

That was her cue. She came barreling out the door and jumped into his arms. "Hiya, gorgeous!"

Calder kissed her as thoroughly as she desired, their tongues battling for supremacy, before he released her mouth. "I keep telling you, that's my line."

"And I'll keep ignoring it. You're a hunk, and it's time you admitted it." Kelly wriggled seductively and laid a hand on his crotch. "Don't make me lead you upstairs on the only leash I can get my hands on right now." For emphasis she gave a gentle squeeze.

"Since the phrase that ends with 'and their hearts and minds will follow' applies here, lead the way." Calder put her down and patted her denim-clad butt. "But I do want to talk later," he added.

"Oh, you look so serious. We'll talk later. I've missed you." She gave one last caress before turning to go up the stairs first.

Calder chuckled. "Since I'm a firm believer in the old 'life's short, eat dessert first' adage, I'm willing." He wiggled his eyebrows when she turned to grin at him, giving Kelly the clear impression she was "dessert."

Feeling suddenly playful, she stuck her tongue out at him and raced up the stairs. "Then you have to catch your dessert!"

God, this was fun. Denny had never chased her around the house, but Calder pounded up the stairs as fast as his bum knee would allow, laughing. "Not fair, wench!" he yelled as she disappeared around a corner. "I've never been up here!"

Kelly peeped out from her bedroom door just as he rounded the corner, stuck her tongue out again, and ducked back. This was it. Her secret self was about to be revealed.

Calder ran into the room and skidded to a halt. "Whoa!" he exclaimed.

Kelly knew what he'd expected. Those few who saw her private sanctum often were expecting elegant, but slightly macabre, decorating. Instead, they saw a tribute to innocent fun.

Unlike the others, who always made a beeline for the poster of Mighty Mouse above her bed, Calder went straight for a movie poster of the Keystone Kops. He stared for a few moments, grinning, then looked down at the small table just below. Her memorial to her father contained a picture of him in his police uniform, sitting astride his motorcycle, and his posthumous medal for bravery. He touched the frame of the medal reverently, then turned to Kelly. "Your dad was a cop?" He had a funny look on his face.

"Yes, in Columbus, Georgia. It's where I grew up."

"I see." Calder paced up and stroked her cheek. "We do have a lot to talk about."

Kelly was more puzzled than she'd ever been before about a man. "You have more twists in your brain than a pretzel factory, Calder. Everyone else comments on Mighty Mouse, or my alarm clock." She pointed to her Scooby Doo alarm clock.

"Baby, if there's one thing I've learned about you, it's to expect the unexpected. It doesn't surprise me in the least that your private sanctum would be cartoons and laughter." He looked around the room. "I see heroes. The quirky ones. Your room says, to me, 'I need a fun hero.'" He pointed to a stuffed Hong Kong Phooey sitting in state in her chair. "You don't get any more fun than him."

"You don't mind?" she asked, flabbergasted that he'd read her so well.

"Mind? Why should I mind?" He snatched her up in his arms and tossed her on the blue and gold stars of her bedspread.

She managed one good bounce before he was on top and pressing her down into the mattress. "Oh! Well, then!" Kelly wrapped her arms around his neck and let him unbutton her blouse. "Want to prove how heroic you are?"

Calder laughed and buried his face in her chest. "Yep! Let's see if I can match Hong Kong Phooey's energy before Sadie calls us for dinner."

There was a laughing tangle as clothes were mutually ripped off bodies and tossed haphazardly on the floor. Kelly noted that one of her pink socks covered her father's picture before she managed to get Calder's briefs off him.

At the end of it all, she wound up on top and took advantage to tickle Calder's exposed ribs. And there, she found a weakness. He was ticklish and dissolved into helpless laughter, crying "Mercy! I give! Help!"

"No quarter!" she yelled, and dragged her nails over his ribs.

"Wicked! Evil!" He laughed, and threw her down among her pillows. "I'm the hero! I must vanquish the evil villainess!" Grabbing her hands, his knee went between her legs. "And since you've discovered my secret weakness, I must protect myself by holding your hands." His other knee pressed her legs further apart.

Kelly, loving the game, pretended to fight and kick while helpfully spreading her legs and raising her hips for impalement. "Oh! Oh! I must find a way to get to my secret weapon!"

Calder buried himself in her and murmured in her ear, "You're a secret weapon. And I just found your trigger."

Kelly couldn't think of a suitable rejoinder while being so thoroughly fucked. "I guess you did," was all she could gasp out.

It was wonderful to have a secret fantasy fulfilled. Calder's playful style had her undone completely. The mattress bounced them both like it was a trampoline, adding to the sense of fun while ensuring Calder buried himself deeply inside her with every impact.

She was building up to a screaming, tear-up-the-sheets orgasm when Calder suddenly withdrew. Kelly looked up and growled, "I'm gonna kill you!"

"No you're not." He snatched her off the bed and into a fireman's carry.

"This is not dignified or romantic, Calder!" she muttered while her face banged into his strong, muscular back.

"Dignified? Nope, pretty dolls like you don't have dignity." She heard scraping sounds, as if something was being moved. Orienting herself upside down was difficult, and before she could figure it out, Calder dumped her on top of her highboy dresser, sitting on her naked butt like a doll on display.

"What the..." she started to exclaim, but Calder spread her knees apart and attacked her pussy, since it was right in front of his face. Her exclamation ended with a moan of pure pleasure.

Calder's agile tongue was nearly as inventive as his mind, she decided. She fisted a hand in his hair and leaned back to enjoy the interrupted orgasm building again inside her. When it was finally ripped from her, she let it fly like Mighty Mouse, who grinned across the room at her.

While she still panted and shuddered, Calder stepped away and wiped his chin with a smug smile. "I think I've vanquished you, lovely villainess. But, just to make sure..." He grabbed her hips and tossed her over his shoulder again.

This time, she hit the bed face-first, right into a star-shaped gold pillow. Calder was on top and inside her before she could do more than squeal with delight at being so...so...Mastered.

Calder lifted her hips from the mattress and began to pound furiously. All Kelly could do was continue to orgasm and squeal into her star pillow. "I give! I give! You win!"

"Good!" He thrust harder and deeper with every word. "Because...I'm...not... sure...who...vanquished whom!" He let go his own orgasm, and conquered her completely.

They both waited, breathing hard, regaining enough energy to think about moving. Kelly moaned as he softened and slipped out, giving her one last intimate caress. Calder fell off to lie beside her, still panting and grinning.

Kelly rolled away. "I'll get you a washcloth. Stay there." She wobbled in the direction of her bathroom, and tripped on his pants.

"I'll just throw these on the chair," she began, but a small white card fluttered out of one of the pockets. "Whoops." She bent down to get it. When Kelly straightened, her eyes were blazing. "Press Club?" she growled.

Chapter Fifteen

Calder sat up in bed, knowing it was too late, but hoping to forestall the inevitable. "Now, Kelly," he began.

"Don't you 'now Kelly' me!" she shouted. "I trusted you! All I wanted was a happy little roll with a handsome guy with no strings, no need to be 'The Infamous Black Widow' one more time." One fat tear rolled down her cheek, unheeded.

She still was magnificent, even when naked and pissed off. But Calder knew that wasn't what she wanted to hear. "Please, Kelly, let me explain."

"Sure, why the fuck not?" Kelly tossed her head and stalked to the armoire, getting out a thin black robe of some silky material. "It's the least I can do before I toss your ass out on the street to ruin me."

"I won't ruin you!" he shot back, stung that she'd think so little of him.

"No? Why do you think we Dommes avoid publicity? Because the press is constantly painting us as whores, that's why! I never, ever sleep with my clients. Why do you think I have special release forms I make every client, no matter who they are or how well I know them, fill out every time they visit? To avoid lawsuits, and so I have a leg to stand on in court!"

"And very fine legs they are, too," Calder muttered, getting up to put on his clothes. The screech that resulted from his compliment should have shattered glass. He pulled on his pants faster. Unless he talked his way out of this one, he might be out on his ear minus the rest, and consider himself lucky if he got them tossed out after he landed. "Do you want to hear what I've been writing before you toss me out, or not?"

The glare she gave him would have etched steel. "Not really, but I will anyway. And it's not because you're a hottie in bed."

He couldn't find his shirt. He gave up and grabbed his jacket, and slid into his loafers. "You're pretty damn hot yourself, beautiful. Let's go into your throne room." Calder gestured to the door.

A snort accompanied another toss of the head, and Kelly regally sailed out the door. "It's not a throne." She sniffed haughtily.

Calder followed her out and down the stairs to the basement. He threw his jacket on a chair, just in case he still had to leave. He could feel the little burgundy box in the pocket. "It damn sure looks like one. And I'll tell you right off that I'm doing this so you have the upper hand, Kelly. I want you sitting on your throne, knowing this is your home. Knowing you can turn on the ice princess BW in her proper setting. I want you that way."

"I know the psychological game. Don't tell me how to play it," she replied with a growl.

"I know you do, and that's one reason why I'm here." Instead of taking one of the chairs, Calder deliberately took one of the pillows on the floor. Kelly's eyes narrowed as he sat in a tailor's seat. "Yeah, so I'm graceless at this. Gimme a break, willya?" he muttered.

"Not on your life." Kelly altered her tone and spoke in an affected accent, "Lucy, you got some 'splaining to do." Her eyes were hot and full of restrained violence.

"God, I love your sense of humor." Calder waved to her position in her chair. "You look like a queen, and I am the supplicant. We've set the psychological scenario now, right?"

"So we have," she said, not at all mollified.

"But that's what my article was all about, Kelly. Psychology. Not an exposé into the sinful nature of our local population." He snorted. "I couldn't care less about what the morality of this whole business of BDSM is. Last time I looked, this was a free country. There's nothing illegal here."

"Except what some might term criminal assault," she snarled. Her fingers started drumming on the chair in a rapid tattoo.

"That's why you have the release forms, right? So you can prove they came willingly to you for a service?"

"Get to the point, Calder. You aren't making a case here. All you're doing is interviewing me again."

"Sorry, bad habit. Okay, from the beginning, then." He sighed. "Yes, I'm a writer. A free-lancer. I don't work for the newspaper, TV, or radio. Let's get that clear up front."

Kelly cautiously nodded, her fingers still drumming, but more slowly. "So, that proves what? You could be working for any gossip rag in the nation. I can see that headline now: 'Infamous Dominatrix Exposed!'"

"Psychology Today."

"What?"

"Psychology Today. That's the magazine that hired me." Calder ran his fingers through his hair. "Look, I know it sounds weird. Hear me out, okay?"

Kelly stood up, and Calder's blood ran cold. Was she going to toss him out now? "All right, Calder. I'll hear you out. But first, I want a brandy."

He sighed with relief and cautiously begged, "May I have one, too?"

"You'd better stick with coffee, Calder. I'm still not convinced I shouldn't throw you out of here with a flea in your ear."

Kelly walked to the basement's kitchen, her long legs flashing in the low lighting. Calder struggled to keep from running to her and begging for mercy. His only hope lay in logic and compromise now. He heard mutters and bangs as cabinet doors slammed.

"What? You think I'm serving you?" she called out. "Get your gravity-defying, journalistic ass in here and get your own!"

"Now who's good with words?" Calder asked. "That didn't sound like you wanted to compliment me, but I'm taking it that way anyway." But he moved to go get his coffee before she threw it at him.

Kelly gave him another one of those fulminating looks, and handed his coffee over. Calder considered himself fortunate that only a tiny portion splashed on his hand.

"Okay, back to explaining," he stated, getting serious. *"Psych Today* has been trying to get information on the BDSM thing for some time. The shrinks have all had their say, but they needed the other side. But contacting people and getting them to talk hasn't been easy."

Kelly swirled her brandy for a moment, inhaling the intoxicating scent, and walked back to her chair before drawling, "I wonder why?"

"Sarcasm is appropriate, yeah." Calder had the sense to put his coffee down on a nearby table before folding his legs up to get back on the pillow. "Someday, I hope you'll explain how this is supposed to be comfortable," he muttered.

"Your comfort is not my concern right now, Calder. So you decided to—infiltrate—the BDSM world on assignment?" The ice princess BW was back.

"Not exactly. I asked my college buddy Brad to help me. I knew he'd been into it back when we shared a dorm room. Brad said the best way to learn was to observe." Calder looked up regretfully at Kelly. "That's all I was supposed to do. Observe. I…"

"Didn't expect to get invited to my home and get the rare opportunity to see how I played?" she supplied in a dangerously low voice.

"No. I didn't expect to find myself lusting after or falling in love with the beautiful Kelly, who just happens to be The Infamous Black Widow."

"You can't be in love with me. You don't know me." Her voice rose to close to a squeak.

"Besides in the biblical sense?" Calder joked feebly. "No, I don't know you well. But I can tell you this, Black Widow. You weave one helluva web around a man's heart."

Kelly got up and began to pace, sipping her brandy. "I'll let that go for now. I still don't believe you. But what about your article?"

Calder smiled wryly. "I need to do a lot of research before I can present a fair and unbiased article to the bosses. And I can't write the article, or the book, until I understand every aspect of your art."

One winged eyebrow arched at him from over the rim of her snifter. "Oh, really?" she said to her brandy.

Calder concentrated on his coffee cup for a few moments. "Yes, there is a lot of research left to do. I'm not without some knowledge, Kelly. I majored in psychology in college. Master's program. You've only shown me the tip of the iceberg, and I've been on fire since I first met you." He put his coffee cup down on the table and got up to pace.

Kelly sat down on her chair arm to watch him walk back and forth. "Fire and ice are my specialties," she commented, putting her brandy down beside her.

Calder shot her a look that was a combination of lust and pleading. "That's obvious. But I want more than that, Kelly. Much more. I want your mind, too. I'm becoming—pardon the pun—painfully aware that I can't write the article, or the book my agent wants on BDSM without you. And I don't want to learn from anyone else. I don't want to work with anyone else." He gestured, pointing at her legs displayed from the front of her robe. "Look at you. You're so incredibly beautiful, so skilled, and dammit, so intelligent!"

He reached up and ran his fingers through his hair. "I'm fixated, that's what I am. And I'm so tangled up in my own emotions I couldn't write that book if I tried." He grabbed up his jacket from where he'd thrown it.

Kelly uncrossed her legs and stood. "Let me make this clear to you, Calder. You lied." She poked a finger into his bare chest, her nail cutting his skin. "Most was a lie of omission, but a lie nonetheless. I don't take well to deception in any form."

"Not even when you neglect to tell me you've been training me to be a Dom, even to the point of hoping I go through the submission process?" Calder asked shrewdly.

Kelly's mouth opened and closed a few times. "That's not the same thing. You have to want it. You have to ask."

"A deception is a deception, beautiful. You didn't put qualifiers on your statement of hatred of them. Did you think I wouldn't figure it out? My logic and knowledge of human nature goes beyond being able to put two and two together. I'll go, for now. But you need to decide if I have a place in your life that goes beyond Dominance and submission."

He turned to leave, then abruptly turned back around. Striding purposefully to Kelly, he grabbed her by the arms and kissed her thoroughly. "I couldn't leave without at least thanking you for the best times of my life," he murmured, rubbing his lips against hers.

Calder released Kelly, and gave her cheek one last stroke with a knuckle. "And I'll never forget you, no matter what you decide." He turned to go, and strode up the stairs.

The soft bang as the front door closed echoed even down in the basement. Kelly snatched up her brandy and gulped it down, hoping the fiery liquid would drown out the tinkle of her heart breaking.

"Mistress?" the tentative voice of Sadie called down. "Are you down there?"

"I'm coming up," Kelly called. She carried the snifter up, deciding she would be courteous when she wanted desperately to shatter it up against the fireplace like some dramatic movie queen.

Sadie stood in the foyer near the dining room doors, waiting. Her watchful gaze told Kelly Sadie knew what had taken place downstairs. Sadie shrugged. "You were kind of noisy coming down the stairs and shouting. I came out to see what the ruckus was."

Kelly gave a shuddering sigh and forced herself not to burst into tears. "It's not eavesdropping when the whole world can hear, I know."

"Come on." Sadie put out a hand. "Screw dinner. You don't need food. You need a hot cup and an ear to bend. Let's go into the kitchen."

A hot cup of coffee, liberally laced with the thick chocolate creamer she saved for special occasions, did help Kelly's hands to stop shaking.

Sadie stirred her own steaming black brew, enhanced only with a dollop of molasses in what she called Creole style. Her big brown eyes were sympathetic. "You gonna tell me what happened or am I gonna get out the thumbscrews?"

It was a feeble joke in this household, but Kelly's lips twitched. "Calder is a journalist," she blurted. It still hurt.

Sadie jumped up, her eyes wide. "No shit? A reporter?" Her stream of invective would have amused Kelly any other time.

"In all fairness, no, not a reporter; a freelance writer. Believe it or not, his assignment this time was from *Psychology Today.*" She sipped her coffee and tried not to sniffle. "Why am I defending him? He still deceived us."

Sadie slapped a handy box of tissues down in front of Kelly. "Besides the obvious reason that he would have never known who you were without the deception, I'd say he had a good reason to hide his profession once he got involved with you." She sat back down and stirred her coffee needlessly while Kelly blew her nose. "And we haven't got any room to talk, truthfully. Much as I hate to admit it, we weren't exactly honest with him either, giving him Dom training. We knew, and he didn't, how that might affect him."

Kelly looked up in surprise. "That's what he said."

"Damn! That man is way too intelligent. I suppose he figured it out from his books?" When Kelly nodded, Sadie asked, "What else did he say?"

Struggling to remember, Kelly shut her eyes. "I had a bit of a red haze on, but he said he wanted to write a book on BDSM and he couldn't do it without me." Her breath hitched. "And he told me I had a decision to make."

"Yeah? What kind?" Sadie had an odd, closed look on her face.

"He said I needed to decide if he had a place in my life outside D&s." Now that she had to repeat it, Kelly admitted to herself that Calder did indeed have a place in her life that went beyond the dungeon. But she couldn't get around the fact that he'd deceived her. "But I have my pride. He lied. And he might ruin me, still."

"You don't believe that any more than I do," Sadie stated flatly. "Girl, you're as full of pride as an egg's full of meat. And so is he, if I'm not mistaken. You both lied to one another. You were both wrong. And pride is the only thing you have. So where does that leave you both?"

Kelly folded her arms and stuck out her chin. "Impasse."

Chapter Sixteen

Another ball of paper sailed across the room, impacting the wall before landing in the vicinity of the overflowing trashcan. The locker room language that accompanied its flight should have blistered the paint on the apartment wall.

Calder forced his reddened, bleary eyes back to the monitor. "It should be easy, dammit. The outline is there, right in front of your face, asshole. Concentrate!" He poised his fingers over the keyboard once more. "This is paint-by-numbers. Just fill in the blanks."

The silence between his ears was deafening, as it had been for two weeks. He gave up. Stomping to his mangled and lumpy couch, he threw himself down on its length.

His heart ached. Calder had never believed in that worn-out cliché until his own chest hurt with every breath, sore with fighting the urge to do something so weak as cry.

The apartment he'd cherished as his private retreat now looked dingy and dull. Okay, the pile of dishes in the sink and the inch of dust on all horizontal surfaces didn't help. The only shine in the whole place was his computer; sleek and glistening like a recrimination.

Calder snarled at the winking display of his screensaver. "Oh, be quiet. I'll get back in the groove. Eventually."

The normally soothing Mobius strip of colored lines flickered endlessly, lulling him into the first sleep he'd had in three days. He dreamed of holding Kelly and telling her insistently and repeatedly how much he loved her. "I'd do anything, literally anything, to keep you!" his dream self shouted over a pounding rock beat.

Calder jerked awake, still hearing the pounding. It took him a moment to realize it wasn't music's backbeat he heard, but his apartment door being hammered on.

"Keep your shirt on, I'm coming!" he yelled, combing his hair with his fingers.

He yanked the door open to find Sadie leaning in the doorframe as casually as an old friend. "I doubt seriously if you're coming, and I will, thank you," she teased as she brushed past him. Sadie stopped just short of the center of his apartment, wrinkling her nose as the odor of unwashed male and equally unwashed dishes hit her.

Calder closed the door carefully. He let Sadie look her fill, knowing she saw the pile of discarded balls of paper and the neglected computer with the same sharp eyes that spotted every speck of dust.

"How can I help you, Sadie?" he asked cautiously.

"You already did, Master Calder. You told me what I came to find out." Her white teeth flashed in the late afternoon sun. "Actually, you were shouting it to the neighborhood." She nodded toward the open window.

Calder winced. "I was?" His embarrassment was enough to make him want to move. "I, uh, was having a bad dream."

"I figured." Her tone dripped with sarcasm. "But I figure there's some truth in dreams." She marched over to the kitchen sink, muttering about getting a sub in here. "Now what are you going to do about your desires, since you aren't denying them?" She turned on the water and started loading the dishwasher.

"Stop doing my dishes. I'll get to them eventually." Out of courtesy, Calder remained a decent distance away. He could smell himself, and that was bad enough. "And I assume Kelly told you everything?"

"Yep. Not surprising, all in all."

"Would have been, if I'd been allowed to tell on my own," he muttered. He pulled the ring box out of his pocket, where it had not left his side since he'd walked out of Kelly's house.

Sadie's breathless "Ohhh!" as he opened the box was a tiny consolation. She looked up at Calder, her face serious. "Okay, now I really believe you. And I ask again, what are you gonna do about it?"

"I don't know, Sadie. I'd do anything. Even submit." He shuddered, but squared his shoulders. "But I'll bet she would slam the door in my face."

Sadie shook her head. "And I thought you were smarter than that, Master Calder." She pulled her cell phone from her jeans pocket. "I got a plan." There was a knock at the door. "And Step One just arrived," she added smugly.

Calder opened the door, admitting Brad, who was lugging a heavy suitcase. "Geez, Calder, you stink. I got the stuff, Sadie." He flung the suitcase on the coffee table.

Sadie shoved Calder toward the bedroom. "Go bathe!"

"What did I agree to? I don't remember agreeing!" Calder yelped when Sadie swatted his ass.

"You said you'd do anything, sugar. Well, I'm going to make you prove it!"

* * *

Kelly wandered listlessly into her office. Sadie had been handling all her business transactions for the past few days while Kelly moped.

"I have to get over this," she muttered to the china kitten holding down the paperwork that needed her personal attention. The cat didn't answer, but it was sitting on a new client file. Kelly flipped open her appointment book. The client was for that night, nine o'clock. The client numbers from the book matched those on the file, so the cat got moved.

The file was distressingly thin. "No previous Mistress to consult," she commented to the cat. "Oh, boy. I got a virgin. Shit. Where the hell is Sadie?"

"I'm here. Figured you'd be looking, since it's after five." Sadie strode in, looking disheveled.

"What the hell happened to you?" The file was momentarily forgotten.

"I ran out of milk. Had to run to the store." Sadie set a glass of milk on the desk. "I know better than to make you eat, but I can hope you'll at least drink something nutritional. You can't live on coffee and air."

"I don't feel like eating." Kelly felt her lip tremble and reined it in by biting it—hard.

"That's obvious. You haven't eaten enough to keep a mouse alive. I'm just grateful you aren't one of those stress eaters who sucks down a half-gallon of ice cream when she's depressed." Her smile was gentle. "Not only would that mess up my carefully organized kitchen, but I don't think we could let out your costumes."

"Speaking of, what's this with the new client?" Kelly flipped open the file once more. "Limits list is signed, but nothing checked." She couldn't read the signature, but that wasn't unusual.

"According to my conversation with him, he doesn't have limits." Sadie crossed her arms and looked firm.

"A virgin with no limits? Get real!" Kelly scoffed.

"I questioned him closely. Made him define a few terms to make sure he knew what he was getting into. Perfect score. Come on, Mistress. How long have I been your sub? I know this stuff." Sadie looked slightly offended.

Kelly turned the page to the Scene Request. "Scene request is blank. Open?"

"Yup. Dealer's choice. He did request that the scene start with him hooded, naked, in chains, and the room candlelit. He won't speak. Says his voice is recognizable." Sadie was amused.

Kelly sighed. "Damn. This one is being secretive." She flipped to the front. "Pseudonym for the evening is Supplicant?" She raised puzzled eyes to Sadie. "What's his shtick?"

"Dom training. Full program."

"Aw, shit. Does he understand how much money he'll be forking out and how long that might take?" Kelly was awed. Normally, she knew potential Doms, sometimes for years, before they took training. And a male Dom went to another male most of the time.

Sadie pointed out a receipt clipped to the back of the file. "Paid in full. I understand he borrowed it. Bank certified check. I deposited it while I was out."

"You're pretty positive of this one. Normally you wait until I've put him through his paces," Kelly commented, slightly disgruntled.

"I'm sure. This one is so Dom, I'm amazed he's submitting." Sadie chuckled. "He's just what you need right now."

Kelly choked back a sniffle. "Yeah, I guess so. I need to get over Calder." Even saying his name hurt. "But he's not called or even left a goddamn dandelion on my doorstep." She gave up and let the tears come. "Guess I blew it. He's probably pounding on his keyboard in that damn dingy apartment, setting out to ruin me."

Sadie reached for one of the many boxes of tissues she'd set strategically throughout the house and handed her Mistress a tissue. "I doubt that. But one of you is going to have to give on your damned pride, and that's the truth."

"I can't, Sadie. I just can't. I won't be used again." Kelly blew her nose. "Never again."

"And what would you do if Calder came to you with a fistful of posies and an apology?" Sadie's voice was intense.

"I don't know. It would have to be a pretty powerful apology. Something I could really believe." She stood and turned fully on Sadie. "And don't you go matchmaking. He's got to do it on his own!"

"I won't. I'm not leaving this house!" Sadie threw up her hands in self-defense.

"Fine. Long as we understand each other. I'm going to take a long bubble bath. Since Devon is off tonight, you get to prepare Supplicant. I'll see what he's made of." Kelly squared her shoulders and walked sedately to the door.

"I'm sure you will, Mistress."

* * *

At nine PM sharp, Kelly descended to the dungeon. She could smell the wax candles, and the rooms were all dark except the pain room. There, the glow of candles told her that this was where Sadie had put Supplicant.

Kelly pulled at her costume. The bustier with the black widow hourglass didn't fit as well as it had a month ago. "Sadie's right," she muttered. "I need to eat. Can't have my shorts falling off my ass." She gave the shorts a tug as well.

She stopped at the doorway of the pain room. Barely visible in the meager candlelight, a naked man waited on the cross. A hood covered his face, but his back and buttocks were beautifully on display.

"Yum, yum!" Kelly commented aloud to let the man know she was there.

The man jerked upright as much as he was able, since he was firmly cuffed to the cross.

Kelly walked over to her toys, noting that his skin glistened from the preparation formula Sadie had sprayed on him. Those butt cheeks could have been sculpted out of marble, and the fine muscles of his back would have made any Domme sigh. "You're very beautiful, at least in the body. If your face matches the rest of you, I'm going to be forced to train you separately. You realize other Dommes will covet you, don't you?"

Supplicant's head nodded again, slowly.

"I understand you want the full program of Dom training. Do you understand that means submitting to me, completely?"

Another nod. This time, it was accompanied by a shudder that shook him from his toes. It was hard to see him in the candlelight, but that shudder told her he knew what he was getting into.

Kelly's heart softened a little. "Are you afraid, Supplicant?" she asked softly.

The answering nod was jerky and short. Then the head fell forward slowly to rest on the V of the cross. The collar Sadie had put on his neck, complete with spider medallion marking him as hers, winked in the candlelight. Sadie had neatly tucked the hem of the hood under the collar, in case Supplicant needed to be leashed.

"I'll take it you are, but understand, you must feel everything a sub feels to be a good Master."

She got her answer in his tiny nod, his forehead never leaving the cross where it rested.

"Very well, then, Supplicant. You can rest easy tonight. I start training at the sensual level. No pain, I promise."

That got a reaction. His whole body jerked. In fact, he damn near tried to flatten himself against the cross. Just as she suspected, he thought that included sex. Well, she'd flatten that idea.

Her voice hard and cold, it was BW who answered. "Don't even think about it, Supplicant. I don't have sex with my clients, or my trainees. You'll have to seek release elsewhere if you need it."

The reaction was the oddest she'd ever seen. Instead of radiating disappointment or even confidence, Supplicant's body relaxed.

"I see relief in your body language. Are you gay?" If he was, she was sure she could find a gay male sub to help Supplicant along with some of the training. Subs would trip all over themselves for this body, even if Supplicant's face were uglier than a homemade mud fence.

A strangled sound came from the hood while the head shook violently back and forth.

Laughter? "Well, okay, whatever. Your problem," she replied indifferently. No matter how pretty his body was, she told herself she wasn't interested. A small, horny part of her mind did wish wistfully she could see the whole of it in full daylight. She told her pussy to shut up and behave. It was on short rations, no matter what her battery bill looked like.

Kelly walked over and picked up a rabbit fur. "Let's begin, Supplicant." She stepped close to Supplicant's back. "This is a rabbit fur mitt. It is used to stimulate the skin."

His body tensed against the cross.

"You're so weird, buster. I tell you something won't hurt, and you plaster yourself up to the cross like you're in agony." The mute nod was slow, and almost pitiful. "Now hold still. Virgins!" she muttered, exasperated.

The shuddering began almost immediately. Kelly was ready to freak out when she glanced down at Supplicant's hardening cock. Even in candlelight, she knew who it was.

"Calder," she growled.

Chapter Seventeen

Calder sighed in relief, as much as he was able, when Kelly reached up and snatched off the hood. It had been difficult to breathe easily.

Kelly's harsh bark of laughter yanked him back into reality. She studied the ball gag in his mouth, and even checked the buckle holding it on. "A ball gag!" she chortled. "Well, that ensures your silence, doesn't it?"

Calder nodded in answer to what he hoped was a rhetorical question. All he could do was plead with his eyes. The gag was well designed. The red ball in his mouth assured he could do nothing but make small inarticulate sounds. Another person would have to remove the black straps that held the ball in place as long as he remained cuffed to the cross.

She tapped a finger on her chin thoughtfully, her eyes full of anger mixed with mischief. "Well, we certainly don't need the darkness and candlelight anymore."

With that, she marched over and flipped on the overhead light. Calder winced as his eyes adjusted. Out of his line of sight, he heard her noisily blowing out the candles that littered the room. His back still tingled from the effects of the spray.

Kelly stomped back into his line of sight a little bit to his right, but close enough to touch him. All he could see over his arm was her face and the top of that mind-blowing leather bustier. His cock remained rigid in response.

"Let me see if I can puzzle all this out," she purred, her tone dangerous. Her arm moved, as if she was fiddling with something in her hands.

Calder prayed it wasn't any of the many pain-inducing devices decorating the walls of the room. But the point was to be helpless, so he steeled himself for whatever she chose to dish out.

"Sadie had to know who you were when she put you in here. I'll make her pay later," Kelly swore. "Additionally, it goes without saying that you put yourself in this position voluntarily. That was a big risk, Calder, knowing what I am. It implies a lot of trust, as well as a certain level of desperation."

Calder nodded vigorously in agreement. All he could do was speak with his eyes and his body. He continued to plead, and knew she could read that.

"Very well. I must say it's an effective way to get my attention, and a start on convincing me of your sincerity." Her arm moved. "However, Calder, I have some issues to work out. I never wanted your submission, but I'll take it now." Her eyes glittered. "Do you still submit, Calder? Are you sure?"

He nodded, this time more slowly. And he let her see the small amount of fear he felt. What was she going to do to "work out those issues"?

Kelly was all Black Widow when she held up a red ball. "You see this, Calder? Do you know what it is for?"

He knew. It was a "safe word" of sorts. He flexed his right hand in answer. She would give him the ball. If ever he chickened out or couldn't take anymore, all he had to do was drop the ball. But this time, dropping the ball meant more. It meant he gave up on the relationship. He opened his cuffed hand slowly, to signify a thoughtful response.

"I see you understand." She put the ball in his hand and watched him grasp it tightly.

Calder decided he needed to let her know fully of his decision. He bowed his head and lowered his eyes. It was, in the language of BDSM, an offer of full submission.

"Hmph. We'll see if you can hold to that, Calder. You've lied before. Two lies, as a matter of fact." Black Widow held up a pair of glittering nipple clamps. Calder recognized them and shuddered, but nodded. "That's right, Calder, one for each lie. The first for not telling me you're a journalist."

The clamp was put on his right nipple. It stung, then settled into a dull ache.

Black Widow moved behind him, coming around to his left. "The second lie was not telling me you're an ex-cop." The second clamp stung just as much. "Did you think I wouldn't ream Brad and find out about that?"

Calder looked into her impassive blue eyes. How could he say he found that detail unimportant? The best he could come up with was a shrug and a shake of the head.

"I see. You figured since your career was over, it was a dead issue?"

Calder nodded. His nipples throbbed with every heartbeat and were impossible to ignore. Worse, his arms were going to sleep. Soon, he'd be in severe pain. He set his jaw as best he could around the gag. He could take it. Kelly would not do permanent damage. But he couldn't help the small adjustment his body made in response to the growing discomfort.

"Getting uncomfortable, Calder?" Kelly asked in a dangerous voice. "It's about to get worse. You see, I accepted your submission, and I now accept your wish to take training. I can both punish you for deceiving me and train you simultaneously." She stepped out of sight.

Calder felt her soft hand on his left buttock. She was stroking it. Her hand moved to the right cheek, repeating the caress. He shut his eyes and tried to reconcile the soft, pleasant strokes with the discomfort of his chest. When she moved her hand to caress the underside of each cheek, the pain went away. "Very nice, Calder. You can take more than I might have given you credit for." The purr in her voice was back. "You lied, and I lied. The rest of this is all for the purpose of making you hit subspace. I want you to see and feel what it is to submit, totally. Then, we'll talk."

The rabbit fur replaced her hand. He kept his eyes closed and stood rigidly still. With his legs spread almost to the level of discomfort by the ankle cuffs of the cross, he wasn't surprised when the fur caressed between his legs and squeezed his balls tenderly. His eyes popped open, and his cock swelled further.

Kelly moved around to his right again, but her head was bent to look directly at his hard-on. "Hold still, Calder. Be very still," she cautioned.

Her small hand grasped his cock firmly and pulled it away from his body. It had been nearly flat against his pubic mound. It felt so good that he had to groan.

He couldn't see, but something slipped down just below the head of his aching erection. A cock ring, perhaps? No, it was soft and flexible. His hips twitched before he could stop himself.

"It's only cotton rope, Calder." Kelly's voice held a touch of amusement. The rope wound around his cock, down to the base, firmly holding him up and hard. "This will restrict blood flow just enough so you can't lose your erection, no matter what happens."

Calder thought he'd lose his mind when she positioned the rope carefully between his balls, separating them. He felt them try to move inside his body for protection, but the rope trapped them in their individual sacs. The pleasure was close to excruciating. He couldn't stop the moan that escaped around the ball gag.

"There's more, Calder." A rope cinched around his waist. It didn't seem to be connected to the first, until BW pulled the first firmly and attached it to the "belt." A knot now rested expertly against his anus. His eyes flew open wide.

Kelly moved back to his right, and leaned casually up against the wall where he could see her clearly. "You see, Calder, that knot serves a purpose," she began conversationally. She reached over and tugged at his rope belt, and the knot moved, rubbing his ass. His breathing hitched. "Did you know that the male G-spot is in a man's ass? Makes sense, doesn't it?" *Tug.* Calder's eyes glazed. "Oh, by the way, Calder. The rope around your cock ensures you can't come, either. I can stimulate you all night, and you'll never get a drop of release until I permit it. Understand?" *Tug.*

Agonized, Calder could only shut his eyes and nod. He now understood pain and pleasure, in combination. His entire body screamed. It was like passing through a barrier, and he floated in a world where both resided simultaneously, where the pleasure was winning.

From far away, Kelly's voice still came in loud and clear. "You're writhing, Calder. You've hit subspace. Good." Distantly, he felt the fur caress the head of his cock, and he rode a new wave of pleasure.

Kelly's voice floated in. "Now, everything I say will be imprinted deeply within your memory."

Every fiber of his being heard her. He thought he nodded, but he couldn't be sure anymore.

"You never asked, but I'm telling you about my husband anyway. I don't think Denny really loved me. He said he did and showered me with gifts, but he never showed it with the little things that are free and easy to give. A spontaneous kiss, a flower plucked and handed to me fresh, all the small romantic things."

All the things Calder had done. It made him happy to hear it, and he floated further.

"Denny was an investment realtor. He only worked with the wealthy, making million-dollar deals. He was gone a lot, and when he came home he didn't want to hear voices, or a phone ring. He demanded absolute quiet, not even music. And he certainly didn't want to hear about his wife's day.

"The only time he wanted me to talk was when I was beating him. Yep, I was the Domme, not Denny. I tried now and then to interest him in switching, just for me, but it didn't work. He was a lousy Dom. It was probably the only thing we had in common."

Calder attempted to nod. He'd dominated Kelly, just the once. He'd be happy to do it again. Especially now that he understood subspace.

She shrugged. Were his eyes open? He guessed so. "What did I have to talk about anyway? How I burned the biscuits daydreaming and had to make a fresh batch? How I went shopping? He didn't care if I redecorated, as long as I hired a professional and it looked elegant and expensive.

"And as long as I remained elegant and expensive, too. I had to be the perfect decoration—discreet, quiet, and well-dressed. I ran from shopping, to the gym, and back home to either cook dinner or get dressed for an evening out with clients."

God, that sounded boring, Calder mused absently. The furry caressing had stopped.

"Finally, my brain was turning to mush. I craved human conversation and feeling intelligent. I also was rebelling against that vapid, perfect little wife who never stepped a toe out of line." Her voice hitched, like she was trying to hold back tears.

"So, I turned pro. Worked for an escort service, since I was already great arm candy. But, when my client went back to the hotel room, I picked up my kit and performed BDSM services. Never sex. Never. Denny couldn't be jealous of that.

"It took a year to build up the client base and the infamous little black book. I renovated the basement into a professional dungeon, and took clients there. Denny loved it. Not only was I making money hand over fist he could invest for me, but also the dungeon was his little playground. Managing both our businesses was a nightmare of organization, but at least I was busier than I ever thought possible. My appointment book was full of dinner parties with Denny in the early evening, clients late into the night, and I slept all day while Denny worked." Her voice was contemptuous.

Something in Calder's brain snapped into awareness. He was coming back.

"The hell of it all was I was still neglected emotionally. Denny figured since I was so busy, I didn't need any romance. My clients brought me flowers, didn't they? Yeah, just before they hit their knees and begged for a beating.

"I've been the vapid trophy wife, and I've been the Black Widow. Never an equal. Never just a woman with a brain and a heart."

A tear tracked slowly down her cheek. "You did that for me, Calder. You were innocent of Black Widow's influence, and didn't need or want a status symbol."

Calder writhed violently in the cuffs, no matter what the cost was in pain. He wanted, more than he'd ever wanted anything, to cuddle Kelly. He thought his hands would fall off, but he clutched the ball so tightly he thought it might burst. His eyes glazed, and he thought he might pass out.

Kelly's eyes narrowed, and she regained some composure. "No, Calder, not yet. I've made my decision, as you suggested. I want you in my life, but you get to choose how. And I'm not removing the gag until you know the full scope of your choices. Deal?"

Calder nodded, so weak he could barely hold himself upright. The logical part of his brain was clicking online. This must be the shock portion of submission. It didn't help to know that. The rest of him didn't give a damn.

"Fine. Fight to stand upright, Calder. I'll release your ankles first." She suited words to action. As tenderly as she'd treated her first sub, she unbuckled his legs and held them until they found solid purchase on the floor.

Calder couldn't describe the relief. The rope belt still had him in discomfort, but at least he was standing, if a bit wobbly. He was now grateful for the cuffs on his wrists that kept him upright.

"Calder. Calder, listen to me," came the gentle voice of Kelly. "I'm going to release your wrists. You will have to remain upright as best you can. You're too big for me to carry. Once you're free, I'm going to make you kneel right at the base of the cross. I won't make you walk. Can you do this?"

Calder forced himself to nod. He felt like his bones were jelly. It was an effort to plant his feet firmly and make them take his weight. He felt Kelly release his left cuff. He leaned on the cross, sacrificing pride so he wouldn't fall on her.

"Okay, Calder. I'm going to release your right wrist." She touched his hand, and took the ball. In his muddled state, he tried to grab for it. It was his lifeline to Kelly.

"It's all right, Calder. It served its purpose," she crooned into his ear. "You proved your sincerity and didn't drop it. I've got it now." She unbuckled the cuff.

Calder sank to his knees slowly, using the cross to make it a controlled fall. Kelly caught him halfway down, and eased him into the kneeling position. He took the ball back as soon as it came into range of his vision.

Kelly brought him a cool cola, its sides dripping with condensation, and a chocolate bar. She set them near him.

"Here's your choice, Calder. Before I un-gag you, you must decide. If you choose to continue the Dom training as it stands now, we will be no more than friends. I don't have sex with my subs. There are too many complications.

"However, you have a second choice. You can be my partner. I will teach you all the aspects of my business, but privately, and in my own good time. I don't need a sub. I'd prefer a partner. In exchange for this, I'll help you with your book. And, we can enjoy a healthy sexual relationship."

Calder allowed the gag to be removed. He still couldn't speak, so he pointed to a table in the corner. There, hidden from casual sight, was the burgundy box. He waited, and opened his cola can with trembling hands.

Kelly went to the table, and found the box. Glancing once at Calder with an unreadable expression, she opened the box.

Calder slugged down the cola to get his throat wet. "I accept the partnership offer. But I'd prefer a partnership based on marriage, if you'd accept." He swayed, but didn't fall over.

Kelly closed the box and knelt in front of Calder, then put the chocolate in his hand. "Eat. You aren't far enough out of subspace to make a marriage proposal at this time."

Calder took the candy, but smiled weakly. "No, I had it in my jacket pocket the night we discovered the truth about each other. But things got out of hand. I love you, Kelly. All of you. And I want you to be in my life. More than a partner. More than BDSM. It's all or nothing."

Kelly bit her lip. She reached over and removed his nipple clamps. The rush of pain/pleasure was indescribable. Calder closed his eyes and forced himself not to tremble. He bit into the chocolate, hoping it would help.

Kelly pondered, and fingered the worn little box in her lap. "All of me? Not just Black Widow?" she asked in a small voice without looking up.

"I admit to a fondness for other aspects, like the girl who watches Bogart with me at three AM and has a Scooby Doo alarm clock, but yeah, you're a package deal." He quirked a smile. "And I'm looking forward to more, uh, training, but as your partner. I've got a lot left to learn." He put down his cola and took another bite of chocolate. It was helping.

Kelly made a sound that was somewhere between a snort and a snigger. Her arm reached behind Calder and released the rope between his legs.

The immediate rush of circulation made Calder yelp. Before the sound echoed back off the walls, Kelly had pounced, tossing Calder on his back. "Then I accept! And your training continues right now!"

Calder moaned as she kissed him very thoroughly, and slowly unwound the rope from his still hard cock. He moaned again and wrapped his arms around her. The release from the rope was close to an orgasm. "Does this mean I get to come now?"

"What? Do you think I'm going to make you wait until our honeymoon?"

Epilogue

Ruben Grimes sat in the back of the room and sniffed happily at the aromas coming from the reception banquet. It was worth the trip to Denver to see his newest best-selling author team finally tie the knot. *The Tie that Binds* had hit the NY Times Extended list incredibly quickly. Ruben had found it both funny and very profitable.

At least the wedding march was traditional, but Ruben was having trouble adjusting to a large portion of the wedding guests being dressed either in leather or nearly nothing at all. *Good thing Calder warned me not to bring the missus.* Ruben chuckled to himself. Cassie would have started with a conniption and worked up from there.

Calder appeared, flanked by the best man. Both were in leather tuxes, and Ruben smothered another chuckle. Calder had certainly relaxed in recent months.

The bride swept by, marching on her own, with one attendant following. Ruben had to gasp as he nearly broke his neck at the attendant's lack of attire. He didn't call that scrap of red cloth covering the bare essentials anything like clothing.

The bride's black leather bustier, bouquet made of leather strips on handles, and tiny thong wasn't exactly traditional either, but Ruben wasn't about to complain. He wasn't going to complain about anything, not when fully half the crowd carried nasty looking whips and things he didn't want to name.

"Who comes before us this day?" boomed the official.

"I am Kelly Forsythe, The Black Widow."

"And I am Calder Burgess, now called Demon Lord."

The official called out to the crowd, "If there be any here who object to this bondage, give tongue that we may hear and consider what you have to say."

There was a pause. Ruben could have sworn he would have heard a mouse sneeze, had there been one with the temerity to interrupt. The official smiled and continued. "This bond is not meant to be a fetter. We have enough of that."

The crowd chuckled, and some even laughed.

"A bonding is a partnership, not two people becoming one. Two minds cannot fuse, two souls cannot merge, and two hearts cannot keep to the same time. If two are foolish enough to try this, one must overwhelm the other, and that is not love, nor is it compassion, nor responsibility. You're two who choose to walk the same path, to bridge the differences between you with love. You must remember and respect those differences and learn to understand them, for they are part of what made you to love in the first place.

"Love is patient. Love is willing to compromise. Love is willing to admit it is wrong. There will be hard times; you must face them as bound Dominants do, side-by-side, not using the weapon of your knowledge to tear at each other. There will be sadness as well as joy, and you must support one another through the grief and the sorrow. There will be pain, but pain shared is pain halved, as joy shared is joy doubled, and you must each sacrifice your own comfort to share the pain of the other."

"We know of pain," Calder and Kelly answered together. "We pledge to face it, with joy, together."

"And yet you must do all this and manage to keep each other from wrong actions, for a bonding means that you also pledged to help one another at all times. You must lead each other by example. Guide and be willing to be guided. Being bonded does not mean that you accept what is truly wrong; being bonded means that you must strive that you both remain in the right. You must not pledge yourselves thinking that you can change each other. That is foolish, and disrespectful, for no one has the right to change another. You must not pledge yourselves thinking that there will be no strife between you. That is fantasy, for you're two and not one, and there will inevitably be conflict that will be up to you to resolve. You must not pledge yourselves thinking that all will be well from this moment on. That is a dream, and dreamers must eventually awaken. You must come to this bondage fully ready, fully committed, and fully respectful of each other."

"We so pledge these things," the couple intoned.

Ruben had to marvel at their perfect unison. He didn't get this BDSM thing at all, but apparently they did.

"Bind each other, then, as you have pledged," commanded the official.

Kelly handed her attendant her bouquet and exchanged it for a leather collar with a leash. Calder got his collar from his groomsman, and it too had a chain leash.

Ruben forced his eyes not to bug out as Kelly and Calder put the collars on each other. He supposed it was the BDSM equivalent of wedding rings.

"I will now say a version of the Apache Wedding Blessing." The official took a deep breath. "Now you will no longer fear the storm, for you find shelter in each other. Now the cold cannot harm you, for you warm each other with love. Now when strength fails, you will be the wind at the other's back. Now the darkness holds no danger, for you will be the light to each other's path. Now you will defy despair, for you will bring hope to each other's heart. Now there will be no more loneliness, for there will always be a hand reaching out to hold you when all seems darkest. Where there were two paths, there is now one. May your days together be long upon the earth, and each day blessed with joy in each other."

A smattering of applause broke out, and ended as soon as the official acknowledged it. "You may exchange your gifts to one another," he intoned.

Calder and Kelly each received a bundle of leather strips on a handle from their attendants. Floggers, Ruben suddenly remembered from reading *The Tie that Binds.*

Kelly handed Calder a blue and gold one. Ruben didn't get it when Calder chuckled and handed Kelly a red and black one.

The official smiled, and pronounced them man and wife. The cheers that erupted didn't stop Calder from yanking Kelly to him for a kiss that should have raised the indoor temperature by ten degrees.

When the kiss finally broke, Calder and Kelly turned to the crowd and said, "Let us proceeded to the reception!" They grabbed each other's leash and paraded down the aisle to applause.

Ruben leaned over to the lady next to him as the happy couple led their guests to the sumptuous wedding feast and reception. The cool-looking matron sitting next to him was regally waiting for the crowd to thin.

"Pardon me, madam," Ruben asked, "but could you explain to me why no one escorted the bride to give her away?"

The silver-haired matron raised one perfectly sculptured eyebrow. "The Black Widow gives herself away, young man!"

~ * ~

Lena Austin

Lena Austin is a "fallen" society wench with a checkered past. She has been a licensed minister, hairdresser, and realtor, radio DJ, exotic dancer, telephone service tech, live-steel medievalist swordswoman, BDSM Mistress, and investment property manager. Not necessarily in that order. She never finished that degree in archaeology, but did learn to scuba. After a life like that, gardening is pretty restful. Of herself, Lena writes, "I'm tall, moody, and I look like an unholy mating between an Amazon and a librarian."

To find out more about Lena and her books, please visit http://www.lena.realmsoflove.com/lena.htm

OTHER TITLES NOW AVAILABLE In Print

ROMANCE AT THE EDGE: In Other Worlds
MaryJanice Davidson, Angela Knight and Camille Anthony

CHARMING THE SNAKE
MaryJanice Davidson, Camille Anthony and Melissa Schroeder

WHY ME?
Treva Harte

THE PRENDARIAN CHRONICLES
Doreen DeSalvo

HARD CANDY
Angela Knight, Morgan Hawke and Sheri Gilmore

SHE BLINDED ME WITH SCIENCE FICTION
Kally Jo Surbeck

ASK FOR THEM AT YOUR FAVORITE BOOKSELLER!

Publisher's Note: All titles published in print by Loose Id™ have been previously released in e-book format.

Printed in the United States
38730LVS00004BA/1-96